nosedive

B. R. Fleming

****

Nosedive

Fleming, B. R., 1949—
　　Nosedive/ by B. R. Fleming—1st ed.
　　　　p. cm.
　　ISBN-13: 978-0-9838201-4-7 (trade pbk.)
　　ISBN-10: 0983820147 (trade pbk.)
　　　　1. Coming-of-age—Fiction. 2. Teen years—Fiction. 3. 1960's rock music—Fiction. 4. Teen angst—Fiction. 5. Sexual awakening--Fiction. I. Title.
　　　　　　2012903467　　　　　　　　813.6

Cover Design by Jeremy Fleming.
Book Design by Murdock Malone.
Photography by @BRImagery
　　　　http://brimagery.wix.

'63

'64

'65

'66

'67

Nosedive

'63

****

Almost ten o'clock. My night had started later than usual. Mom and Dad usually went out to eat before going to the bowling alley. But tonight Mom had fixed fried chicken, and my Dad would kill for Mom's fried chicken. When they left at about seven, I immediately went to the bathroom and pulled my Playboy out from behind the clothes hamper.

This month's copy of Playboy contained a special section on "Sex in the Cinema" with some of the newest Hollywood starlets showing off their boobs and butts to make a name for themselves. Just thinking about opening to that section gave me a boner that wouldn't quit. I didn't even need to turn to the centerfold or the boobs that didn't make it to the centerfold to get a hard on.

Seeing their boobs was what turned me on the most. I could remember being in the bathtub with my Mom when I was just a little boy and seeing her boobs. I couldn't hardly not see them with me squeezed in the tiny bathtub in front of her and with them sticking right in my face. When the baby-sitters would come to watch my brothers and me, I would sneak in and peek through the keyholes in the bathroom door every time they went in there. I couldn't see their boobs, but I could see their hair before they pulled up their panties when they stood up after pissing. I had no clue what I was looking at, just that it was hairy, and it was in one of the areas that girls kept hidden from us guys, so I guessed it was something special.

Now, I not only could see their boobs and butts, but I could jack off dreaming about squeezing them, about having them play with my boner and jack me off. Boobs and beating off. No matter what any mother wants to think, that's what thirteen year old teenage boys think about.

After my secret date with Ursula Andress, I put the Playboy back in its hiding place and went down to check on my brother. My oldest brother, named after my Dad, was sprawled on the couch in his usual position watching Gunsmoke. He wasn't asleep yet; still picking his nose and wiping the little treasures on the arm of the couch. I never sat on any furniture in the family room. You never knew what disgusting remains might stick to you. Seeing my brother's friends sit there, though, gave me immense pleasure after all the crap they put me through.

He would be asleep soon from eating his fill of the chicken and mashed potatoes, at least four helpings. He was usually out with his friends and was just hanging around until the fall, when he would be off to college. My next oldest brother and the pride of my parents was out with his friends and wouldn't be home until late, if at all. He would be off to college soon too, studying to be Daddy junior. My parents always took my little brother with them, so I was pretty much left on my own, as usual.

I went back up to the bathroom, removed the screen from the window, and climbed onto the second level of the house. Our house was one of the nicer in the neighborhood since my Dad was the partner of the builder. Dad sold the houses and his partner built them. They had been doing that for about five years and had built all the houses in our neighborhood and lots in North Little Rock. That was the main reason we had moved from our chicken farm south of

Little Rock three years ago to North Little Rock, commonly called "Dog Town" by the people south of the river.

It had been a lot different for me, moving from the country, where my closest friend lived half a mile away, to the city where my best friend lived right across the street. Fortunately, the neighborhood was filled with kids my age, and all of the stuff we did together helped me get used to it. But I still felt the need to be alone sometimes, like I had been in the country, climbing the bauxite hills behind our house or climbing the trees in the woods all around us. Our neighborhood was on the northern edge of the city right next to an old army base and had woods and creeks on the hills around us, so I could still wander off into the woods by myself or go camping and fishing in the creeks with some of the other guys in the neighborhood who also liked that kind of stuff.

After climbing onto the second story of the house, I replaced the screen and climbed up to make the jump to the third level. My lawn chair was still there behind the chimney from the last time I had come up. I unfolded it and set it on the top of the roof with the back side over the edge to keep it from sliding down, spread the quilt over it with enough left over to cover myself, and pulled my transistor radio out of my pocket.

I stood there just looking out over the city and the open sky. It was so different being able to see for miles around like that, and it made it even better that we had the only two-story house in the neighborhood. Our house in the country had been surrounded by trees and was set down from the road. I had to climb the trees around us to see any more than a few hundred yards and could at least see the woods that surrounded us and the bauxite hills behind us from my tree house. Now I was surrounded by the sounds of the city, the lights, the billions of stars, the steady stream of music, usually

WGN from Chicago, and it excited me to feel all of those sensations all at once.

The night was clear which made the music come in better than usual. I couldn't remember a time when music didn't fill my head or wasn't a part of my thoughts. As a young boy, I would get into my Dad's records and listen to his Tommy and Jimmy Dorsey, Benny Goodman, and big band records. My favorite was Gene Krupa though, and I would play along with him on the songs.

Now, here I was, on the roof, listening to "It's My Party," gazing at the stars and the occasional airplane, thinking about my ex-girlfriend, Phyllis, and how much I'd wanted to squeeze her boobs. I'd almost felt her up through her panties once and had rubbed her boobs and we'd kissed; but that was the extent of my having sex with her, except for in my fantasies.

My mind began to wander, to a girl in the neighborhood who was a real fox, Debbie McIntyre, and who liked to tease all us guys down at the neighborhood swimming pool, letting her top ease down a little further than her mom would have liked, or sitting on the edge of the pool with her legs open to let the pubes poke out from the edge of her bikini bottoms.

Then Donna filled my thoughts, another fox who was my age and dated high school guys. My buddy Darryl and I had peeked through her window one night while she was getting fingered by her boyfriend in her bedroom. We had seen her parents leave earlier with her little sisters and had then seen her boyfriend's car pull in a little later. We walked down the street from her house and then went into the woods to sneak to the back of her yard. The light was on in the family room, and we saw a dull glow from her bedroom. We quietly moved across the yard to the window and peeked through the blinds and there they were, studying, on her bed. She wasn't quite as hot as Debbie, but she was older and less of a tease, and she was my first look at a pussy with hair and was my first real experience with sex. The sight of her and her boyfriend filled my mind every time I jacked off and could get a boner going pretty easily.

"Let There Be Drums", a Sandy Nelson drum song almost as good as Gene Krupa's songs, came on, and I wished I was sitting at the drums playing it. I had started singing while in elementary school and had begun playing the clarinet in the sixth grade. Mr. Haslett, he'd played trombone with my Dad and uncles in dance bands, was the band director and talked my Dad into switching me to sax. I wanted to play the drums, but I also wanted to please Dad, so when seventh grade started I switched to alto sax. That didn't keep me from wanting to play the drums though, and I took every opportunity to go back to the drum section and play the snare drums when Mr. Haslett left the room. I became friends with the drummers, and they would let me borrow their old drum sets sometimes to mess around with them. For now, though, I was stuck in the sax section, in last chair usually, barely able to play any of the songs.

My Dad's family was very musical. His father had been a violinist and made violins. My Grandmother, who I never knew or remembered that well, had played piano. Dad and two of his brothers had played sax together in bands during the Depression, and Dad was the state harmonica champ during the twenties.

My mother wasn't a musician, but she loved all kinds of music, especially Broadway show tunes and movie music. She had lived in New York City during WW II, where she met my Dad who was stationed there in the navy, and her mother had been a costumer for Radio City Music Hall and the Rockettes. She had her own collection of Robert Goulet, Tony Bennett, easy listening, movie hits albums and always had the radio going. And she always took me along with her when she went to see the new movies, even getting me up late at night to go to the late night showings. By the time I was ten, and we had moved to our new house, the love of music, going to the movies, and staying up late at night had definitely become a big part of me, almost like a curse.

The night was getting cooler, cooler than usual for summer in the south, so I decided to pack up a little early and go to my room, actually the room I shared with my little brother, though he almost always slept in the big bedroom. The room was fairly small, with bunkbeds, me on top, and had a desk that was always covered with the current model I was building or my comic books or sci-fi book I was reading, or with the current issues of my brother's Popular Science or Popular Mechanics magazines or with all of that stuff at once. It was now covered by a '63 vette convertible, red with black walls and chrome mags, that would be a nice addition to my sports cars, and waiting in my closet was the "Tiger" tank that Mom had bought me.

My parents would be returning soon. Dad would go straight to bed, after a smoke and maybe a nightcap of a glass of milk filled with chunks of white bread. Mom would stay up and watch Johnny Carson and would maybe have an ice cream float, after she roused my brother from his camping on the couch. She would often fall asleep on the couch with the video noise going full blast, but not loud enough to drown out her snoring. Or was that Dad snoring?

My light was always the last to go off, if it went off at all. During the summer especially, when I didn't have to worry about getting up for school, I enjoyed working on my projects with the peace and quiet, just my music going constantly, and hardly ever went to bed before two or three in the morning. When I got hungry, I would go down to the kitchen, make a bologna and ketchup sandwich, grab a bottle of coke and some potato chips, and head back. No one was awake to bother me or tell me what to do or what not to do or keep me from doing what I wanted. I felt very independent and happy.

The Vette was coming together very well. The most fun part of putting the model cars together was that they had great detail and everything came unpainted. You were left completely on your own to make the car look the way you wanted it to look. The wheels were rubber and would roll, the doors opened and closed, the hood and the trunk would open and close, and on some the steering worked. The only problem was my little brother would play with them sometimes and break them.

About three o'clock I started getting sleepy. I began gathering up the paints and parts and glue and instructions and put them into the model box and put the box up in the closet, so my little brother wouldn't mess with the stuff. Back at the desk, with everything gone, I could again see the envelope I had received earlier in the week from the local university medical center.

I had written to the Microbiology Department at the school to find out about how to become a Microbiologist and this was the reply I had received, the booklet Microbiology In Your Future from one of the professors outlining the classes I should take in high school to prepare for college and the kind of jobs that Microbiologists could get. I opened the booklet again to the page I had marked. A man in a white lab coat was sitting on a stool at a counter covered with beakers and other scientific-looking instruments and was looking into a microscope. Each time I saw that picture, I knew that that would be me in about ten years. I'd be in ninth grade at the end of summer, then high school for three years, then college for at least four years, and maybe a few more, and then there I would be, sitting on my stool in my laboratory, discovering germs and bacteria and whatever else I could discover.

Next year in school would be great because I'd finally have my first science class. Science and science fiction were two of my favorite things. I was always reading books or magazines or watching television shows or movies or anything that had to do with science or science fiction. The first novel I ever read was Twilight World, by Poul Anderson, and I loved the shows on television like The Twilight Zone and The Outer Limits. The Outer Limits shows were so cool, especially the first show. In that one, a guy who owns a radio station brings this creature from another galaxy to earth with microwaves, and the creature goes around exposing people to radiation until the guy gets the creature back into the transmitter and back to his galaxy. It was kind of like The Day the Earth Stood Still, because the creature has to save the guy's wife from dying after she's shot, the same way the robot, Gort, has to save Klattu after he's shot by the army. And the creature tells the earthlings who try to kill him how they have to keep from using violence if they want to make it to the future.

I loved anything to do with Biology too, and last Christmas I had gotten a Biology Kit which had a microscope and dissection tools and scales and a book on Biology. I had already used the microscope and tools a lot to look at plants and bugs and anything I could fit on the slides.

I especially liked the dissection tools, because I felt like a doctor when I was using them. I had used the dissection tools earlier in the summer to dissect a sick cat that my friend Darryl had found in the woods and killed. He could be a little strange sometimes, and when he saw the cat he decided that he was going to put it out of its misery. He went back to his house and got a rope and went back to the woods, made a hangman's noose, put the cat's neck in it, and threw it over a limb of a tree, breaking the cats neck, of course. Then he came to get me to show me what a hanged cat looked like.

My Mom had cats, Siamese, and so I was kind of disgusted by the sight of the cat hanging there, but I also saw it as an opportunity to use my dissecting tools.

I went back to the house and got my tools and some jars and went back to the site of the hanged cat. I got Darryl to cut it down and laid it on the grass under the tree. I didn't know exactly what to do first so I just started by making a slice down the middle of the body. I was fascinated with every step of the dissection and pretended that I was a doctor saving a patient's life. I removed each organ one at a time with Darryl acting like my assistant, putting the parts in the jars after each of us had completely analyzed each one. By the time we finished we had the heart, liver, kidneys, lungs, and some of the intestines in the jars. We buried the cat, or what was left of it, and he helped me carry the jars to the house. Then he went home.

I didn't have formaldehyde to put in the jars, so I poured water in with the parts and planned to do something with them the next day, Saturday. To keep my Mom from seeing them, I hid them in a storage room in our garage, one of the dark corners where you needed a flashlight to see anything. I went into the house and got a coke from the fridge and sat down to watch The Three Stooges and heard my Mom pulling into the driveway. She and my little brother came in, and she went straight upstairs, and I heard my Dad's car pulling into the driveway. He stuck his head in the door and called for me.

"Peter, come and help me. We're going to the lake this weekend."

Going to the lake actually meant going to the cabin that Dad shared with his partners, who were actually the sons of his partner who had died a few years back. I loved going to the lake and fishing. It was one of the only times I got to spend any time at all with my Dad, and so I jumped up and helped him pack our Dodge station wagon with the fishing tackle and blankets and clothes and food that my Mom got ready.

We spent the weekend at the lake and came back late Sunday evening. My parents were exhausted from waking at sunrise and going out in the boats and drinking beer and the late nights of playing poker and drinking bourbon and coke or vodka and orange juice, with an ice chest full of crappie, bream, and bass that I had helped my Dad clean. All my parents could think was to get into the house, have some dinner, take a shower, and go to bed. Dad got out first and started unpacking the car as Mom went to the garage door and opened it. My Mom jumped back and grabbed her nose and began screaming.

"My God! What is that?"

My Dad ran over to her, and then he grabbed his nose and scrambled away from the garage opening.

The odor from the garage quickly reached me, and I almost doubled up and puked. It was the most awful thing I had smelled in my life, and probably the most awful thing my parents had ever smelled. My parents raced to open the other garage door and the windows and began searching the garage to find out what was making the horrible smell that was now getting the attention of kids riding their bikes and people walking past our house.

Hearing my Mom's next horrific shriek from deep inside the garage, I immediately knew the cause and didn't want to see what I knew she had discovered. One at a time she brought out the jars to the middle of the garage floor, each one containing a now cloudy mixture of water and rotting cat insides, holding them as if they were radioactive. The look she gave me was worse than any words she could have screamed at me, and I knew at once that I'd better get those jars as far as possible away from the house, in the shortest time ever, if I wanted to live to see another day of thirteen.

Anytime I didn't want to face my parents, or anything else for that matter, from as far back as I could remember, I would go off by myself, ride my bike, climb to the top of a tree, lose myself in the woods, and this seemed like a good time to do just that. I put the jars in a bag and got on my bike and rode toward the woods to a trail that followed the railroad tracks through the woods to Five Mile Creek, where Darryl and I would go fishing and camping sometimes. Except for a rare train coming through and the sounds of nature, the creek was absolutely quiet and peaceful. It was an excellent place to think, escape, or just get away from the traffic and noise of the city.

Back in the country, living on a seven acre chicken farm in Sweet Home, south of Little Rock, I'd always been able to run off into the woods, or climb the bauxite hills, or go swimming in the bauxite holes to find peace and quiet. I'd climb to the top of one of the hills and sit there and just look around and think. More like ask myself questions about why this was like this or that was like that. It helped now to have the woods and the creek around our house so I could do the same thing here.

The creek seemed like a good place to empty the jars, mixing the cat remains with the running water and then washing the slimy liquid out of the jars, and it seemed right that the cat would be returning to nature fully after being stuck in our steaming hot garage over the weekend. I opened the jars one by one and let the remains mix with the water, watched as the parts drifted down the creek, bounced off rocks and got stuck on sticks, and washed out the jars. Dead stuff looked a lot different than live stuff. Smelled different too.

I finished cleaning off the desk, turned off the light, and was getting into my bunkbed as Franki Valli and the Four Seasons came on the radio singing "Candy Girl." Damn, he could hit some high notes. Immediately, I thought about Rhonda, a girl I had met at my cousin's cabin on the lake down in Hot Springs, about fifty miles southwest from Little Rock. My Dad's cousin and her husband, Will, who could always entertain us telling us stories about fighting in the war in France and Germany with General Patton, had a nice little cabin on the lake that my Dad pretty much had an open invitation to visit, and my Dad would always take his vacation there in the Spring when the bass and crappie were moving up the streams to spawn. They had a speed boat and fishing boats and a party barge and that's where I learned to water ski and slalom and where I met Rhonda.

Her family lived in Kansas, and her dad and my cousin were good friends. They had come down earlier in July for a fourth of July weekend party that had also included our family and some other relatives. The second I saw her I fell for her big time. She was so cute, with big blue eyes, fairly short cut strawberry blonde hair, freckles that you could just barely see because she was so tanned, and she looked great in her two-piece bathing suit. On top of that, she had one of those outgoing, bubbly personalities that I liked and that drew me to her like she was a magnet. But, I had a hard time talking to her or letting her know how much I liked her, because I would always get so shy around girls. And that pissed me off big time. I couldn't understand it, and I didn't know what to do about it or who to ask to help me with it. I did get her phone number and address, and I called her a few days after we got back from the cabin.

"Hello." A man answered the phone, probably her dad.

"Hi, is Rhonda there?"

"Who is this?"

"Oh, this is Peter. We met at--"

"I know. That was just a few days ago. I'll see if she's available."

I waited and felt the sweat beading in my palms. What would I say? Well, of course I would first say "Hello" and "How are you doing", but what would I say after that? I heard the phone being picked up, and then I heard her voice. I panicked.

"Hello." Her voice sounded so sweet.

"Hi." I stammered. "This is Peter, from Hot--"

"Oh, hi! Yeah, I know. You're Keith's cousin in Hot Springs."

"Well, I kinda don't live in Hot Springs."

"I know. You live in Little Rock, and you're thirteen, and you're going to be in the ninth grade next year, and you ski very well, and you like music a whole lot, and--"

"Yeah, I guess you do remember."

"Now, you tell me what you remember."

Oh hell, I thought. What if I screw up?

"Well." Great, dumbass! "You're name is Rhonda--"

"Oh, that's a good start." At least she was laughing when she said it.

"Okay, and you're going to be in the eighth grade, uh, and you live in Kansas City, uh, and your dad is good friends with my cousin, and, uh, uh . . ." Hell, here goes, I thought, "and I sure had a lot of fun this weekend." I hoped that last one would get her.

"I did too. What are you doing now?"

"I just finished eating dinner and wanted to see--"

"I don't mean right this minute, silly, I mean now that you're back in Little Rock. Are you in summer school or taking lessons or anything like that? Have you been going to the pool?"

"Oh. Yeah, I usually go to the pool every day and practice diving and race with my friends." Was she expecting me to say more. Panic again! She must have realized I was done.

"I usually go to the lake with my parents on the weekends and take a few of my friends along. We ski and go to the movies and go to the skating rink they have there at the lake. They have those paddle boats and a big water slide . . ." She told me everything I'd ever want to know about the lake, and I wished that someone would teach me how to talk with girls.

The conversation went on like that for about twenty minutes. She would ask a question, I would give the shortened answer, and then she would start again with a short story of what she and her friends were doing, and I would sweat wondering what the next question would be. What I wanted to do more than anything was tell her how much I liked her, that I wanted to marry her and live my life with her forever, the same way we had spent the weekend together at my cousin's cabin. Of course, then she might say "no," and I would have to kill myself.

Then came the words that always seemed to come when I started getting up my nerve to talk. "My dad needs to use the phone now, so I have to go."

"Oh. Okay." Now I was kicking myself that I hadn't talked more.

"I'm really glad you called. Maybe we can talk again soon."

She sounded like she meant it, and I asked her when I could call again. She told me to call anytime I wanted, and if she was there we could talk. I waited for a few days and called, but she wasn't in. Then I called several days later, and we talked for a few minutes, but she was going to a movie and had to go. We hadn't talked now for several weeks, but I had written her and asked for a picture and had been checking the mail every day to see if she had sent one, but nothing yet.

Lying on my bed now I wished that I had that picture of her. Better yet, I wished that she was sitting beside me the way she had in the boat while we were skiing. The water had been fairly cold while I was on the skis, and when I got in the boat after my turn, the seat next to Rhonda was empty, so I sat next to her. Her body was so warm and had immediately warmed up that side of my body, and I felt a tingle in my dick sitting that close to her.

Now, she was hundreds of miles away, it seemed more like across the universe, and I probably would never see her again, and I felt lonelier than I had ever felt before I met her. Maybe they would come to the lake again next year, and I could go there and see her. I would make a point of keeping in touch with her in case they decided to come again the next year. Next year seemed like a universe away too, and she might find a boyfriend by that time, and then I would be sunk. I tried to not think about that and concentrated on the radio.

The Miracles were singing "You've Really Got a Hold on Me," and I knew that would only make me think more about Rhonda, so I felt for the tuning knob and started searching for another station. "You're the reason I'm living," sang Bobby Darin on the next channel, and The Beach Boys were singing "Surfer Girl" on the next channel, so I turned the radio off and tried to think of something else.

As usual, when I tried to get myself to go to sleep, my mind raced with all kinds of split second images complete with the music of all the songs that I liked at that time. Cars, Rhonda in her swimsuit, bacteria in slides, spaceships, Rhonda, the robot Gort, boobs, drum sets with me sitting behind them, Rhonda, motorcycles, riding my bicycle in the woods, Rhonda, tanks, all the stuff I did during the day was in my thoughts. I would have to do something to get myself to sleep.

I slipped out of bed and went to the closet, got my flashlight and the copy of "Spiderman" I'd been saving for just such an occasion as this, went back to bed, slipped under the covers, and began reading Peter Parker's newest adventure. In order for this to work I would have to be on my stomach with the flashlight shining from the side onto the comic book. That way, when I got tired, I would just put my head down on the bed and fall right to sleep. Within a few minutes my eyes would begin to burn, and I would have to shut them for several seconds to wet them, and then I could open them again to continue reading.

After a while, I laid my head down on the pillow and fell sound asleep, the flashlight still shining on the page. I'd have to get Mom to get more batteries, and of course she would ask me the same old question.

"What do you do, eat those things?"

****

The next morning, I awoke with the sun shining brightly, kids playing in the street below my window, the attic fan going, and an empty house. During the summertime, I slept until anywhere from ten to twelve in the morning, unless Mom needed me to go somewhere with her, or I had somewhere to go before that. Today I had nothing planned and would just get on my bike and ride around the neighborhood and see what was going on. First, though, I was starved.

The kitchen was on the middle level of the house, with a counter and four barstools, a telephone and intercom, and, of course, the refrigerator my parents kept filled with enough food for me and my brothers. Breakfast, when I fixed it myself, was Sugar Pops or Frosted Flakes with banana. It was only ten o'clock, so Sugar Pops it would be. As I got the bowl from the cupboard, I could see my Mom in the backyard hanging clothes on the clothesline, even though she had a clothes dryer in the garage.

"They smell so much better when they're hung on the line to dry," she would say. I knew I'd better get going quickly, or she might think of something for me to do.

I scarfed down the bowl of cereal, went back upstairs and got the rest of my clothes on, jumped back down the two flights of steps to the garage, grabbed my bike and took off down the street. My Mom with her mother eyesight saw me leaving.

"Where are you going?" She yelled as I rode by on the street. One thing Mom never had any problem with was being heard when she wanted to be.

"I'm gonna go and see what Darryl and Billy are doing." I yelled back to her and kept going down the street.

"You be careful!" She yelled back.

Darryl and Billy lived right next to us, but I could tell they weren't home because their bikes were not in their carports, so I kept going up the street to the baseball field we had all made out of the field on the other side of the houses. When we had first moved here, we only had enough guys in the neighborhood to put about four on each team, including me, Darryl, Billy, Larry, Ronnie, Steve, and Philip. Now, the houses were growing up around us like weeds, and we had enough guys to make two teams that filled each position on the field. A lot of times we would play the guys from the down the street on Wood's street.

No one was at the field, so I kept going up the dirt road after the pavement stopped, to the pond, which was our next favorite place to hang out. Here we would go swimming, sometimes, if the water wasn't too muddy and we'd had enough rain, we'd make rafts and have raft fights, or we'd just bat rocks across into the mud on the other side. That was where I found Darryl and Billy, batting rocks. They saw me coming up the road.

"It's about time you got up." Darryl grinned as he hollered at me. They always teased me about sleeping late, because they got up every day at sunrise, but they would go to bed by ten o'clock every night too.

"I was working on my Vette last night and got to bed late. It's turning out so cool." I picked up a good size stick and starting batting along with them.

"I heard your brother and some of his friends got caught sneaking into the pool and can't go down there for the rest of the summer." Billy grinned like he got a big kick out of that.

"Yeah, my parents were real pissed off about that, my Dad especially, since it was him and Harold."

Harold Jr. was the youngest son of my Dad's dead partner, and also lived in the neighborhood. He and my brother and some of their friends who were all seniors were always doing stuff to get in trouble, and they didn't care one bit, because they all worked for the construction company my Dad's partner had owned, which was now owned by the oldest son, and they knew they wouldn't get in much trouble. If they didn't go swimming at our pool, they could always go to the swimming lake in Lakewood or to someone else's pool or to one of the many lakes around town.

"What are you guys going to do today?" I was having trouble hitting the rocks that early.

"We were thinking about going to the river and climb the cliffs." That was one of Darryl's favorite things to do.

"I'm getting hungry too." Billy could eat three sandwiches easy, like me. "I'm gonna go home first and get something to eat."

"Why don't we just get it and take it with us. It'll take us about an hour to get there, and I need to be home by four when my dad gets home." Darryl's dad was very strict and wanted him to be there when he got home from work to help around the house. Both his parents worked though, so the day was his time to hang out and have fun, after he had done all the stuff his parents made him do.

"Okay, let's all go get something to take with us and meet at your house." Billy was ready to go.

I wasn't very hungry yet, but I knew I would be soon, especially after the hour ride to get to the cliffs.

We jumped on our bicycles and raced down the dirt road, dodging the potholes and rocks and flying through the air each time we came to a dip in the road. We made it to the concrete pavement and raced even faster down the street to our houses, each of us laying rubber in the driveway when we slammed on our brakes.

I jumped off my bike and ran into the house to make my bologna and ketchup sandwiches. My Mom's car was home, but she was nowhere to be seen, so I slapped the sandwiches together as quickly as I could to avoid having to explain my coming mission to her. She didn't normally question me about where I was going, but she didn't much like it when I traveled very far from our neighborhood, when she knew I was doing it. Sometimes these missions of ours would take us all the way back to Little Rock, a good twenty miles away through busy streets and across the Arkansas River bridges, and, had she known about them, she would probably not have let me go that far on my bike alone. This time we would be going to the North Little Rock side of the river, still a good fifteen miles away, but we'd be riding through less crowded streets and would end on the dirt road that followed the cliffs along the river's edge.

I saw Darryl and Billy riding up the street to the house, so I stuffed my sandwiches, apple, chips, and bottle of coke into a bag and headed down the steps to the garage, jumped on my Apache, and met the guys in the street.

Darryl and Billy were already eating their first sandwich, so I stopped and stood there with them while they finished and ate some of my apple. We finished and stuffed our lunches in the carriers on our AMF's, and started down the road.

Whenever we rode through town we tried to take back streets as much as possible, and we rode single file to try to keep from getting side-swiped by the cars travelling on the two-lane streets. Most of the streets in the areas outside of the housing areas had no curbs and no sidewalks, so if you rode off the street you were in a drainage ditch, and some of the ditches could be pretty deep with mud and rocks at the bottom.

Darryl always led the way, since he was the oldest and the biggest of the three of us. He would be in tenth grade next year, and Billy and I were going into the ninth grade. When Billy went with us, he usually rode next, and I would follow in the rear. We moved fast and were extra careful along the streets, keeping the mission in mind. We knew the route perfectly and didn't need to stop and rest, so we just kept moving and talked as little as possible, if at all.

The closer we got to the river, the more we needed to travel on the busier streets of town. The main street on the west side of town followed along beside the Missouri Pacific railroad yards, several miles from beginning to end. Every time I rode my bike by there or went by in the car, I thought about the trip my Mom and my brothers and I had made to California to visit my grandmother when I was nine.

We had taken this train called the *Super Chief* from Little Rock to San Diego, and I had loved every minute of the ride. It was so different going through the desert and through the mountains, and I liked it more and more the farther we travelled that way. The only thing I didn't like about the trip, besides having to leave the beaches in California, was that I had lost my false teeth one day at the beach after being hit by a huge wave that knocked the wind and my teeth out of me. I didn't even know that it had happened until I got up and started walking back to shore and felt with my tongue that the bridge was not there. I panicked, jumped back into the water to try to find the teeth, but we never found them. My mother asked the lifeguards to please keep a look out for them, and we did get a call one day about some teeth that had been found in a shark's gut, but it was a full bridge from an adult, and I came back to Little Rock with no front teeth. I always wondered if that shark had eaten the person.

That was the second plate that my parents had had to buy for me since being tripped in third grade by Leon Riley and cracking my two new permanent front teeth on the corner of one of the classroom desks. Instead of fixing my front teeth, the butcher dentist had talked my parents into pulling what was left of the teeth and putting in a partial plate to fill the space. So there I was, a little third grade boy who now had to worry about losing his teeth or about them being broken any time he played baseball or football or did anything outside.

The first plate lasted about eight months before getting flushed down the toilet after I puked the night before starting fourth grade. My parents were so upset with me losing the second plate, that they refused to buy me another, and I spent the entire fifth grade with no front teeth. So, I spent fifth grade learning how to smile without opening my mouth and talked very little with my classmates, not because they made fun of me, but because I was so embarrassed of the space that was left by the missing teeth.

A year later, my parents finally felt sorry for me, I guess, and took me to the dentist to get another plate, but by that time, the space had closed so much that where I had once had two normal teeth, the dentist could now only fit one huge tooth or two small teeth. I didn't want to look like a beaver, so I told my parents I'd rather have the two small teeth. They looked a little odd, but I was just happy to have something there, and, anyway, I had already learned how to smile and talk with no front teeth. I guarded those teeth like they were gold from then on.

We passed the railroad yards and were again travelling on side streets until we came out on the river road. We were able to stop for a moment and relax, pulled our lunch sacks from the carriers on our bikes and sat in the grass on the side of the dirt road to enjoy our sandwiches and bottles of coke.

"Damn it's hot." Darryl would sweat in the winter time in the snow.

"Hey, what do you guys think about going up to Fort Roots and seeing what we can find in the buildings." Billy wasn't in any hurry to get back to his empty house.

Usually, when we came to climb the cliffs, we would just climb up and then come back down, but if we went further down the road, we could climb up and get into the old part of Fort Roots, and, hopefully, not get caught by the guards.

"I can't. I've got to get back home. You guys can though, and I'll just leave when I need to." I wasn't about to let Darryl go back alone.

"No. We either all go, or we all don't. Nobody's going home alone." Billy shook his head yes.

With that settled, we finished our lunches and got back on our bikes and headed down the tree-lined dirt road. The breeze felt good riding along the road next to the river. We could see the cliffs about half a mile down the road in front of us. If we'd had time, we probably would have gone to the banks of the river and hit rocks. We didn't dare swim in the swift currents of the river, and the junk on the banks made the water kind of nasty anyway.

The cliffs rose to around a hundred feet above the dirt road reaching straight up toward the sky, with a stretch of wild grass and weeds about thirty feet wide along the road in front of them. They were completely rock, with plenty of crags and notches for us to use as footholds for climbing. We didn't use ropes or any kind of gear, just our sneakers and blue jeans to keep from scraping our legs up if we fell. No one ever fell.

We parked our bikes off the road where they would be hidden in case anyone came by while we were up on the cliff and then waded through the wild grass to the bottom of the cliff.

"Who's goin' first." I knew Billy wanted to go first.

"I went first last time. Why don't you go first, Darryl?" I knew Billy wouldn't complain about Darryl going first.

"Okay. I'm gonna go up the crack and then across at that ledge up there," he said, pointing to a ledge about fifty feet up to the left of the crack that ran from the bottom to the top of the cliff. "Then I'm gonna go straight up the rest of the way from there."

The climb he chose was fairly dangerous, especially after we got to the ledge, but that was one of the reasons I wanted Darryl to go first. He always chose the most dangerous climbs, even if he didn't mean to choose it because it was dangerous. None of us thought about anything being dangerous to us or for us. The fact that we could have fallen from the cliff onto the dirt and rocks below and broken our necks never even crossed our minds while we were climbing, not even the first time we had come upon the cliffs and had immediately dumped our bikes on the side of the road and had raced each other to climb to the top. I had been climbing trees and cliffs like this, maybe not as high as these, since I was a boy in the country climbing the pine trees that surrounded our house and the bauxite hills all around our property. One of my favorite spots to get away from everything, mainly from my brothers chasing me, was to climb in the top of the pine tree next to our house.

I had built a small tree house there, which was actually only a few boards nailed across two tree limbs, and I'd sit there and enjoy the only open view I could get of the surrounding countryside, the rolling hillsides filled with pine trees, the field in front of our house with the few horses who were always grazing, and the bauxite hills behind our property. I couldn't see any of this from the yard or house because of the woods that surrounded the house and the woods across the highway in front of our house.

The only other place where you could see for more than about seventy-five yards was on "Skull Mountain," a bauxite hill that looked like it had risen out of the ground in the middle of the bauxite pit behind our property. I'd climbed it several times, always ending up with skinned legs and arms from sliding on the loose bauxite, before it was finally leveled by the mining company.

Darryl and Billy had made it to the ledge and sat there resting while I climbed the few feet needed to step onto the ledge and squeeze next to them to rest for a minute before we finished the climb. Sitting there, looking out over the river and across to Little Rock on the other side I felt like I was in my tree house again enjoying the countryside, except now, the view seemed to go on forever and included the Arkansas River and the hills on the other side of the river. This was nothing like seeing the Pacific Ocean, though, and I thought back to being on the beach again, this time with my teeth still in place.

After a few minutes, Darryl got up, followed by Billy, and then me, and started the climb up the rest of the cliff. The rest of the climb would be a little more difficult, since the rock wall went straight up with no cracks like we had had on the first part of the climb. But the wall had plenty of footholds and handholds to let us climb pretty easily to the top.

When we reached the top we just sat and looked out over the same view we had seen from the ledge, but now completely clear of the trees along the road.

"What are you guys doing this weekend?" I didn't have any plans yet.

"I think we're going to the lake this weekend." Darryl and his dad went fishing a lot on the weekends during the summer.

"I don't know what we're doing yet." Billy's mom and dad were divorced, and he didn't always know when he would be going to his dad's for the weekend.

"I just thought you guys might wanna go up to Five Mile Creek and camp out one night."

"Maybe next weekend." Darryl got up. "Better get going." Billy and I followed. We couldn't go back down the way we came up, so we walked along the cliff edge and down the hill to the road and then back down the road to our bikes.

An hour later, I pulled into my driveway and waved to the guys.

"See you later."

They both waved and rode their bikes to their own houses.

I opened the garage door and put my bike in the garage and checked the door to the house. Open, as usual; no need to lock the doors around our neighborhood. Everyone knew each other and knew what was going on at everyone else's house, and everybody had pretty much the same stuff, so nobody much worried about break-ins.

I went up to the kitchen and got a coke out of the refrigerator. I couldn't hear anyone.

"Anybody home?" No answer. Good opportunity to visit the bathroom and get out my "Playboy."

I climbed the steps, entered the bathroom, locked the door, put my coke on the counter, and sat on the toilet and pulled the Playboy out from underneath the clothes hamper and began thumbing through it. I skipped the first few sections and went to the back of the magazine which I hadn't looked at yet. Lots of boobs to look at here. Why didn't I ever see girls like this around? Then I came across a picture of a girl that looked just like the older sister of my friend Petey Peterson.

Petey was my age, but was in the fifth grade when I was in the sixth because I had started school early, and he had been my first real, best friend when we moved to North Little Rock. He lived right across the street, and his dad and my Dad were good friends. He had an older brother and two older sisters, who we used to watch getting dressed, and his mom was pretty too. His real name was Ralph Peterson, but he hated the name Ralph, and most everybody called him Petey anyway.

Petey stayed in trouble most of the time for playing jokes on people, usually his sisters, and, being best friends, I usually got pulled into the trouble. Watching his sisters get dressed got us in trouble a bunch, but we also had tried smoking cigarettes, drinking beer with his older brother, and sneaking out his dad's Playboy magazines. It wasn't anything that bad, but it was enough to get our parents mad at us. He also had a motor bike which we would ride around all over the place. My Mom hated when I rode on that thing, but I loved riding up and down the streets on it. He loved science fiction movies as much as I did, so we went to the movies a lot whenever new sci-fi movies came out, and he'd go with us a lot when we went to the drive-in movies.

His brother would do this thing with us where he would grab us around the chest and squeeze and hold us up. Then he would let us go, and we'd try to stand up, but we'd get this rush that would make us dizzy, and we'd usually fall to the floor. When my Mom found out about it, she got so pissed and said I couldn't go over to Petey's anymore if just his brother was there.

Petey moved away after the sixth grade and now lived in another subdivision that my Dad and his partner had started. We didn't get to see each other very much anymore, because he had gotten a lot wilder in junior high, and he was even in more trouble, a lot. I had spent the night with him a bunch of times after he first moved, but his parents had stopped letting him do much after he began getting wilder, and now I hadn't seen him or heard from him in over six months. I missed him a lot too. Thinking about Petey had gotten my mind off of beating off, and so I put the Playboy back under the hamper, got my coke, and went downstairs to see what was on television. The Three Stooges were on, so I settled into the bean bag, the only chair I figured wouldn't be covered with my brother's disgusting remains, and watched the show, drank my coke, and knew that the rest of my summer would be pretty much the same as this until the coming fall when I would start ninth grade.

'64

****

Except for finally having my first true science class, General Science, ninth grade had been fairly uneventful. One major highlight had been going to the state band competitions in Hot Springs, where I had won my first medal for band and where I had made out with one of the flute players, Lynn, and had rubbed her boobs through her shirt on the bus going down there and coming back.

Mr. Haslett had taken me off alto sax and had put me on baritone sax, which was much easier for me to play and was less of a problem for me because I was the only baritone sax player in the band. The year had been one of the best I'd ever had in band, especially because playing the baritone sax meant that I didn't have to move my fingers as quickly, and I had made marching band and got to go on all the trips and played at the football and basketball games.

I made two new friends who were also sax players, Dennis and Terry, and we played in the sax quartet that won the first-place medal at state. They were both excellent sax players, Dennis on alto and Terry on tenor, and the only reason I was playing with them was because I could easily play the bass notes to their lead parts. The weird part of it was that I was only five feet five inches tall and weighed one hundred and twenty pounds and was carrying around a four foot, thirty pound baritone sax. The only way I could play it was to put it on the floor directly in front of me during band rehearsal with the mouthpiece perfectly in line with my mouth. I was still a drummer at heart, though, and would still go back to the drum section any time I got the chance to play the snares or would borrow Mark's old drums to bang around on.

One of my most fun classes had been Film Crew. Ninth grade boys were allowed to sign up for Film Crew and during that class time would take movie projectors to rooms and show films for the teachers. When we weren't showing films, we'd repair the films and take care of the equipment. It was lots of fun, and I got to see all the films that were shown in all the classes. For a movie nut, that was great.

The teacher who was in charge of the Film Crew was also my Algebra teacher. Algebra was not a fun class for me. I knew I needed it if I wanted to be a Microbiologist, but it was hard for me, because the x's and y's didn't make any sense, and it didn't make sense to try to figure out what a number was when the other numbers weren't there to help you figure it out. My brothers had been good at math and would be using it a lot as an engineer and an accountant, but they weren't around to help me, if they even would have, and my parents never bothered that much about whether I had my homework done or not, and they hardly ever asked me if I needed help or offered to help. They were too concerned about my Dad's company.

Dad's new partner, the son of his dead partner, had gotten pretty wild after his father died and had bought a new T-Bird and the cabin on the lake with new boats and equipment and was always having parties at his house, which I loved to go to because he had the best bands around playing at them, and I could watch the drummers play and hear them and sneak drinks at the bar, and I would hear my parents talk about him and his girlfriend and how he was spending so much money on her. I would also overhear my parents talk about how they were worried that something might happen to the construction company and that that would mess up my Dad's real estate company.

Algebra had given me my worst grades on my report card, C's and D's, but I had done pretty well in Science and English, and I had liked my English teacher a lot. She was young and pretty, and she taught us grammar and poetry. I made B's in English, because I didn't do my homework very much, but I did well on the tests and class assignments, and I put together a poetry notebook that the teacher had liked a lot.

I had been looking forward to summer the whole year, because Rhonda's family had planned to come down again for the fourth of July. We had talked several times, once at the beginning of school, once when President Kennedy was shot, and then more recently when she had told me that her mother planned to come early and that she might come with her. Her dad would come later in the week, because he had to work at his business.

I had daydreamed a lot about how the meeting with Rhonda would be, and every time the song "We'll Sing in the Sunshine" came on the radio, I would immediately see Rhonda. Chad and Jeremy's song "A Summer Song" did the same thing to me whenever I heard it, and I would put those 45's on our stereo in the living room and lie in front of the speakers in the dark, while everyone was downstairs watching television or up in bed, and would listen to them over and over and dream about being with Rhonda, feeling her warm leg next to mine, holding her close to me, feeling her boobs push into my chest. The year had definitely been very long and very difficult just having the memories of the one weekend with Rhonda and the few letters she had written to get me through. One way or another, I would get myself down to Hot Springs when she was going to be there, and all the better that we would be there for a few days before everyone else got to the cabin.

When school was out, I began working on my mother.

"Why don't we go to Hot Springs for fourth of July this year?" I put the bug in her ear one day.

"We thought we might go camping at Bull Shoals instead this year. Daddy was just in Hot Springs fishing in the spring for vacation. We don't even know if they'll have room."

"You know they always let us come down if we wanna go. There's always room either at the cabin or in town."

"Why go to the lake if you're going to sleep in town?" She thought about that for a minute. "Who's going to be there that you want to see? Is it Rusty and, what's his daughter's name, Rhonda?"

"She said they might be going. I just like it there better than camping sometimes, especially on the fourth. It's not as crowded as it is camping at the lakes."

"I'll see what your father thinks." She gave me that look of knowing that something was up but didn't want to get into it for the time being.

"Okay."

I didn't think I'd better say anything just yet about going up early. That would be pushing things a little. At least she was now thinking about it, and I could just ask her in a day or two what Dad had said. If Dad thought it was okay, then I would see if Mom wanted to go early and maybe do some bowling with Mary Ann, Will's wife who bowled on a traveling league sometimes with Mom. They and Rhonda's mom could do some women's stuff, and Rhonda and my cousins and I could go to the movies or to the bowling alley with them or just stay at the house or the cabin and listen to music and walk around and stuff. At least, that's the way I would tell it to Mom. She always used to walk around the house calling herself a "Dumb Polack", but she was actually pretty sharp, and she would understand what I truly wanted but would let me think that I was getting something out of her.

She was usually pretty easy with me anyway but still pretty protective. She would always tell the story of my birth.

"When you were born, you weighed five pounds and four ounces; but then you got sick, you had diarrhea and wouldn't hold anything in your stomach, and you lost so much weight, you were only about three pounds, and you looked so pitiful lying there in your crib in the hospital."

By this time she was usually squeezing me to death with one of her mother hugs, but she would go on with the story.

"And we thought we were going to lose you. And then, Dr. Miller brought in this specialist who was the only one who could feed you by putting a tube into the vein in your head. And you started gaining weight and got better, and we were finally able to bring you home. But we were so afraid there for a while that you weren't going to make it." She would still be squeezing me, if I hadn't managed to break free from the mother squeeze grip by that time. Then she would end the story. "And always remember what Dr. Miller said about being short: It doesn't matter how tall you are, what matters is what you do." Of course, Dr. Miller was short too, but I was so short when I was a little kid, five to be exact, that I had to be lifted up onto the first step of the school bus to go to school the first year.

That was another of the stories my mother would tell, seeing me off that first day of school and having to lift me up onto the step. That called for another mother hug when that story was retold. No one ever retold the story about my teeth getting knocked out though, and I never got a mother hug for that. And no one ever retold the stories about me falling on a broken coke bottle in the back yard and having the bottom of it stick in my stomach, leaving a two-inch long scar, or about when I jumped off my best friend Jesse's outhouse and caught my palm on the nail latch and almost ripped my thumb off.

Those stories had nothing on the tales of my brothers in championship baseball and football games and playing first chair clarinet in the high school marching band and graduating from high school to become an engineer or an accountant. My dream of being a Microbiologist never was discussed or mentioned in any stories or at family gatherings, but everyone knew that I had almost died as a little baby and that Dr. Miller had saved my life and had always told me not to worry about being short.

A couple of days passed before my Mom got back to me about the fourth.

"Honey, your father said that it would be okay to go to Hot Springs on the fourth, but he'll have to work until Friday. It's just too busy for him right now. He may not even be able to leave until Saturday morning."

My Dad worked all the time, but I guess that came from growing up during the Depression and having to support his mom and brothers after he kicked his father out of the house for hitting his mom. He was sixteen and had to quit high school and go to work, and he and his brothers had paper routes with the Arkansas Gazette that helped to bring in money too. I think that's when they started playing sax in bands at night too to make extra money. He and my uncle started working for an abstract company, and that's how he got started in the real estate business, but he still played music too. Then he got married, not to my Mom though, yet. I didn't even know that until last year when his ex-wife came over to the house.

It was weird to meet her. She was pretty and kind of short, like Dad, not like my Mom who was a little taller than Dad. She only stayed for a little while, and Dad never said anything else about being married to her after she left. He did tell us that she didn't want to have kids and he did, and he divorced her when he left for the navy during World War II, and then met Mom.

My Mom was working for the navy too when he met her, and she did want to have kids, and now they both got what they wanted, four boys who could eat a house in one sitting. I kind of got the feeling that my Mom wanted a girl too though, because when I was in grade school she was always getting girls that I liked in my classes to come and spend the night. She especially liked my first real girlfriend, Judy, in the third grade, and had had her over a lot to spend the night. That was kind of weird too, that these girls were coming over to spend the night with us, but Mom would treat them like little princesses, and they would eat it up.

Mom had come from a screwed-up home too. Her mother, my Grandma we went to see in California, was a good-looking woman and had had three or four husbands and lots of boyfriends and worked in the theatres on Broadway, and so my Mom basically grew up with her aunts and uncles and her grandmother in Pennsylvania.

During the Depression she had had to work as a maid to help her family, but she did finish high school and then moved to New York when the war started. Mom would get out the pictures every so often and show me Grandma, my aunt, and her when they lived in New York, and pictures of her family when she was a young girl, and when she and Dad were in New York. She still had relatives in New York, her aunts and uncles and cousins from Grandma's family, and she said we might go to visit them that summer. I'd never met them before, so I thought that would be fun.

When Mom told me that we could go to Hot Springs for the fourth, I figured I'd better start Operation Rhonda.

"Hey, Mom, how long has it been since you and Mary Ann went bowling?" Bowling was always a good topic to bring up with Mom.

"Our travelling league was finished in April. It's been since then. Why?"

"Oh, I just thought you might wanna go down and see Mary Ann and go bowling or something."

"We'll be going down for fourth of July weekend."

"But we'll be at the lake, and you won't be able to go bowling or do anything except sit around the cabin and cook and clean up."

"We don't just sit around and cook and clean up. We play poker, we visit, Daddy and Will and the guys go fishing--"

"While you're sitting around cleaning up and cooking--"

"And we go out on the pontoon boat and go skiing." She stopped and gave me the look. "What is it? What are you trying to get me to do?"

"Well, I just thought maybe we could go down a little early that week, and I could do some stuff with Keith, cause I don't get to see him very often--"

"You just spent the weekend with him a couple of months ago when you went on that band trip."

"But that was a couple of months ago."

"I have a summer league starting in a couple of weeks on Tuesday nights, so I couldn't go down until Wednesday. When is Rhonda going to be there?" She knew what I was doing.

"She and her mom are going down on Monday, and then her dad and little brother are coming on Friday."

"Okay, we'll see. It might be fun to visit with the girls for a day or two before we go out to the cabin for the weekend. I'll see what your father thinks about it."

I already knew what Dad would say. "Honey, if you want to go down early, that's okay. I'm going to be working anyway, the boys will be gone, and you can take the kids with you. I'll come down on Friday so I can do some fishing Saturday morning." Dad pretty much let Mom run things around there.

Operation Rhonda was in full swing, and, for the next few weeks, I counted down the days until the fourth. I went to the movies a few times and saw the new James Bond movie, *From Russia, With Love*, and liked it even better than *Dr. No*, which I had gone to see last year when it came out. I had started reading the James Bond books after that and liked them a lot, so seeing them as movies was great. I didn't even care that the movies weren't just like the novels, because Sean Connery was James Bond to me.

I had also gotten a chance to play drums for the first time in a group one Saturday. Well, almost a group. It was just a few of us guys, Darryl, Larry, Ronnie, and me, dressed up as The Beatles and playing along with Beatle records. Ronnie was Paul, and he even looked like him, and Darryl was George, and Larry was John, and, of course, I was Ringo.

We had gone to Woolworth's and picked up some Beatle wigs and dressed in suits with our collars turned under, and I borrowed some drums from one of my friends in the band, and we set up in Darryl's family room and all the kids in the neighborhood came over to watch us and listen to us. I was the only one playing any at all, and the others were just hitting the strings and didn't have amps or real microphones to use. Ronnie was singing, though, and was pretty good. It was a lot of fun, and it made me even more determined to get some drums and play in a band.

The kids thought it was great, and one of the girls, Cathy, who was a friend of Debbie McIntyre's who was visiting her, was coming up and talking to me each time we stopped playing. She asked me to call her before she went back home, and I got her phone number and planned to call her after the fourth, which was coming up the next weekend.

All I could think of at all, though, was seeing Rhonda, but every time I thought about her, I couldn't help but feel jittery. As much as I liked girls and wanted to talk with them and be with them, I had a hard time starting a conversation with them. If they came up to me and talked, I was okay, and could usually keep things going with them for a while. But, I always had a difficult time making the first move with one that I thought was cute or that I wanted to meet, and that happened much more often than one coming up and talking to me first. And, of course, it was always the cute ones that I wanted to talk with or meet, like Rhonda.

I had only talked with Rhonda a few times since last summer, and we hadn't gotten much further than just small talk, so I didn't want to get my hopes up too much or let my daydreaming about her make me think that she was going to be madly in love with me or something. She seemed glad that we would be seeing each other again, so I felt I had a pretty good chance with her. Maybe, I would even have a chance to be alone with her and get to kiss her. That would be great! Our first kiss, maybe on the dock, with the moon shining on the water, so I could see her face in the moonlight and see how pretty she was. I wondered if she had changed much since we last saw each other. If she was any prettier I wouldn't be able to stand it.

Throughout the rest of the week I tried to keep occupied with anything I could so I wouldn't go nuts thinking about the fourth. One night I sat in my parents' bedroom, in the dark, while they were gone bowling, I thought, or it might have been somewhere else, and talked on the party line. The party line was pretty cool. It was this number that you called, and you would be able to hear all these people talking at the same time, and you would have to be loud enough to be heard, and maybe someone would hear you and answer you. People would talk about meeting somewhere or about sex or about school or music or just about anything you could think of. I usually just listened to see what people were talking about or try to catch some girl's number so I could call her. It was easy to get the numbers, and then all you had to do was tell the girl that you were the guy she was talking to on the party line. I had tried it a couple of times, but I didn't know what to say after we got past the first few questions.

"Hi. Where do you go to school?" That was the way I'd usually start.

"I go to Sylvan Hills Junior High. Where do you go?"

"I'll be going to North Little Rock High next year."

"Oh, yeah. What grade are you going to be in?

"I'll be in tenth grade. What about you?"

"I'll be in ninth grade."

"What kind of music do you like?"

"I like the Beatles a lot, but I like American groups too, like the Four Seasons and the Supremes and the Beach Boys. Who do you like?"

"I like all those groups too. And I like Manfred Mann and the Dave Clark Five and Chad and Jeremy and the Four Tops. I like a lot of different music. I wanna play drums and get in a band."

"Oh, yeah. Do you play drums?"

"I don't have any yet, but I wanna get some."

From here the conversation would usually start going down hill. My parents always told me not to brag about myself or talk a lot about myself, and so I wouldn't say much more than that about me. Then, I wouldn't be able to think of anything else that I thought a girl would want to talk about, so I would just sit there, waiting for her to say something.

Then she would finally say, "Well I have to go now. Maybe we can talk again some time."

"Okay. Bye."
"Bye."
And that would be that.

****

Wednesday finally came, and we packed the car to go to Hot Springs. Mom always packed everything she thought she would need, plus everything she thought she might need, and then she would pack the things that she would never need but just wanted to have with her. She packed some clothes for me and my little brother, so all I had to do was take the swim fins and goggles and books and comic books and things I wanted to do when I didn't have anything else to do around the cabin or at my cousin's house.

I would definitely have my AM radio with me too, especially for when I went to bed at night. I would listen to it in bed every night to help me get to sleep, since I didn't have my models or other stuff to do there at night. Sometimes I would go down to the dock and fish until I got tired or go walking down the country road that led to the cabin, or, if we were in town, I would walk around the streets with or without my cousins, who weren't quite as much night owls as me.

I loved the ride down to Hot Springs. Once you got a little ways out of Little Rock, you were driving through forests of pine trees on rolling hills, and, during the summer months, you could smell the different flowers and weeds and plants and the heat, and the cool breeze through the open windows felt great. We would drive along for mile after mile like that until we got close to town.

The closer we got, the more I wanted to just turn around and go back home to my room and work on my model or read my comic books or go out into the woods. My stomach was in knots, and I could feel my pulse beating in my temples. What would I say to her? Would I make a fool out of myself? Would she be happy to see me? Would I have a chance, and have the nerve, to tell her how I felt about her? All of this went through my mind as we pulled into my cousin's driveway. The only car in the driveway had an Arkansas license plate, which made me wonder if Rhonda was there yet.

Mom parked the car, and we got out and went to the front door. Before we could ring the doorbell, Mary Ann was opening the door to greet us.

"Hi, Annie." She was a hugger like Mom.

"Hi, Mary." Hugs all around.

"Hi, Mary Ann." My turn to be hugged. "Is Keith here?"

"No, he's not here right now. He's with Pam in North Little Rock at mom and dad's. They're coming down tomorrow after Pam gets off work. Come on in."

"Are we going to stay here tonight or go on out to the cabin?" Mom didn't want to empty the car if we were going to the cabin.

"It might be easier to just stay here tonight and then go out to the cabin in the morning. We're the only ones here tonight, so we'll have plenty of room."

Without asking I knew that Rhonda was not there yet and wouldn't be there tonight. Operation Rhonda was already starting to fall apart.

"Help me get some stuff out of the car then, Peter." I followed Mom out.

We got one of the suitcases and Mom's overnight case and took them into the house. Mary Ann was in the kitchen. I liked their house a lot, because it was two story and had a big game room and patio downstairs from the main living area which had the kitchen, living room, and several bedrooms. Whenever I spent the night, my cousin and I would sleep on the sofa bed in the game room and would stay up as late as we wanted playing pool, watching television, and listening to the radio or records.

"Make yourselves at home." Mary Ann was already in the kitchen. "You can have Pam's room tonight, Annie. Will's out at the cabin this week. Connor can take Keith's room, and you can sleep downstairs, hon."

That was what I was hoping she would say. My cousin's bedroom upstairs wasn't very big, and I enjoyed being downstairs away from everyone else anyway.

"I thought Rusty and Barbara were coming down this week." Mom knew I was hoping she would ask about them.

"Barbara and Rhonda will be down tomorrow some time. Rusty and Joey will be down probably Friday some time. They're going to stay until Tuesday or Wednesday."

I was already wondering how I might get to stay a few days longer, in case things went well with Rhonda. At least now I knew when she would be there.

That evening was fun. We went out to eat pizza and then went to the bowling alley. Mom and Mary Ann bowled, and I played the pin ball machines. I was a pretty good pinball player and usually could keep myself going all night on just a few quarters. I wanted to play pool, but only older guys were there playing, and they weren't about to give up their tables to a little runt like me.

I could always get money out of my Mom, so I got some money from her and went to the snack bar and got a chocolate shake and a hamburger. The pizza had been okay, but I was a hamburger nut and could eat a hamburger any time of the day or night, and would. And we didn't have them at home that often anyway, unless I cooked them myself for lunch.

My Mom usually fixed supper each night, chicken or meatloaf, or spaghetti, or something like that, or we had leftovers. Sunday night was the night she would fix roast and potatoes usually, and would bake a lemon meringue pie, my favorite, or a chocolate pie, my Dad's favorite. And she would always fix a lot. But she wouldn't waste any of it, and she wouldn't let us either. You ate everything on your plate before you got anything else. But one thing about growing up with older brothers was that you learned to eat everything on your plate, because you didn't know if you'd even have a chance to get seconds. My oldest brother, particularly, would normally eat three or four helpings of everything, so we would fight with him just to get seconds.

We got back to Mary Ann's house about ten thirty, and she and Mom sat at the breakfast bar, drinking beers and smoking cigarettes and talking, after Mom put my little brother to bed. I went downstairs and turned on the television to the "Tonight Show with Johnny Carson" and played pool. At midnight, the National Anthem started up and the channel went dead, so I turned on the radio. "You Really Got Me" was playing by a new group I liked a lot called The Kinks, from England.

Ever since The Beatles had become popular, the radio stations were playing a lot of music by English groups, and the music was a lot different from the music of the American groups. The drums always seemed to be a big part of the English music, where with the American music the drums seemed to be more in the background, except with Sandy Nelson. But even his drumming was less like rock and roll and more like Gene Krupa stuff. The British music was full of guitars too that sounded a lot different from the guitars in the bands like The Beach Boys or Jan and Dean or other California groups. The Dave Clark Five was another group I liked too, because the drummer was also the lead singer of the band, and I had never seen that before with a group.

I stayed up till about three that night, playing pool and listening to the radio, making a trip to the refrigerator upstairs to get a bologna and ketchup sandwich, and I visited the bathroom to beat off thinking about Rhonda, and Phyllis, and Lynn, and Debbie, and Cathy, who I was going to call when I got back. But, it was seeing Rhonda take off her bikini top and her hand grabbing my boner that helped me finish. I finally went to sleep, listening to the radio, dreaming about the next day and seeing Rhonda again.

****

I awoke about nine the next morning with my Mom yelling down the stairs at me to get up so we could go to the cabin. That was fine with me. I was ready to get out there and do some fishing and wait for Rhonda to get there.

We packed up the cars and headed out of town to the lake. The cabin was on Lake Hamilton, which was not that far away, but we had to travel down a lot of county two-lane roads which made the drive slower. The last part of the drive was a mostly dirt road that led to Mary Ann and Will's cabin, near the end of the road.

The cabin wasn't actually on the lake but was situated on a hill above an inlet that ran into the lake. The fishing was especially good there, because the fish, bass and crappie and bream mostly, would come up the inlet during the spring to lay their eggs and would stay in the area until summertime, when the baby fish would be growing and would be food for the larger fish.

Dad would always return from his annual Spring fishing vacation with an ice chest full of filleted bass, crappie, and bream, and we would have fresh fish for months. The lake itself was more of a skiing and swimming lake too, so the fishing wasn't as good on the lake with all the speed boats and party barges zooming around. But the location of Will's cabin made swimming and skiing and fishing very easy, especially with the party barge and ski boat and fishing boats he had at his dock.

Will was sitting on the screen porch, beer in hand, fishing hat pulled down over his face, when we pulled into the driveway. He must have been napping, because he didn't move until we opened the screen door and the spring pulled it closed with a loud bang.

"Hey! Hey!" Will yelled as he shot up out of the chair, dropping the beer on the concrete floor. "Look there, dang it, I just wasted a good beer." Will was very good-natured and a lot of fun. He loved to party, play pool, drink beer, play poker, gamble, and fish, so the weekend at the lake was always an adventure. During horse-racing season, in the early part of the year, Will worked at Oaklawn Race Track in town in one of the windows, taking people's bets on the races. He would also make trips to other cities to work their race seasons and would go to Las Vegas a lot to gamble and work. Needless to say, when Mom and Dad, Mary Ann and Will, and Rusty and Barbara got together, you could count on a lot of beer-drinking, poker-playing, and laughter and fun.

"Hey, Annie." He was a hugger too and hugged Mom. He reached out and shook my hand. "You ready for some fishin', bud?"

"Yeah, how are they biting?" I couldn't let him know I was more worried about when Rhonda was getting there.

"The small mouths have been runnin' in the morning. I've been gettin' some big ones in the late afternoon up a ways. The water's been cooler this year, so they're stayin' up there longer. Been gettin' some rock bass hittin' lures up there too. It's too dang hot down this way this time of day for anything more than what I was doin' just now, unless you kids wanna go skiing."

"Yeah, I'd like to go."

"I know Keith and Pam wanna go, and Rhonda will be here soon, and she'll wanna go. We can go out tomorrow after we drown a few worms in the mornin'."

I liked going with Will to "drown a few worms" when we came here. Dad was always so intent on his fishing that he wouldn't hardly even talk. He'd just sit there and mess with his fishing tackle and with his lines, or he'd want to go trolling for bass. Will would talk and tell stories and give me some of his beer sometimes. Mom and Dad would let me have a sip every once in a while too, and I would sometimes sneak beers out and drink them while I was walking around at night. It was easy as hell to get them at the lake, because they were all over the place, in the fridge, in the ice chests, in the boat coolers, almost everywhere you went.

"Come go with me, and we'll fill up the gas tanks." Will led me out the screen door and down the steps to the dock.

We loaded all the gas tanks on the party barge and headed out to the marina. The trip took about thirty minutes because the party barge didn't move very fast, and Will was never in any big hurry anyway. That was another thing I liked about him. I didn't care either, because I was enjoying the warm breeze and the sun beating on me. It would feel great to get into the water and do some skiing.

After the tanks were all filled, we headed back to the dock. I helped Will put the tanks back in the boats and followed him up the steps to the cabin. When we reached the top, I noticed two more cars in the driveway. My heart raced and a huge lump came up into my throat. One of the cars was my cousin Pam's Corvair. The other was a Cadillac, and I could only guess that it was Rhonda's mom's, because I couldn't see the license plate. Will answered the question for me.

"Looks like Barbara and Rhonda made it. Pam and Keith got here too."

This was the moment that I had waited for for a year now. I was going to see Rhonda again. I could feel the blood pumping in my veins, and I felt like I was going to pass out. Why did I always get like that around girls? It pissed me off so much that I felt that way, but I couldn't help it.

We walked up to the porch, and there they all were, sitting on the picnic table and lawn chairs, Pam and Keith, and Mary Ann, and Mom, and Barbara, and then I saw her. She was even prettier than I remembered her being. Her hair had grown out a little longer and was more blonde than strawberry blonde, and she was wearing a top and shorts which showed that her body had filled out since last year. "Hi's" and "hello's" were thrown all around, and I gave my cousin Pam a hug and said "hello" to Keith, and then I turned and walked over to Rhonda.

"Hi." I walked up and sat on the picnic table near her chair.

"Hi, how are you doing?" She was smiling and seemed happy to see me.

"Fine. How was your trip?"

"Tiring. We had to leave early this morning, and I didn't want to wake up. I tried to sleep a little in the car, but my mother kept waking me up to help her with the map. How long have you been here?"

"We came last night and stayed in town. Mom and Mary Ann went bowling, and I played the pinball machines. Have you been here long?"

"We just pulled up a few minutes ago. I still feel like I'm moving in the car."

Before I could say anything else, Rhonda's mom called to her. "Rhonda, come help me with the bags."

"Okay, Mom." She got up and went to the car to help her mom.

"Need any help?" She didn't know that I would do anything she asked. Anything.

"That's okay. We don't have that much. Thanks, though."

My eyes were glued to Rhonda as she walked to the car and stood there waiting for her mom to hand her something to carry. My cousin Keith broke the spell.

"Hey, let's play frisbee." He threw the frisbee at me, and I caught it as I jumped off the table.

We went out into the yard to play, but all the while I was stealing glimpses of Rhonda and was watching her walk to and from the car to the cabin. She didn't look my way, but when she finished, she came back out and sat in the same chair, talking with Pam and watching Keith and me throw the frisbee, or at least I thought she was watching us. Of course, then I had to make sure that I didn't do anything wrong, like miss an easy catch, or throw the thing too wildly, or run into a tree or a ditch and kill myself or bust my head open and end up like the kid at school last year who had to wear a football helmet all the time to protect his head. I didn't think I would be too good looking to her wearing a football helmet all the time.

Rhonda and Pam were laughing and talking and seemed to be having a good time. It was amazing to me how girls could just sit and talk and talk and talk about what seemed like absolutely nothing at all, while guys had a hard time saying anything more than "Hi, how're you doin?" Keith and I had said little more than "Hello" and "nice catch" since we had first seen each other and started playing frisbee, and we probably wouldn't say much more than that before the night was over, unless we got involved in a card game or Monopoly or some other game. But there Pam and Rhonda sat, talking away, and Pam was even six years older than Rhonda and had graduated from high school two years ago. One day, I thought, maybe I would understand girls.

After throwing the frisbee for a while, I motioned to Keith to go sit down with me by Rhonda and Pam. They were still laughing and talking as we sat down next to them.

"What do you wanna do tonight?" I already knew what I wanted to do.

"We were just talking about maybe going to the drive-in. One screen has *A Shot in the Dark* and *The Pink Panther*, and the other has *Dr. No* and *From Russia With Love*. I knew which ones I wanted to see.

"I've already seen the James Bond movies, but I'd see 'em again if those are the ones all of you wanna see. What is *A Shot in the Dark*? A murder mystery or something?" I hadn't heard of that one.

Pam was looking through the paper now. "That's another Pink Panther movie. It has Peter Sellers in it. The advertisement in the paper said he's Inspector Clouseau again in this one, and he's zanier than ever."

"Isn't he in that movie *Dr. Strangelove*?" I hadn't heard of that one either.

"Yeah, he is." Pam seemed to know all about him. Rhonda had been sitting there listening to the movie talk.

"I've seen the James Bond movies too, but I haven't seen the Peter Sellers movies. But I'll go to whichever ones everyone wants to see."

"Well, since I'm driving, I'll choose and say Peter Sellers." I liked Pam's choice.

We were set and decided we'd get ready and go to the Sonic drive-in and get a hamburger before the movies. All I could think about was maybe getting a chance to get closer with Rhonda, and I hurried in to take a shower and get cleaned up.

Keith and I were dressed first and went outside to wait and play frisbee again. It was going to be a great night for the drive-in. The sky was bright blue all over and a nice warm breeze blew through the trees. We could take a blanket and sit outside in front of the car to watch the movies, and if I worked it right, I might get to sit by Rhonda and maybe put my arm around her. I didn't think I could hope for more than that at the movies, not with my cousins there too.

Afterwards, maybe we would come back to the cabin and go down to the dock and talk. I might get the chance to kiss her then. But, there I was again, drifting off into my dream world, maybe land, where everything was how I wished it to be, and that world didn't come true very often.

After a while, Pam and Rhonda came out of the cabin, dressed and ready to go.

"Hey, do you have a blanket in the car?" We couldn't hardly sit outside without a blanket.

"No, get one."

I ran to the cabin and got a blanket off one of the cots on the front porch. We all got into Pam's Corvair, Pam and Rhonda in front and Keith and me in the back, and we took off.

As we drove down the road, the radio played the Dave Clark Five's "Glad All Over," and the warm air blew through the car windows, and I felt very free and excited. I had sat behind Pam so that I could see Rhonda easier and would be able to talk to her directly. It was especially hard not to stare at her the whole time. Pam and Rhonda kept the conversation going pretty much, talking about movies and clothes and music and all kinds of stuff, with Keith and me adding a comment here and there and talking about school and Razorback football.

Sonic was already getting crowded, but we managed to find a spot and parked the Corvair in one of the slots. We all knew what we wanted, so Pam called our order in on the intercom, while we sat and waited, listening to the radio and watching the constant flow of cars driving in and out. I couldn't wait until I could drive, so I could pick up my girlfriend and go on dates to the drive-in movies and get hamburgers and just go driving around.

Our orders came, and we dug in like we hadn't eaten in months. No one said a word as we gobbled down the hamburgers and fries and shakes and cokes and listened to the stream of songs playing on the radio, the Beatles playing almost every other song, with the Supremes and Roy Orbison and Martha and the Vandells and Gerry and the Pacemakers and the Four Tops and the Dave Clark Five and the Beach Boys and all the others mixed in between. Rhonda liked the Beatles a lot, and she sang along with every one of the songs. I liked them okay but still liked the Four Tops and Dave Clark and the Kinks and Manfred Mann and some other groups better, and I always listened for the songs by new groups, like one that I had just heard recently called "The House of the Rising Sun" by this new group called The Animals.

When we finished eating and had put our trash out on the window tray to be picked up, we pulled out of the Sonic and headed for the drive-in movie, which was located just outside of town. Every time I went to the drive-in now, I remembered the night several years ago when Mom and my little brother and I had gone to the drive-in in North Little Rock to see *The Wasp Woman* and some other movie that I couldn't remember, because we never got to see it. About half way through the first movie, the wind starting picking up, and the car started rocking from side to side.

The wind kept getting stronger and stronger, and then suddenly the movie screen blew into a million pieces that flew toward us and the other cars. Mom pushed me and my little brother into the floor of the car and held us down as the car continued to shake and pieces of the screen hit the car and flew all around us. I looked up through the windshield and could see the pieces flying through the air, and Mom yelled at me to turn over and stay on the floor. After a few minutes, I couldn't even tell how long it was, the wind died down, and the car stopped shaking. Gradually, Mom raised up to see what was happening and pulled us up onto the front seat with her.

When I looked out the windshield, I could see that the movie screen was entirely gone and that pieces of it were scattered all over the ground. Mom started the car and drove around the rubble and back home. The next morning the news said that a tornado had touched down in North Little Rock and had destroyed the drive-in and some nearby buildings and then had lifted off the ground again. One guy on leave from the navy had been killed at the drive-in when a two-by-four board was blown through his front windshield and struck him in the head.

Tonight was nothing like that night though. The sky was perfect, and the wind was warm and was blowing just enough to give a nice breeze to the evening. And there in the front seat was the girl I had been waiting for a year to see again, the only girl I had ever felt this strongly about, even though I hadn't seen her in that long a time.

We got to the drive-in in plenty of time before the sun set and got a good spot in the middle, toward the front. While Pam and Rhonda went to the bathroom back at the snack bar, I got the blanket out of the trunk and spread it out in front of the car and moved the speaker from the post to the ground by the blanket. Keith sat on one side of the blanket, and I decided I would go to the bathroom too and would wait to see where Rhonda sat before I picked a spot on the blanket. I hoped that I would be able to sit by her.

When I returned from the bathroom, I found the three of them sitting on the blanket watching the advertisement for the snack bar. Keith was on one end, and Pam was on the other end of the blanket, with Rhonda sitting in-between them. That was good for me. I could plop down in the middle of the blanket and sit between Keith and Rhonda and could try to get something going with her. I didn't want to be too pushy, so, when I sat down on the blanket, I sat down toward the middle of the blanket, between Keith and Rhonda but not quite right next to either one of them and leaned on one arm.

As the movie started, I thought of how I could get closer to Rhonda. I would wait for a while and keep turning my head to talk to the rest of them, and then would eventually move up and sit up against the front of the Corvair the way they were sitting and would finally be next to Rhonda.

The movie was funny as hell and kept us all laughing and making comments about Clouseau and how ridiculous the character was. After about twenty minutes into the movie, I decided to make my move. I sat up and scooted back across the blanket until I was up against the front bumper of the Corvair and was next to Rhonda. Everyone was watching the movie and didn't even seem to notice that I had moved, or, at least, didn't make any comments or look at me funny.

I had succeeded and now needed to plan what my next move would be. I didn't want to be pushy or hasty, but I needed to know what Rhonda was thinking. Was she as excited to see me as I was to see her? Did she want me to put my arm around her, kiss her? Not knowing was what made me so damn crazy. I was usually okay if I knew how someone felt.

I tried to talk to her, but it was hard with the movie going on trying to think of something to say other than stuff about the movie. She was talking with Pam, and Keith was watching the movie. I started feeling weird and didn't want to be feeling that way. I felt like I needed to climb a tree and sit up in the top of it and watch the sun go down.

I got up and told them I was going to the snack bar to the bathroom but went to the playground instead and climbed to the top of the monkey bars and sat there watching the movie. I felt better after a while and climbed down and did go to the bathroom. The bathroom was full of guys, mostly older guys, who were talking and laughing with each other. I had a hard time pissing sometimes when a lot of people were around, so I went outside and waited until some of them left and then went back and went into the stall to piss.

The movie was ending as I left the bathroom. On my way back to the car, I ran into Pam and Rhonda and Keith.

"Hey, where have you been?"

"The bathroom was packed. I had to wait in line."

"We're going to the snack bar. You want to go with us?" Rhonda's smile made me feel better.

"Sure."

We headed for the snack bar, and, of course, the line was already out the door. We stood in line, talking about the movie, looking at the listing of the snacks they had, and talking about what we wanted. The line went pretty fast, and so we were on our way back to the car pretty soon, with our Junior Mints and popcorn and cokes and Three Musketeers bars.

We plopped down on the blanket and started eating up the goodies. We were all just sitting around in a circle, talking about the movie and the evening and what we wanted to do tomorrow and watching the intermission ads and the coming attractions on the screen.

My visit to the playground and the climb up the monkey bars had helped settle me down some, and I felt more at ease about what I was going to do next or about what Rhonda might do or think or say. But I didn't have any idea what I was going to do next. Nothing had gone even close to the way I had planned yet.

When the second movie started, we moved back up on the blanket, against the Corvair bumper, and settled in, passing the popcorn and drinking our drinks. The movie was just as funny as the first one, and we laughed and laughed at watching Peter Sellers playing Inspector Clouseau.

The movie ended about eleven thirty, and we gathered the blanket and our trash and climbed in the car and headed for the exit, lining up behind the already formed line of cars there. It didn't take long to get to the exit, and we hit the road for the drive back to the cabin. We were still laughing and talking about our favorite funny parts of the movies and decided that tomorrow we wanted to go skiing and swimming, and maybe get one of the boats and go to one of the islands on the lake and sunbath and swim there and dive off the cliffs that some of the islands had.

The cabin looked completely dark when we pulled in the driveway, but as we got nearer we could see the light on over the kitchen sink and our mothers sitting at the table on the porch, drinking beers and laughing and talking and smoking. As we entered the porch, they asked us how we liked the movies and if we had had fun. And, of course, we all started telling about the movie at once, trying to explain every single funny move that Peter Sellers made or all the funny lines that we could remember and laughing so hard sometimes that we couldn't even tell them about it. It was almost funnier when we told it to them than when we had seen it at the drive-in. They got the general idea that we had a good time and that we had enjoyed the movies, and then they told us where we were going to be sleeping and where our clothes and things were.

The cabin only had three small bedrooms, which were reserved for the adults, and then one big play room and living room combination and the screened porch. The play room and the porch had couches with beds in them and room to put up cots, so we kids would always sleep on the cots or on the couch beds.

The couch beds would be where our parents would put the little kids, and the rest of us would usually just put up the cots because they were so much easier to put up and take down. Everybody would sleep in pajamas or in shorts and t-shirts, depending on how cool it was and if you were sleeping in the play room or on the porch. The porch could get pretty chilly in the early morning hours, but we had plenty of blankets and sleeping bags to keep warm.

We all took turns going to the bathroom and putting on our pajamas and then went back to the porch to put up the cots and get ready for bed. Our moms had already gone to bed by the time we were ready to hit the sack. We had a radio on the porch, so we turned it on and lay there on the cots talking and listening to the music.

Pam and Rhonda were doing most of the talking, and I was pretty much just listening to them and the music, and Keith sounded like he was asleep already. After a while, Pam and Rhonda got quiet, and all you could hear was the music playing low on the radio and the crickets in the woods next to the cabin and the bullfrogs on the river below. The only light now was the glow from the moon, and it lit the porch just enough so that I could see Rhonda's face on her pillow. She looked so peaceful and beautiful, and I still wanted so much to tell her how much I liked her and how much I hoped that she liked me too.

I was glad that I hadn't done anything stupid at the movies tonight and had just gone along with what was going on and not tried to make anything happen with her. Tomorrow would be a good day, and maybe I could find a chance to be alone with her and talk. I didn't even know if she had a boyfriend, but I hadn't heard her mention it to Pam, and that was a good sign. I lay there listening to the music and the sounds of the night. The Beatles were singing "Do You Want to Know a Secret," and I thought about how much I wanted Rhonda to know how I felt about her, my secret. As usual, the way I had hoped, dreamed, that things would turn out was not the way it was happening. But we still had a few days left, and I might get to stay the extra days that Rhonda would be here. I hadn't planned that either, so maybe that would work out. After a while, I drifted off into sleep, dreaming about the days to come.

****

I awoke the next morning to the sound and the smell of bacon frying. I loved that smell, and I knew if I opened my eyes I would see my mother standing at the stove with a fork, turning the bacon over in the fry pan. I didn't want to open my eyes yet; I loved waking up that way, hearing the birds talking to each other, feeling the warmth of the morning breeze, smelling breakfast cooking. I wanted to just lie there and take it all in, to lie there and pretend I was still asleep so nobody would bother me.

My Mom would usually just let me sleep until I awoke on my own, at least during summer vacation she would. During the school year, she would be yelling at me to get up so I wouldn't be late for school. It didn't matter, though, I would be late anyway, even if I got up three hours ahead of time. My Mom was always late, so I was always late.

I finally opened my eyes and looked around the room. Everyone else was up and their cots were put away, and the blankets and pillows were gone back to the closet until tonight. I was the only lazy bum still in bed, but I wondered where they had all gone. I sat up on the cot and stretched and looked around the yard. All the cars were in the driveway, but nobody was to be seen, and I didn't hear any screaming or anything from the dock down below.

I got up and went into the kitchen, and, there, just as I had seen in my daydream, was Mom, standing at the stove with the fork in her hand, turning the bacon.

"Well, sleepyhead; you finally decided to get up?"

"Yeah; where is everybody?"

"Will went fishing with your little brother, and Mary is in the back getting dressed. Barbara went for a walk, and Pam took everybody else out in the speedboat for a ride until breakfast. They should be back any time, so why don't you go ahead and get dressed. Just put on your swim trunks and a shirt; we're going to go to the island after breakfast."

"Are we going to get to ski?"

"Of course. We're planning on staying out there for the afternoon."

"Why didn't Will wake me up to go fishing with him?"

"He tried to wake you, but you wouldn't get up. Connor woke up when he was trying to get you up, so he took him."

I grabbed a piece of bacon from the plate on the counter and went to put my cot away. I folded the cot and put it in the corner with the others and took the blanket and pillow to the closet. By the time I had changed into my swim suit and shirt, I heard the sound of the speedboat coming up to the dock down below, and I could hear laughter and shouting when the engines shut down.

I walked out into the yard and to the top of the steps and looked down toward the dock. Rhonda was standing on the dock beside the speedboat talking with Pam, wearing a two piece which showed off her cute body. I felt the blood racing through my veins, and my dick started to tingle as I watched her. I began walking down the steps and called to them.

"Hey, why didn't you guys get me up?"

Rhonda looked up at me. "Oh hi, good morning. We didn't want to bother you. You looked like you were sleeping so peacefully."

Now I started to wonder if they didn't want to bother me or if they just didn't want to bother with me.

"That's okay. You could've gotten me up." I reached the bottom of the steps.

"We just wanted to take a little ride around the lake to see what was going on." Pam loved driving the boat. "We're going to the island this afternoon."

"That's what Mom told me."

"And we're going to do some skiing." Keith and I had skied since we were little.

"That's what I was hoping." As long as Rhonda was there.

"Let's go get some breakfast." Rhonda started up the steps.

We all followed her up the steps to the cabin. I couldn't help but watch Rhonda's ass as she climbed the steps ahead of me. I had to be careful that I didn't let anyone see me staring at her though, especially our parents, but I couldn't help but stare. I was beginning to think I'd be walking around with a boner the whole weekend and wouldn't be able to do anything about it.

All our moms were in the kitchen now, getting the bacon and eggs and pancakes and coffee and juice and all the other stuff on the table. Will and my little brother weren't there yet, but the moms said to sit down and eat while it was hot. It didn't take much to get me to eat, so I sat and filled a plate with the pancakes and plenty of syrup, Aunt Jemima's of course, eggs, bacon, toast, and some coffee with lots of milk. It must have amazed people that I could eat so much and still be a skinny runt, but that's the way it was.

About the time we were finishing breakfast, Will and my little brother came walking up to the cabin from the dock.

"You finally got up, I see." Will sounded in a good mood as he opened the door.

"Sorry, Will, I did wanna go with you. Did you have any luck?"

"Tell 'im, Connor."

"We caught eight bass; Will caught a four-pounder, and I caught a three-pounder, and we caught some more smaller ones." My little brother was grinning like the village idiot. Damn! I thought. Just my luck that I miss out on something like that.

"He's kidding, isn't he." I was hoping it was just Will playing a trick on me.

"I'm not kidding. Go look in the ice chest."

I went down the steps to the dock and opened the ice chest sitting on the dock. There they were, the four-pounder, the three-pounder, and a bunch of little bass. I had kind of hoped that they were kidding, because now I felt like the morning had been a waste. I had slept late, and everybody else had been up doing stuff and having fun. I had missed out on going on the ride with Rhonda and had missed out on catching a bunch of nice bass. Now I wondered which one or ones I might have caught. And if I had gone fishing, I still wouldn't have gone with Rhonda. Now I was more confused than ever. The whole morning had been shot.

I walked back up the steps to the cabin. Connor and Will were eating some breakfast, and everyone else had finished and had gone to get ready to go to the island. The moms were now busy cleaning up after breakfast and were getting the food ready to take with us to the island.

"Pretty nice catch, huh." Now Will was grinning.

"Yeah, some nice ones there."

"Your dad would have had fun with those. He likes catching 'em with his fly rod."

"Maybe they'll be hitting again in the morning when he's here."

"You ready to do some skiing?"

"Yeah, I'm ready." At least that was one thing I wouldn't miss out on today.

"Let's go get the boats ready." Will got up from the table and headed toward the door.

We went down to the dock and got the party barge and the ski boat ready, and Pam and Keith and Rhonda started bringing down the food and stuff we would take to the island. Before long we were packed and ready to go.

Pam was driving the speedboat, so Keith and Rhonda and I rode with her. Will and the moms and our little brothers loaded onto the party barge, and we took off.

The trip over to the island drove me nuts, mainly because I was sitting behind Pam and could lean over and see down her top and see her nipples on her boobs, and Rhonda was sitting across from me in the front seat and was sitting sideways with her legs up in the seat. I was just glad I had shorts on over my swim trunks.

Pam drove the speed boat pretty fast and took a spin around the lake checking out the islands to see if we could find a good one without a group already camped out on it. She knew all the spots, especially the ones that people who hadn't been there before wouldn't know, since she lived there in Hot Springs much of the time.

"Anybody want to do some diving?" I knew Pam and Rhonda wouldn't but I wanted to.

"I do." I had to yell over the sound of the motor and the music.

She immediately turned the boat around and went back to the party barge, which was chugging along slowly behind us.

"Dad, we want to do some diving." Now she had to yell over to Will.

"Okay, I know where you're going. Go on and save the spot until we get there, then we'll do some skiing after we dock the barge."

Pam revved the engines on the speed boat and took off across the water at full speed. It was great fun going so fast and sitting on the edge of the boat, feeling the warmth of the sun and the coolness of the water spraying up from the boat hitting the waves, both at the same time. It was still early, but the sun was already beating down pretty hard. I wasn't too worried about burning, because I'd already burned earlier in the summer and had a tan from going to the community pool.

We reached the spot in no time, and it was great. A twenty foot cliff, with a straight drop into the lake, a small beach for the moms and our brothers, and a place to park the barge and the boat. The cliff was rocky with lots of crags and ledges to climb up to jump off. Why hadn't we come to this place before? It was Thursday, so maybe that was why nobody had staked out the spot yet.

Pam stopped the boat, and Keith and I jumped out and onto the beach. The beach was more rock than sand, but it was soft enough to put a blanket or towel down and be okay. I didn't care much about that. I would be spending my time diving off the cliffs and skiing.

We pulled the boat up onto the shore, and Pam and Rhonda started getting their stuff out. I immediately started climbing the cliff to take the first dive into the clear water below. Keith scrambled up the cliff behind me, and we started racing to see who could get to the top first.

At the top, we moved to the edge and looked over. It wasn't that far up, but it was enough to have some fun and do a few dives. We didn't have much room for running toward the edge, so our dives would have to be from standing on the edge and just jumping out. It wasn't anything like the ten meter board we used to jump off at the Community Center in Little Rock.

When we lived in the country, Mom used to take us to the zoo and the Community Center during the summer. It was so far from our house that we made a day of going to the zoo in the morning while the weather was cooler, and then heading for the pool in the afternoon when the sun was heating things up. It was packed usually, but it was a huge pool, and it was a lot different from going swimming in the bauxite pits behind our property.

Keith and I had finished our scouting of the area and looked at each other, yelled as loud as we could, and jumped, cannonballing the cold morning water onto the boat and Pam and Rhonda as we hit.

"Hey, that's not fair!" Now Pam yelled at us. "We're getting the stuff out, and you're already in the water!"

"You better watch out. We'll get you when you least expect it! Just remember who's driving the boat!" Rhonda could do anything she wanted to me, and I would love it.

We looked at each other and dove down under the water. In water this deep in the lake, you could see pretty well, even without goggles, and one of our favorite things to do was to dive down to the bottom and explore. Here the water was too deep for that, but we could explore the rock cliffs under the water.

The cliffs were pretty bare, and when I resurfaced, the party barge was there with Will and the moms and the little kids. The barge rested close to the shore, next to the beach, and Will had started unloading the chairs and other goodies we would need for the day. Will saw us in the water now.

"You two get out of the water and help me here."

I climbed onto the barge, and Keith went onto the shore, and I started handing him the chairs and beach towels and bags of snack stuff our moms had put together for the day.

It didn't take long to unload the stuff, and our moms started getting the food ready for lunch. We went back to the cliffs until Mom called us to come and eat. We scarfed down the food so that we'd have plenty of time to ski.

Pam and Rhonda jumped into the front of the boat again, and Keith and I grabbed our life belts and jumped in the water to get ready to ski. We had both been skiing since we were big enough to fit the skis on our feet, and we were now good enough to slalom.

Pam pulled the boat out away from the shore and stopped the motor. She and Rhonda grabbed the skis and threw them out to us, and we quickly pulled them on and waited for the ropes to be thrown out. Pam threw the ropes to us and went back to the driver's seat and started the engine, revving it and holding it a fast idle.

"Ready?" Rhonda would be watching us while Pam drove the boat.

We gave the ready signal, and Pam gunned the engine. We both made it up first time and went to our side of the boat as Pam pulled out into the open area of the lake. Pam was a good driver and knew that we liked to jump waves and go fast, so she drove the boat at top speed.

As we sped across the lake, I felt a thrill at moving so fast and being in control of my movements. I loved to move to the side of the boat, up with the front seats, and lean to my side until I was almost touching the water. Then I would raise up and pull on the rope and speed to the back of the boat, jumping the waves as I moved across behind the boat. Keith and I had skied enough together to know when to let the other do his thing, and we took turns doing tricks and just playing around.

After about fifteen minutes, Pam waved to us to let go of the ropes, so we dropped them and sank into the water. Pam pulled the boat around and zipped between us, and we took off our skis and left them in the water for Pam and Rhonda. When we got to the boat, they jumped in the water to have their turn.

Keith got in the driver's seat and started the engine, moving the boat forward so I could throw the ropes out to them. After a few minutes they were ready to go. Keith slowly pulled the boat forward to get the slack out of the ropes, and they signaled they were ready to go. Keith rammed the throttle forward, and the boat shot out into the lake, pulling Pam and Rhonda out of the water onto their skis.

I couldn't keep my eyes off of Rhonda. She looked so great on the skis, her hair blowing in the wind, the sun beating down on her, reflecting off the lotion on her skin. I could feel the tingle in my dick as it started getting hard. Her swim suit looked pasted to her body, outlining her breasts and the "v" between her legs. My dick was tingling like crazy now.

I took my eyes off of Rhonda and watched Pam, hoping that that would help stop my hard-on, but Pam looked good too. Her skin was always tan looking, since she was part Cherokee, and she had a nice shape. Her boobs were sort of small, but she still looked good on the skis.

I finally had to look forward for a few minutes to try to get my mind off the girls. I concentrated on the song playing on the radio, "Do You Love Me," and that helped the tingle go away, but it also made me wonder about Rhonda and how she felt about me. I turned back around then to watch the girls and make sure nothing happened to either of them. If they decided to drop off, I would need to tell Keith so he could turn around to pick them up.

We spent another couple of hours taking turns on the skis. I took a turn at slaloming and made some pretty decent jumps on the waves. Then I crashed and burned and decided that was enough for me for the day. Everybody was starting to get a little drained from the sun and heat and wind and water, so we headed the boat back to the island.

The moms and Will were sitting on the party barge, drinking beers and talking and laughing. Our brothers were standing on the top of the cliff, throwing rocks down into the water. Pam pulled the boat up alongside of the barge, and we tied the docking lines to the barge.

"Back already." Will and the moms thought that was pretty funny for some reason, and they all laughed at this. I think they would have laughed at about anything at this point. Pam turned off the engine, and we all looked at each other and shook our heads.

"You kids hungry?" My Mom would get silly after just one beer.

"Starved." Mom knew I was always hungry. Keith agreed.

"I need a coke." Rhonda jumped down to the beach, followed by Pam.

"Me too."

We all jumped aboard the barge and started raiding the bags and ice chests of food and drinks. Mom got out some sandwich stuff and made Keith and me sandwiches, while Pam and Rhonda got cokes for all of us. We sat with the grown-ups and devoured the food and drinks, telling our stories of jumping waves and falls and spills and wondering what we would do that evening. Our parents were planning on going to town to the bowling alley. They would take the little guys with them. That would leave us at the house by ourselves. I started thinking that this could turn out to be an interesting evening.

The parents left about six thirty for the bowling alley, taking the little kids with them and leaving Pam in charge at the cabin. We got the poker chips out and set up the poker table and got some cokes and chips and started our poker game. One thing we had learned from our parents was how to play poker. We had been around it for as long as we could remember and could hold our own in a game.

My only problem was that I couldn't stop once I got started betting. I would play until I lost all of my chips and would try to get more chips to keep playing. I was always going for the big hand. And we didn't play the sissy games with all the wild cards and stupid combinations of cards to win. We played down and dirty stud poker or blackjack.

Rhonda sat across the table from me, with Pam to my left and Keith to my right. That was great because I could look over my cards at Rhonda, watch her every move, memorize her every expression, see if she was watching me. She wasn't. We were playing and talking, mainly about the game. I got up and searched for a station with some good music on the radio. We couldn't get WGN out so far on the lake, especially with the mountains around us, so I settled on a local station that played mostly American rock and roll - Lesley Gore, Jay and the Americans, the Beach Boys, Jan and Dean. "Where Did Our Love Go?" was playing at the moment. The music helped liven things up a little. But, I hadn't been able to talk to Rhonda the way I wanted to talk to her, with her, yet, and I wondered when I might get the chance.

I knew I wouldn't be able to get my nerve up without a little help, so I got my glass from the table and went to the kitchen. I knew where the parents kept the whiskey, so I sneaked the bottle out of the cupboard, poured a good amount in my glass, put the bottle back, and filled the glass the rest of the way with coke. I took a sip and felt the warmth of the whiskey as it glided down my throat. I usually would sneak beer when I was at home, but I figured I needed something a little stronger now to get me settled.

They were waiting for me to start playing when I got back to the table. I took a few sips off the drink, and it didn't take long until I was feeling the effects of the whiskey. I was getting louder and saying things I wouldn't normally say, making jokes and throwing more "damns" and "hells" into what I was saying.

I finished off the first glass and made another drink, this time putting even more whiskey in the glass before I filled it the rest of the way with the coke, thinking that I was doing so much better with a little bit that a lot more would be even better. I grabbed some potato chips for everyone on my way back to the table. I was getting pretty loose with my betting now and was getting low on poker chips, but the way I was feeling, the poker game didn't matter that much anymore. I was starting to feel the effects of the whiskey now, and I was thinking more and more about Rhonda and what I'd like to be doing with her. With Pam and Keith there though, it would be difficult to get anything going. I needed a plan.

I thought that if I lost all my chips that they would not want to play any more with just three people playing. Then, I might be able to talk Rhonda into going outside with me for a walk. I started betting my chips double what I would normally bet and losing them even faster. At last I bet the last chip and lost. I was out.

"Well, that's it for me," I said. "I think I'll go outside for a bit. Anyone for going for a night ride in the boat?"

"I want to see who the big winner is." Pam wasn't helping me.

"Yeah, me too." That wasn't what Rhonda was supposed to say either.

"I'm staying." And of course Keith was staying too.

"Well, I'm going to go down to the dock."

"Okay, be careful."

My plan hadn't worked. I was hoping by now I'd be walking down to the dock with Rhonda. It sure is hard to get girls to do what you want, I thought.

I went down to the dock anyway, got into the speedboat, and put the radio on. I sat back in the seat and watched the stars in the pitch-black sky and listened to the music playing on the radio. The back of the seat was just low enough for me to lay my head back and stare at the stars, while I propped my feet up on the dash. The Four Tops were singing "Baby I Need Your Loving," and I tried to sing along with them, but couldn't because I kept getting teary eyed and choking up thinking about how much I needed Rhonda to be there with me, to kiss her and hold her and feel her next to me. I stopped singing and just sat back and listened.

The boat swayed gently with the waves from the lake, and my eyelids grew heavy from the rocking motion. I closed my eyes and could feel the rocking of the boat even more than before. Back and forth. Back and forth. The more the boat rocked, the more my eyes seemed to roll under my eyelids. The rolling moved from my eyes downward, and I was feeling a wave move down my throat and into my stomach. I tried opening my eyes, thinking that would stop the motion in my stomach, but it didn't work. My stomach kept tumbling and turning, and now I could feel my stomach getting fuller and fuller. The fuller it became, the more I felt like emptying it.

Then suddenly, my stomach felt like it was exploding. I sprang forward in the seat, feeling the gurgling liquid bursting into my throat. I had just enough time to hang my head over the side of the boat and let everything in my stomach spew into the lake. It felt like my stomach came up into my throat as I kept emptying the liquid into the lake. The wave slowed. My throat burned from the liquid, and I sat back in the seat to rest. It didn't take long for another wave to hit me, and my head was hanging over the side of the boat again. This time, not much. My guts were now trying to escape my body. But my body was holding onto them. Barely.

I finished and sat back again. The boat felt like it was still rocking, even though the water on the lake was calm. I rested for a few minutes. My stomach was still tumbling and rolling, but nothing was left in it to come up. I knew I'd better get back up to the cabin before the parents got back and found me gone. I tried to get up and felt the wave hitting me again, so I sat back down. I figured I'd better rest for a few more minutes before trying to make it back up the steps to the cabin.

Then, I heard someone at the top of the steps.

"Peter?"

"Are you down there Peter?"

It was Pam and Rhonda. Oh, great, I thought, Rhonda's going to be so impressed seeing me like this. At least all the puke had gone into the lake. I leaned over the side of the boat and scooped some water and drank it. I at least wanted to get the smell and taste out of my mouth. I might be able to hide the fact that I'd been puking my guts out if my breath didn't smell too much like it.

"I'm down here."

"What are you doing?" Pam sounded worried.

"Just sitting and listening to the radio."

"Are you okay?" Rhonda sounded worried now.

"Yeah. Just sitting here in the boat."

I could barely answer and call up to them.

"You want us to come down?"

"No. I was just on my way back up." I didn't want them to see or smell the puke.

Now I would have to make it back up the steps on my own. I stood up and started moving toward the other side of the boat to the dock. The boat tossed and turned as I stepped across the seats, but I was able to step up onto the dock. I saw Pam and Rhoda at the top of the steps.

"I'm coming."

I could see them move away from the steps and back toward the cabin. Good, I thought, I could make my way up without them seeing me hanging on to the rail for dear life to keep from slipping on the steep steps.

I started up the steps, holding the rail with both hands. It wasn't as bad as I thought it was going to be. I slowly moved up step by step until I made it to the top. I was still feeling a little dizzy, and my stomach still felt like it was rolling and tumbling, but I was able to walk across the yard to the cabin.

As I got closer to the cabin, I could see Keith, Pam, and Rhonda sitting at the kitchen table, drinking cokes and eating and talking and laughing. I didn't feel at all like facing them at this point. As I opened the door to the porch, I saw my empty cot and decided the best thing for me to do was to lie down on it and try to get over the dizzy feeling. I flopped down on it and shut my eyes. I could hear them laughing and talking in the house. Soon, their voices faded, and I was totally out.

****

A jack-hammer and construction equipment woke me the next morning. I hadn't seen any heavy equipment on the road lately and wondered how all the equipment could have been brought in so quickly. I tried to raise my head to see what was going on. That's when my head felt like it was going to rip itself from my neck and roll across the floor. I then realized that the construction noises were coming from a woodpecker and the birds in the trees around the cabin.

I wouldn't call what I had a headache. It was more like a space being was inside my skull kicking and screaming to get out. I flopped back down on the cot, hoping that if I just lay there for a little while, the kicking and screaming would end.

It didn't help. I couldn't hear anything else in the cabin, no talking, radio, or anything else. Where was everyone?

I got up and started searching the cabin, to see if anyone was around and to see if I could find some aspirin. No one was there. I found the aspirin in the bathroom. I didn't know how many to take, Mom usually gave us any medicine we took, so I just emptied four into my hand and took them. I stuck a couple in my pocket just in case the four didn't help. I went back into the kitchen. It was ten o'clock. I wasn't much hungry, but I was thirsty as hell. I grabbed a coke from the fridge and gulped it down. I felt a wave of dizziness from drinking the coke and sat at the kitchen table. After a few minutes, I began to feel better. I got up from the table and went outside.

One of the cars was gone. I went and looked at the dock, and the boats were gone too. What had I missed this morning? Where were Keith and Pam and Rhonda? Where were the moms and Will and the little kids? When would Dad be getting there?

It didn't take long before all my questions were answered. In unison, the car pulled in the driveway with the moms in it, followed by my Dad in his car, the speedboat pulled up to the dock from the lake, with Keith, Pam, and Rhonda, and the fishing boat pulled up to the dock from up the river, with Will and the little brothers. Everyone was talking and shouting and laughing and asking me how I was doing and if I had a good sleep.

Dad and Will immediately started talking and grabbed a beer and went down to the dock. The little brothers got some gloves and a baseball and went to the yard to play catch. The moms brought bag after bag of groceries to the cabin and talked and gabbed about who knows what. And Keith and Pam and Rhonda went into the cabin calling to the moms to get something ready for lunch. I stood and watched all the movement and activity and wondered to myself how it was that I always seemed to be on the outside of what was going on, to be there but then not be there. All I could do was just sit at the picnic table in the yard and listen to the laughing and talking.

From that point on, the weekend just went more and more down hill. I did go out with my Dad and Will a couple of times fishing. Didn't catch anything. Of course, they caught their limit of bass and crappie. I went skiing again with my cousins and Rhonda, but we only stayed out for a while, because Rhonda and Pam were going into town to do some shopping. Keith was going to a friend's house Saturday night and left with Pam and Rhonda. So, there I was, pretty much all alone. I was glad I had brought some comic books with me. I spent the rest of the weekend reading comics and eating the hamburgers Dad and Will cooked.

We went home on Sunday, everybody hugging and kissing and saying goodbye and how much fun it had been. I said bye to Rhonda and told her I hoped to see her again. She said she'd keep in touch. We got home late on Sunday, and I went to my room and crashed on the bed. It had been a long week that hadn't gone the way I had hoped it would go. What had gone wrong? Why were things always turning out so different from the way I wanted? I had no answers and no idea. I fell asleep, dreaming of how it might have been.

We made one more trip that summer, to New York to visit my grandmother and cousins and to go to the World's Fair. My Dad wasn't able to go, so my Mom took us kids and one of my brother's friends, Doug, in our new Dodge station wagon. Doug and my brother drove most of the time, and I had my spot in the very back by the window, where I could read my comic books, listen to my radio, and look at the countryside through the rear window.

New York was fun, even though I didn't get to go on the tour with my brothers to see the Empire State Building and the United Nations. But I did get to go downtown and to the Fair, and we got to ride on the subway from my cousin's house in the Bronx to the park where the fair was being held. The fair was like going to Disneyland again. We went on rides and saw displays of space rockets and new cars and ate food from different countries. We spent the day walking around and buying souvenirs and went home late that evening to my cousins house.

I wasn't ready to go to bed, so I went out for a walk around my cousin's neighborhood. It was neat to see things going on all day and night. I walked along the street for a while, watching the activity and listening to the sounds of the constant traffic and the subway overhead. After not too long, I got tired and went back to my cousin's and went to bed.

We left for home the next day. Most of the trip back was pretty calm until we stopped in a little town in southern Indiana, Terra Haute, to eat dinner. We stopped at this Italian restaurant and all had spaghetti and meatballs. We got back in the car after eating and got back on the road. We didn't have a lot further to go and would probably be home the next morning by driving all night.

By the time we arrived home the next morning, we were all ready to hit the bathroom. Something we had eaten the night before, probably the spaghetti, had made us all sick, and we were taking turns trying to get the stuff out of our systems. It took a couple of days to get back to normal.

The rest of the summer was filled with going to the pool and riding my bike and going into the woods. I thought a lot about Rhonda, but I didn't hear from her again that summer. I didn't try to call either, remembering how lousy the week at the cabin had turned out and thinking she probably wouldn't want to talk to me anyway. So, I spent my time getting ready for my first year of high school and felt a wave of panic every time I thought about it. But the panic left me when I remembered that this would be my year to take Biology and would be the year that I would start on my goal to be a Microbiologist.

'65

****

Tenth grade had been an interesting year. I turned fifteen, probably the youngest student on a campus of over two thousand, and I had learned that being small was both an advantage and a disadvantage when you were playing dodgeball in P.E.

I had started out in band in the fall, but the band at North Little Rock High was very good, and I knew right away that I would have no chance of doing anything with the sax. So after about two weeks of struggling with alto sax and the band director, I talked my parents into letting me out of band.

The only other option they and the guidance counselors could offer was P.E. I hadn't had P.E. in junior high because of band and the film monitor class. I had actually tried out for football in the seventh grade, all five feet, four inch, one hundred pounds of me, and had had a short-lived experience when two weeks into practice I was cleated in the head by Ricky Biggs and needed seven stitches to sew up the wound. That was the extent of my experience in athletics, except for swimming and diving at the neighborhood pool.

So, it was quite a shock to walk into the locker room with big, hairy seniors and juniors and sophomores changing their clothes into the P.E. clothes and then taking showers after P.E. The only thing that kept me from being creamed by some of the older students was that they knew my big brothers, or knew who they were, and so they didn't mess with me. And if anyone did mess with me, my brothers' friends would set them straight. The coaches, however, didn't even care who you were or who your family was, unless you were a jock. And if you weren't a jock, then you were a weenie.

My other classes had gone pretty well. I was a little disappointed with my Biology class, though. Mr. Ward, the teacher, didn't seem as interested in Biology as he was in telling jokes and getting the students to laugh, or telling stories about what he and Mr. Jackson would do during their summers off. We did get to dissect frogs and insects and stuff, and we did use the microscopes sometimes, but most of what we did I had already done on my own with my microscope and dissection tools at home. The rest was taking tests and doing the homework assignments, which was not very exciting. I ended up making B's in the class.

Then I had the other just normal classes, like English and Math and History. I didn't have much interest in any of them, and so I didn't do much more than what I needed to do to get by. One of my more interesting classes was Humanities, taught by Mr. Porter. It was kind of like History class, except we looked at art and listened to music from different countries. We also studied about what was going on in Vietnam and in China. Mr. Porter had been in the service and told us a lot about what it was like to fight in a war. It didn't sound at all like what you heard from the army recruiters who would come to talk with us. Guys were being sent to Vietnam to fight, and we might have to go after we graduated too. That was still a few years away for me, but seeing it in the news every night kept it in my head.

Probably the scariest part of the whole year was being in a school with that many students, wondering what they thought about me, how they saw me, how I fit in. Since all the high school students in the whole city went to that one school, getting to know people was kind of hard for someone who was shy. One thing helped me more than anything else. My older brother was a senior and my oldest brother had already graduated, and so their friends knew who I was, and some of them had younger brothers and sisters in the tenth grade. I knew many of them and hung out with them at lunch and at the football games and at the rec center after school.

Though I knew a lot of the kids who were the younger brothers and sisters of my brothers' friends, I only made a few good friends, like Andy, who lived on Park Hill, one of the nicer areas of town. He and I would spend the night together on Friday or Saturday night and watch television and sneak out at night and walk around on Park Hill and Lakewood. He lived near the Old Mill in Lakewood, and we would walk down there and hang around. Lots of kids from Park Hill would hang out there on the weekend. It was next to the fishing lake in Lakewood too, and the road next to the lake was a favorite spot for kids parking in their cars.

One thing I was learning in tenth grade about being a high school student was that clothes were important. Gant shirts. Levi's. Camel hair blazers. Florsheim penny loafers and belts. All were necessary for the guy who wanted to be accepted. My parents didn't even care if I had all the popular clothes, so I was usually stuck with the copies from Sears or Penny's. The one guy everyone looked to to know how to dress was Harry Bailey. He was the best dressed sophomore on the campus. I hadn't known Harry before high school, because he had gone to another junior high, but he was in my home room because we were in home room by last name, and so I saw him every morning first thing and knew what all the new clothes styles were by watching how he dressed.

Mostly, the year had been one of trying to figure me out, who I might be, how I fit in, what people thought of me. I hadn't gotten many answers to my questions. By the end of the year I was still as confused and lost as I had been at the beginning of the year.

The thing that remained the same was my desire to be a Microbiologist. Even though my year in Biology had not been what I had hoped or expected, I was still dead set on following my goal. I had done okay in all my classes, keeping a "B" average, and was set to take the classes I needed next year. I would need to take Chemistry for sure and Geometry, along with the other required classes like English and History and an elective and P.E. I'd have to study harder, especially in the math class, but I would need those classes to get into the program at the university.

The university I planned to attend was the same one my father had attended when I was a little kid. At that time though it was a junior college, and he had gone to finish the high school diploma that he had never had the chance to finish and to take classes in real estate and insurance. I could remember my mother packing us into the car to go and pick him up after school at night, and we would sometimes stop and get him something to eat on the way home.

By the end of the school year, I was ready for summer vacation. The year had seemed to go on forever, and I couldn't wait for the time when I could sleep late every day, wake up when I wanted, and do pretty much as I pleased.

Another thing that had changed around the house from the previous summer was that my mother was now working. She had had to go to work when my father's partner had gotten into money problems and had quit the business. I didn't know all the particulars, but I had heard my parents arguing about money and saying that we were in pretty bad shape now that my Dad's company had split up. I had noticed that my Dad was working longer hours and spent the weekends showing houses in the neighborhood. I would go by sometimes to visit him at the houses and talk with him. It was about the only time I got to see him.

So, now my mother worked at a local drugstore in Levy as a clerk and delivery person. My father knew the people that owned the drugstore, and I'd go there with my mother sometimes and go upstairs above the drugstore and talk with their girls.

One of them, Diane, was in my class, and she had two younger sisters who sang in a trio with her, and they sang at different parties and the community events. Diane wasn't too bad looking, but her younger sister, Cathy, was super cute. She had long dark brown hair and was outgoing, just the kind of girl that attracted me. But now that my mother was working at their parents' drugstore, I was more like the son of the hired help.

Working at the drugstore also meant that she could get me all the latest Spiderman, Fantastic Four, Iron Man, Batman, Superman, and other comics that I loved when they came out, and I could go down during the day and sit at the lunch counter too and get malts and hamburgers.

Once school was out, I was pretty much alone at the house all day long, except for when my mother would come home to check on me while she was out delivering drugs. My little brother went to the baby-sitter, and I was left at the house to help my Mom with keeping the place clean. She had made an agreement with me at the beginning of the summer that if I would clean the house for her, she would pay me each week. I wanted to get a drum set, and so I figured that would be a good way to get some money to buy the drums.

So, I spent the days waking up when I wanted, making the beds and doing the dishes and sweeping the floors and listening to my records at full blast. I would make hamburgers or fried bologna sandwiches for lunch, with potato chips and, of course, plenty of Coca-cola. In the afternoons, I would go out around the neighborhood and see what was going on or go swimming at the pool.

We had a new lifeguard at the pool, Nicky, and he was a guitar player. The other lifeguards, Kim and Patti, had been there for several years. I was taking Junior Lifeguard training from them and loved the lessons, because we would get to go in the water and pretend we were drowning, or Kim or Patti would pretend they were drowning, and we would "save" them. It was an easy way to rub against their tits or ass, and they both had great bods anyway and were just great to look at in their bikinis.

Nicky played pretty good guitar and had wanted to get a band together. He already had some guys he practiced with, but they weren't at all as good as he was, and he wanted to play skating rinks and school dances. I would play drums with sticks on the tables when Nicky played his guitar down at the pool. I knew all the surf songs that Nicky liked to play and did a good job of playing along with him. He said that I needed to get some drums so we could "jam," as he called it. I was having trouble though talking my Dad into letting me get some drums. He was still disappointed that I hadn't stayed in band.

I had talked my Mom during the school year into letting me get a snare drum from the music teacher that lived across the yard from us and taking lessons. I figured something was better than nothing, but that hadn't lasted long. I could play some of the Sandy Nelson songs I liked and some other simple songs, but whenever I tried to do more than just the snare, I got frustrated and would just give up. I didn't want to take snare lessons anyway. I wanted to play a drum set and play with a band. So, one day I took the snare drum back and left it on the music teacher's front porch. I never went back for another lesson.

The biggest deal I had been waiting for after school was out was the meeting I would have that summer with the school guidance counselor to pick my classes for my junior year. Those classes and my senior year classes were the ones I would absolutely need to get ready for college. I had the class list from the booklet the professor had sent to me and had the booklet if they needed to check it.

When the day finally came, I got up early and got all my work done and then just paced around the house, watching through the window for Mom to get there for the eleven o'clock appointment. Mom came by at eleven o'clock in the drugstore delivery truck. I had learned long ago that you could usually count on my Mom to be late, but I thought for something like this she might make more of an effort.

"Mom, we were supposed to be there at eleven." I piled into the truck.

"I had to deliver some prescriptions before I took my break." One more reason to be late. If it had been one of my brothers going to a game or counselor meeting, she would have been there early.

She pulled out and headed for the school. You could also count on with Mom that if it took twenty minutes to get somewhere, you'd be there in thirty minutes with her driving. It wasn't that she was slow really, she would be distracted, because she was always looking around at stuff, paying more attention to what was going on beside her or behind her than what was going on in front of her.

The school was a pretty good ways from our house, but we made it there in about fifteen minutes. We parked on the street and went in to the main office.

"Oh, hi, Mrs. Bennings." The Office Secretary already knew my mom after having two sons go through the school.

"Hi, Mrs. Clark. We're here to see Mrs. Billington."

"Let me see if she's ready for you."

Mrs. Clark left the office and went into an office across the hallway. Mom stood at the counter while I looked at the bulletin board next to the door. The board had advertisements about tests for students, advertisements for colleges, jobs available for students, a list of important dates for the beginning of the next school year, and an Army recruiting poster. Mrs. Clark came back after a few minutes.

"Mrs. Billington is ready for you."

We walked across the hallway to the Guidance Office and entered. Mrs. Billington stood inside waiting for us.

"Hi, Mrs. Bennings." She shook Mom's hand, then she turned to me.

"Hi, Peter."

"Hi, Mrs. Billington."

"Let's go into my office." She started walked back toward her office as Mom followed, and I followed behind her.

Mrs. Billington sat behind her desk, my Mom sat across from her, and I sat in a chair beside my Mom.

"Now, let's see what we have for you for next year." Mrs. Billington opened a folder on her desk and pulled some papers out of the file and pulled a catalog out from under the folder. She looked back and forth from the file papers to the catalog, making "Hmm" sounds as she did. After several minutes, she began writing on a sheet of paper. She finished writing and turned the paper around to show us what she had written.

"I've looked at Peter's past grades and his test scores, and it looks like this would be the best course for him to follow the next two years." She was speaking to my Mom, not to me. Wasn't it my schedule?

"His math scores are not very good, but, he's done well in English and History and Civics. I would say that he would probably do best by following a course of Business classes, starting next year with Typing I, Accounting, English, and Business Math. He needs to take a foreign language, so we can put him in French I, and then he'll have P.E. as his elective."

I couldn't believe what I was hearing. Business courses? Accounting! Typing! All the classes I hated! I couldn't hold back.

"But I don't wanna take Business classes. I like science, and I wanna be--" Mom cut me off.

"Honey, Mrs. Billington knows what's best for you. She has all of your scores and test results. She knows what will be the best classes for you to take." My Mom sounded like a robot.

"And your scores in Algebra are not very good. You need to take classes where you can do well, and these math classes will be better suited to your abilities." Mrs. Billington had it all wrong.

"But--" I tried to protest again.

"You need to take the classes that Mrs. Billington has put down for you." She took the class schedule from Mrs. Billington and looked it over.

How could this be happening? For the last three years, all I had talked about was going to college to be a Microbiologist. Nothing had ever meant more to me than that. My biology kits, chemistry sets, microscope kits, dissected cat parts, everything I had done over the past years to learn more about science and get ready for being a scientist had been wasted. Now I would be taking business classes and ending up like my brothers, working in an office, selling houses or insurance or something equally as boring.

I followed my Mom out as we left the office and walked to the delivery truck. She kept telling me how my classes were going to be so good, and I would be getting so much out of them, that the guidance counselors knew what they were doing and knew what was best for the students. I couldn't believe she had just sat there and let Mrs. Billington change my life for me. Didn't she know I had been set on being a Microbiologist since before seventh grade? Didn't she realize how much I loved science from all those kits and books and movies that I asked for all the time. She had sat back and let my dream be crushed in just a few minutes time.

The ride home was quiet. I sat looking out the window while my Mom drove and looked around. The ride back seemed to take even longer than the ride to the school. Mom pulled up in front of the house and let me out.

"I'll be home in a while. Did you finish cleaning the house?"

"Yeah. I'm finished all right."

"Okay, I'll see you soon."

I shut the truck door and walked around to the back of the house to let myself in through the back door. The house was quiet and warm from being closed up from the morning. Any other day, I'd be getting ready to have my lunch about now, but today was definitely not just any other day. I went into the living room and put on the radio and lay down in front of the speaker. "What's new pussycat," sang Tom Jones. I liked that song, but it wasn't one I felt like hearing right now.

I got up and dialed through the channels. Wayne Fontana and the Mindbenders were singing about "the game of love"; the Rolling Stones couldn't "get no satisfaction"; and the Animals had to "get out of this place." That was about the way I felt too. As I dialed through the channels, nothing seemed to fit the mood I was feeling. I decided to go out and get on my bike and take a ride up into the woods. I got my bike out of the garage and took off up the street toward the pond and the woods.

As I rode along the street, all I could hear inside my head was Mrs. Billington calling out the classes I'd be taking. "Typing I. Accounting. English. Business Math." What was I going to do now? If I didn't get the classes I needed, I wouldn't be able to enter the Microbiologist program at the college. Didn't my Mom realize how important that was to me? Didn't they understand that? Maybe I could try talking to her and make her realize how important it was. But, how could she not know? All I'd ever talked about was being a Microbiologist. Anytime my parents asked what I wanted for Christmas or my birthday, I would always ask for something like a Biology set or Chemistry set or something having to do with science. Wouldn't it seem that I was interested in that if I always asked for those things? Had I ever said anything to them about wanting to go into business?

I had traveled far from the houses and was climbing the path through the woods that would take me to the railroad tracks and on to Five Mile Creek on the other side of the hill. I stopped at the top of the hill and climbed into the top of a tree where I could look out over the woods and the houses below.

I had no interest in those classes they had put me in, but I would probably not be able to do anything about it. The tears began welling up in my eyes, and I couldn't help starting to cry. Crying was not something that guys were supposed to do, though, and I tried to stop, but I couldn't. I was glad I was alone up there where my friends couldn't see me. But the more I cried, the more I got angry at myself for crying, and the more I got angry at myself for crying, the more I got angry at my Mom and Mrs. Billington for making me cry. I suddenly screamed at the top of my lungs. "Fuck all of you!" I felt better. The scream had helped. I screamed again.

"Okay," I thought to myself, "I've got to stop this and think of something."

So, they thought the best thing for me was to take business classes. Well, no way was that something I wanted to do or was that something I was going to do. I didn't know what I was going to do about this, but one thing for sure, I wasn't going to sell houses or insurance or work in an office like my Dad. I'd think of something.

I climbed down the tree and got back on my bike. I rode off toward the house, and though I had sounded sure of myself when I was on the hill, I was more confused than ever about what lay ahead for me. My thoughts kept going back and forth between being confident and being lost.

When I got back to the house, I put my bike back in the garage and went upstairs to my room. I threw myself on the bed and lay there, trying to think of a plan. I was tired. My mind drifted to thoughts of Rhonda and Debbie. I needed to beat off, but I was too tired, and I couldn't concentrate on it. The last thing I remembered was sitting at the drum set, playing in front of a bunch of screaming girls.

****

I woke up after midnight to the drone of the ceiling fan. All the lights were off, and I could hear the snorchestra playing in my parent's bedroom. I needed to piss.

I went to the bathroom and then went downstairs to get something to eat. A bologna sandwich sounded good. I got a pan out of the cupboard and put a little oil in it, got the bologna and ketchup and mayonnaise out of the fridge and threw a couple of pieces of meat in the hot oil. The bologna smelled great when it hit the oil and started frying. My stomach felt like an empty pit now that needed to be filled. I got a coke out of the fridge and gulped a big drink of it. I got the bread ready and put the sandwich together. I threw the sandwiches on a plate and sat at the counter, taking a huge bite out of one of the sandwiches. That was good.

As I sat there gorging on the bologna, I couldn't help but think of the meeting earlier in the day. I didn't want to think about it anymore. I reached up into the far left cabinet above the counter, where my Dad kept his booze, and pulled down the bottle of bourbon. I got a glass out of the cupboard and put some ice in it and poured some of the bourbon in. I filled it the rest of the way with coke and took a big sip. It just tasted like coke. Maybe I didn't put enough bourbon in it. I opened the bottle and poured more bourbon and took another sip. This time I could definitely taste the bourbon. It burned my throat going down, and I felt a tingle going down into my stomach. I remembered how I felt that night at the cabin. I sure didn't want to feel that way again in the morning. But, right now all I wanted was to not think about the day's events.

I finished the rest of my sandwiches and downed the coke. I poured some more bourbon and coke and went out the back door to the patio and sat in one of the lawn chairs, looking at the stars. I was starting to feel pretty light headed about this time, and my mind again started drifting to Rhonda. What I wouldn't give to be with her right now, her hand on my dick, beating me off, my hands on her boobs, squeezing them and playing with her nipples.

I started getting a boner and needed to go up to the bathroom. I took my drink with me and went upstairs. I quietly shut the door and locked it and set my drink down on the floor. I didn't have to worry about making noise with the ceiling fan going. I sat on the toilet and grabbed my dick, rubbing it as I thought of Rhonda. My mind wandered to thoughts of seeing Donna being fingered and playing with Lynn's tits on the bus at band camp and seeing Rhonda in her swim suit in the boat at the lake. My dick was so hard, I couldn't believe it.

I was stroking now, imagining it was actually Rhonda's hand doing the work. It didn't take long till I was feeling the tingle starting in my balls. I leaned back against the toilet and tightened my grip and stroked harder and the tingle moved up into my dick. The tingle got stronger and my stoking got harder, and then I could feel the tingle moving up through my dick. I stroked my dick feverishly and felt the come spurt out onto my leg. I tried to aim into the toilet, but I had already come all on my leg and on my hand. I didn't care at this point.

My dick was tingling like crazy now, and I was still stoking with the come all over my hand and my dick and my leg. My grip remained on my dick, but the stroking became a lazy up and down movement. I was still resting against the toilet and felt spent. I sat there so long that my hand started to stick to my dick because the come was drying. I took some toilet paper and wiped the still wet come off my hand and dick. My leg was sticky from the dried come.

I got a washcloth and washed off my leg and my dick and washed my hands in the sink. I still felt a little dizzy from the booze, picked up my coke, and went to my room. I turned on the radio and lay down on my bed. WGN was coming in, since it was so late at night, so I lay there listening to the music. It didn't take long before I drifted off to sleep.

****

The next morning I woke up with a nasty headache and just lay there in bed trying to be still enough to keep my head from hurting any more than it did. I lay there for the longest time, or so I thought, my head drifting through so many different thoughts and emotions. The booze had helped me forget for a while, but now I could still hear the conversation from yesterday with Mrs. Billington and hear her say that I would be taking business classes and then hearing my Mom say that the counselors knew what was best for me. When did I get to say what was best for me?

I got up off the bed and went into the bathroom to piss and splash some water in my face, to see if that would help my head stop hurting. I saw my reflection in the oversized mirror and wondered if that was the way other people saw me too. What did people think when they looked at me. Skinny little runt kid with bad teeth? Cute little guy, but no James Bond? Right? Right then I could care less what they thought.

The water helped a little, but my head still pounded. I went into my Mom's bathroom and got some aspirin, took them, and went downstairs to have some cereal. Maybe eating would help.

I downed a couple of bites of Sugar Pops - "Sugar Pops are Tops!" or so the commercial went - but my stomach wasn't ready for Sugar Pops and milk. I tossed the rest of the bowl down the disposal and decided I'd go to the pool for a swim. Maybe the cool water around me would help me feel a little better.

The walk to the pool took me by Darryl's house and Donna's house, nobody home, and then through a wooded, sidewalk area and across a small creek to the pool. The walk was actually fairly relaxing. I usually rode my bike like a maniac down the narrow sidewalk, avoiding any little kids walking to or from the pool, and then would ride up to the fence and screech to a halt at the gate. Today's walk made me, for the first time, realize how nice an area the pool was, against the woods on the outskirts of the housing division my father and his partner helped build.

Kim was getting the pool ready for the day. She had the vacuum going and was skimming the bugs and stuff from the night off the surface of the water.

"Hi. You'll have to wait a few minutes. I just put some chlorine in and need to finish this." I walked up to the covered patio area.

"Okay. I'll just sit here and wait." I didn't mind. I could just sit there at one of the picnic tables and watch her while I was waiting. She looked great in her black two-piece. She must have been about twenty, because she had gone to school with one of my older brothers. What did a guy have to do to get a girl like that to like him? I wished I knew.
She finished going around the pool with the skimmer and put the tools away behind the bathroom building.

"Okay, you can go in now." She walked over to sit in the lifeguard chair.

I left my towel and t-shirt and sandals on the picnic table and went to the diving board. That was my favorite part of the pool, the diving board. I loved to try different dives and jumps. I was pretty good too. I could do a one-and-a-half flip, flip with a half twist, back flip, back flip with a full twist, and a lots of other dives. Right now, I just wanted to get in the water, so I just dove straight in.

The coolness of the water felt great and made my skin and my head tingle. Maybe it was the water or maybe it was the aspirin, but my head was feeling much better now. I surfaced and went to the shallow end and just lay in the water, enjoying it surrounding me. I parked myself in front of one of the water jets, lay back with my eyes closed, and let the water stream against my back. It felt great and relaxed me immensely.

I must have been there for at least thirty minutes, I may have even nodded off, when someone splashed into the water and broke my spell.

I opened my eyes and saw a body swimming under the surface to the other side of the pool. A head popped up out of the water, and I could see it was a guy. He looked about my age, maybe a year older. He shook his hair and looked over at me.

"Hey, how're you doing?"

He swam over to where I was.

"Hi, I'm Allan. I just moved here a couple of days ago."

"I'm Peter. I've lived here about five years now."

"What grade are you in?"

"I'll be a junior next year."

"I'll be a sophomore. My dad works at a television station as a cameraman and show movies at the Arkansas Theatre."

"Wow, that's pretty cool. Do you get to see all the movies?"

"Yeah, I can go with him and get in to the balcony anytime I want. You wanna go some time?"

"Sure."

"Hey, you like the Stones?"

"Yeah, the British groups are cool. The Yardbirds. Them. The Animals. Hey, do you like the Beatles?"

"Yeah, they're pretty good too. But Mick and the Stones are the best." He kind of looked like Mick Jagger a little.

We swam for a while and talked about music and school and girls and lots of stuff and stayed for a couple of hours more before deciding to go and have some lunch. We'd go to his house, because his mom was home and would make something for us.

Allan's house was a block down from our house, in the middle of the block, with a long sloping yard and driveway. We went in through the carport door and entered the family room. His mom was in the kitchen.

"Hi honey. Who's your friend?"

"This is Peter."

"Well, hi Peter." She sounded nice. "Where do you live?"

"I live up the street on the corner."

"You must be Jack's son then."

"Yes, ma'am. That's my dad."

"You can call me Momma. All Allan's friends call me Mama Si and call Allan's dad Papa. Okay, hon?"

"Yes, ma'am."

"You boys want something for lunch?"

"Yeah." Allan looked to me. "You want a hamburger or something?"

"That'd be great."

Allan's grandmother came in from the other room about that time.

"There you are. Where have you been?" She grabbed Allan and hugged him. Another hugger.

"I was down at the pool."

"And who's this?" She was moving toward me.

"I'm Peter."

"Well hi hon. I'm Allan's grandmother." My turn to get hugged.

"Momma, this is Mr. Benning's son, the real estate man." Mamma Si was in the kitchen. I could smell the hamburgers cooking.

"Oh? honey, your daddy is so nice. He's a musician too, like me. I like musicians. Do you play anything?"

"I've been playing sax for a few years, but I'm not very good. I stopped playing in band last year. I wanna play the drums in a band."

"Your daddy plays sax too, doesn't he?" She sure knew a lot about my Dad.

"Yeah; he played when he was younger, but he doesn't play hardly at all any more." I always wondered why he didn't play any more.

"Here you go, boys." Momma put our hamburgers on the table.

We scarfed down the hamburgers and went to Allan's room. His room was very cool. He didn't have any brothers or sisters, so his parents got him about anything he wanted. The walls had posters of Mick Jagger and Keith Richards and The Who. Those were his favorites. His closet was filled with Gant shirts and Levi's. I was impressed.

Then, he reached into his drawer and pulled out a pack of cigarettes. He offered one to me, and I took it. My parents and my brothers smoked, and Petey and I had stolen his sister's cigarettes and taken them to the woods and smoked them. But I had never smoked on a regular basis. He lit his with his lighter and grabbed an ashtray, and I lit mine.

We sat there and listened to the Stones on his stereo and talked more about school and girls and cars, and I started getting a little light-headed from the cigarette. It was a weird feeling, but I was kind of enjoying it. It was a little like taking a sip of the whiskey bottle.

We talked some more and smoked another cigarette, and then he said he had to get going. He was getting his driving permit in a few weeks and was going to be driving his dad's Falcon, even though he wouldn't be able to get his license until next summer, and he was going to go practice with his mom.

I thanked Momma for the burger and said my goodbye's and went home. The house was empty, so I grabbed a coke from the fridge and went to my room and turned on the radio. I still felt a little light-headed from the cigarettes and lay down on my bed. The breeze from the window felt good, and I drifted off to sleep.

****

The breeze had cooled into the evening. I lay on the bed with a boner and drowsily came back to life. The house was quiet except for "She's Not There" playing on my radio. I listened and dreamt of Rhonda. I needed to do something about that. Rhonda was gone. As much as I had wanted her, I knew now it was never going to happen. I remembered the girl that Debbie had brought to the party at Darryl's house. Cathy. She was damn cute and had wanted me to call her while she was in town, but that was during my Rhonda period, and nobody could take my mind off of her. I'd heard that Cathy had moved to North Little Rock and lived not too far from our house. I'd have to get her number and give her a call, maybe invite her down to the pool some time.

Now, I was hungry, and I needed a plan. I fixed some bologna sandwiches, grabbed a coke, and went back to my room. Everyone was already in bed or asleep for the evening, so I wouldn't be bothered. One of my favorite songs came on, "For Your Love," and I imagined myself playing the drums and beat on the desk and chair like they were my drum set. I made up my mind that I wouldn't give up until I had a set of drums. I would talk to Nicky the next time he was at the pool and find out a good place to look for some drums. I'd been saving the money that Mom had been paying me for cleaning the house and had about forty dollars saved. I figured I'd probably need a few hundred dollars to get a decent set, so I'd have to figure a way to get the rest of it.

I was getting excited now, thinking about actually having a set of drums, having girls screaming at me while I played. I wasn't tired at all and was too excited to sit around the room, so I went downstairs, got a coke from the fridge, poured a little bourbon into it and went out onto the patio. The bourbon made me light-headed, like the cigarette had earlier. I went in the house and found my Mom's purse and grabbed a couple of her cigarettes and some matches out of the kitchen. I grabbed my radio from the room and went back outside. I lit one of the cigarettes and sat on the lounge chair. I knew better than to take too deep a drag on the cigarette and slowly drew the smoke in. It felt good and made me tingle. I took a sip of the bourbon and coke and that made me tingle too.

My mind started racing with thoughts of playing drums. What color would I get? I liked the color blue a lot, so maybe I'd get some blue ones. A lot of bands had white or black drums, but blue would be a good color. How many cymbals would I get? I'd at least need a ride cymbal and a crash cymbal. I remembered seeing the Beatles and the Stones on Ed Sullivan. Ringo and Charlie Watts didn't have a lot of cymbals, and they were good drummers. I'd have to start listening closer to the drums and watching what the drummers did. I remembered back to Gene Krupa playing on my Dad's records. He used a lot of tom-toms on his songs, especially on that one song. Damn, I couldn't remember the name of it right now, if I ever even knew the name, but I'd have to listen to that one some more.

I finished the cigarette and decided to take a walk. The neighborhood was so quiet it was like a cemetery. That was one thing you could count on in our neighborhood. After ten o'clock, nothing was happening. Most lights in most houses were off, and only rarely did you ever see a car drive through that late. I could walk the streets with no fear of anyone even seeing me.

I walked around for a while, drank the rest of the bourbon and coke, and smoked another cigarette. I was getting a little tired now and decided to go back to the house.

I sneaked into the back door, grabbed a few more cigarettes out of Mom's purse, and went to my room. I lay on my bed and dreamed more of drums and girls. I'd have to call Cathy tomorrow and see if she wanted to come swimming with me.

****

Friday was Nicky's day at the pool, so I got up early and went down to talk with him. He was cleaning the pool from all the little critters who were attracted to the water and then died from drinking the pool chemicals.

"Hey, Peter." I plopped down on the grass and watched him skim the water.

"I wanna start playing drums."

"That's great. I'm trying to get a band together right now. What do your parents think about you playing?"

"I could care less what they think. My Dad's never wanted me to play drums. Why, I don't know. I quit sax last year, which pissed him off, so I don't give a shit if they want me to play or not. I'm gonna play drums."

"If they don't want you to play, how are you gonna get some drums?"

"I don't know. But I have some friends who play who might let me use theirs for a while."

"I tell you what." He kept skimming the dead bugs from the water. "Why don't you see if you can borrow some drums, and we'll have a jam down here at the pool and see how things go. I'll bring my PA, and we can maybe get someone to sing some songs with us."

"That sounds cool!" I was in heaven.

"Okay. You go work on that. Let me know what you find out before I go today, and I'll bring my stuff with me tomorrow. Maybe we can get some of the kids around here to come down while we play."

I jumped on my bike and headed for the house to start calling people.

I was at the house in no time and was looking up numbers for my friends who had drums. I tried Mark, but he wasn't home, so I called my friend, James, who was also a drummer in the school band. He was home and said I could borrow an old set of his to use. I'd get my brother to take me to pick them up later.

I raced down to the pool and gave Nicky the news. He'd tell all the kids coming down that we were having a party at the pool tomorrow with a band. He'd get some songs together that we could jam on and try to find a singer. My job was to tell everyone I ran into about the party too.

I was excited about getting to play for real with a guitar player but also worried. I'd have to show that I could do something with the drums once I got behind them. It wouldn't be like the party at Darryl's house where I had cloth covering the tips of the drums sticks and was just pretending to play pretty much. Now I would have to play along with a guitar player and maybe a singer. It might be my last chance to show that I could play the drums and should have some drums.

I put on my Sandy Nelson records and listened to some other songs while I waited for my brother to get home. He was home from college for a few weeks, living on the couch and running around with his college friends most of the time. He sometimes wouldn't come around for days at a time. He had a new girlfriend who was an English teacher. They spent a lot of time running around and were always having heated arguments about people I'd never heard of. College stuff. They were pretty wild too. One time I heard them all talking about how my brother and she had gone out one night to find tires for her VW Bug. My brother would lift up the back of the VW's, and she would loosen the tires. They were quite a team.

Later that afternoon, they came to get some of his clothes, and I talked them into taking me to get James' drums. They thought it was cool that I would be playing drums with a band. So did I.

We picked up the drums, and James showed me how to put them together and a little about playing them. It was a small four-piece set with a snare, bass drum, ride tom, and floor tom, and he let me use his ride cymbal, a crash cymbal, and the hi-hat. It was plenty for what we were going to do. He loaned me some of his sticks and said I could keep the drums for a few days, if I wanted. He couldn't have even imagined how much I wanted to keep them those few days. We got them home, and I set them up in the living room in front of the stereo, so I could listen to records and play along. My brother and his girlfriend left, and I was all alone to try out the drums.

I put on the Sandy Nelson record, "Drums are My Beat," and just played along, trying to figure out which drums he was using to make different sounds. After I played around for a while with the record, my feet and hands started just doing things without me even trying. I was actually playing along with the record and sounding pretty good. I had played around on pots and pans and books and desktops and with other friends' borrowed drums sets enough that I had a little bit of an idea of what to do when I got behind the set, and I was having a blast.

I stopped playing when my parents got home from work and explained to them about the drums. They were not real happy that I had borrowed them without asking, but my Mom knew how much I had wanted to play the drums and helped smooth things over with Dad.

Later that night, after dinner, I called Cathy.

"Hello." A woman answered. I guessed it was her mom.

"Hi. I was wondering if I could speak to Cathy."

"Who is this?"

"I'm a friend of her friend, Debbie. We met at a party here."

"And what's your name?"

"Peter."

"Okay. Hang on, please." She put her hand over the mouthpiece.

I could hear her calling for Cathy in the background. I could hear them whispering when Cathy came to the phone.

"Do you know this boy?"

"I met him when I went to Debbie's for that party last summer."

"You have five minutes to talk to him." She sounded pretty strict.

I could hear the phone being handed over.

"Hello."

"Hi, Cathy. It's Peter. We met at the Beatles party."

"I remember. Hi, Peter. How are you?" She had a sweet voice.

"I'm doing great. Debbie told me you moved here after school was out."

"My dad got transferred here. He works for the railroad. We used to live here and then moved to this little town down south for the past couple of years. I'm glad to be back."

"I was calling because we're having a party at our pool tomorrow, and I wondered if you would like to come. Me and the lifeguard, Nicky, are gonna play some music." It felt good to be saying that I would be playing music.

"That sounds like fun. I'll have to ask my mom."

"Okay." I listened while she talked with her mom but couldn't hear what was being said.

"My mom says she'll bring me over for a while. What time?"

"Just come down to the pool about two. We'll probably go to about four."

"Okay. I'll see you then. Thanks for asking me."

"I'll see you there. Bye."

Wow. That was easier than I had expected. She had sounded super sweet on top of being damn cute. This could be the start of something good, I thought.

I got some of my records and went to the living room and lay in front of the stereo and listened to them over and over, memorizing the drum parts and figuring out how the different drums and cymbals were being used. I liked Jan and Dean, so I listened to "Dead Man's Curve" and "Surf City" just in case Nicky wanted to do some of those. I already knew "Wipe Out" and some of the other instrumental songs by the Surfaris and the Hondells, so that would be easy to follow them.

I lay there for hours, unable to get to sleep, so excited about the coming day. After everyone went to bed, I got a coke and poured some of Dad's Jack Daniels in it and laid back down in front of the stereo. After a while, I got light-headed and dozed off. I woke up after the last song on the stack finished and went to bed, thoughts of the next day whirling through my head.

****

Saturday began like a nightmare. I awoke to wind and rain from a thunderstorm beating on my bedroom window and on the roof. "Shit." Now nobody would come to the pool. Would Nicky even bring his stuff with the rain and wind blowing like it was? I became depressed very quickly. Would Cathy call and say she couldn't come now because her mother would be afraid she would be struck by lightning at the pool?

I had slept later than I wanted, almost ten o'clock now, and I scrambled to get my clothes on and snatch some breakfast. I was starved. I hadn't had my usual late night snack of bologna sandwiches, so I poured an extra full bowl of Sugar Pops and sliced a banana over the top. It was gone in no time.

The rain let up a little, so I got on my bike and hurried to the pool to see if Nicky was even there. He was. But I didn't see any equipment. Shit, my debut as a drummer would have to be put off to another time.

"Hey, Peter. Where's your stuff?"

"I didn't know if you were still planning to play with the rain and all."

"A little rain won't hurt anything. We'll be under the patio cover anyway."

A sense of relief poured through me. Even if no kids came, I'd still get to play the drums with a real guitar player.

"Go get your stuff. Allan'll be down here in a little while to sing with us."

"Allan?"

"Yeah. That kid Allan who moved here a couple of weeks ago. He's a good little singer and knows some of the stuff I do."

"Wow, that's cool. I'll be right back!" I screamed and jumped on my bike and sped home.

The rain had pretty much stopped by this time, so I grabbed my little brother's wagon and stacked the drums on it. It was tight, but it worked. Now the only problem would be getting them to stay on as I pulled the wagon over the bumps and holes in the street and the sidewalk going down to the pool. The little bridge over the creek might be a little bit of a problem too, but I'd almost be to the pool by that time.

After only a few minor emergencies, the bass drum was a little too big for the wagon and kept sliding and pushing the tom tom over the edge, I made it to the bridge. From there I just grabbed what I could get in a handful and carried the drums and hardware the rest of the way inside the fence and onto the patio.

I wanted to pretend I was on a real stage, so I set up on top of one of the picnic tables. It was tight, but I got them all on with a little squeezing. I started warming up playing "Wipe Out" on the floor tom.

Nicky was setting up his guitar stuff and stopped to listen. He grinned and finished plugging in his stuff. He joined in playing the guitar part to the song, and we were playing together in no time.

We kept that up for a few minutes, and then Nicky stopped playing, so I stopped too.

"Hey, that was boss, man." He tuned his guitar and set it down on the table. "Allan should be down here any time."

I started playing again, trying to do some of the beats that I had practiced the day before. I could hear the guitars in my head and tried to play along with them.

The pool was pretty empty, probably because of the rain. Nobody hardly came down when it was raining. As long as Cathy made it, I could care less if nobody else showed up. I kept banging on the drums, waiting for Nicky and Allan. I was getting into a Gene Krupa beat when I looked up and saw Cathy sitting at the table in front of me. I froze.

"Don't stop." She smiled. She got up and came over to the table. "I love listening to the drums. I knew when I saw you at the party that you would be a good drummer."

"We were just playing along with the records then."

"No, you were really playing the drums that night. You had the sticks covered, but I could see you hitting them."

I couldn't believe that she had remembered all that or that she even cared about whether I was playing for real or not.

The rain poured down now. Nicky ran under the patio cover and pulled his guitar and stuff closer to the center. The drums were okay on the table where I had set them up.

"You think Allan's goin' to make it?"

Nicky strummed his guitar. "We'll just hang loose and play something anyway."

Nicky immediately started playing a surf song, and I joined in with the surf beat. I could see Cathy staring at me, and I looked away so I could concentrate on keeping the beat with Nicky.

We kept playing for over an hour, while the rain kept starting and stopping. Every time it stopped I thought people might show up, but nobody ever came, and Allan never showed up.

Cathy sat and listened to us and clapped every time we finished a song. Our lone fan. I thought she might be getting a little bored though, just sitting there by herself, and then her mom pulled up and honked for her. She got up and waved at her. We stopped playing, and I got down off the table to say goodbye to her.

"Thanks again for asking me over today, Peter. I'm sorry more people weren't here to hear you. They missed some good music."

"I hope it wasn't too boring for you with nobody else showing up."

"I didn't come here to see anyone but you, Peter. I wasn't bored at all."

Her eyes twinkled when she said this, and I couldn't believe that she was talking to me that way. I started to get brave.

"Hey. Do you think we could go to a show some time?" And I couldn't believe I was asking her out already.

"I'd love to. But I need to ask my mom first. When did you wanna go?"

"How about tonight?" I was amazed at how brave I was getting.

"Sure. Why don't you call me when you get home."
Her mom honked again.

"Bye."

I watched as she ran through the drizzle and jumped in the front seat of the station wagon. She waved and smiled as her mom took off.

I needed to quickly get the drums home and find out if I could go tonight. I'd have to wait until the rain stopped to take the drums back to the house. If I ever wanted to borrow James' drums again, I'd need to get them back to him in good shape. What I needed to do more than anything was get to work on getting my set. Playing with Nicky showed me that I could do it, and I felt like it would be easier to maybe talk the parents into it. Well, at least my Mom. I didn't think I'd ever talk Dad into it. Mom was the one I needed to work on. Nicky was packing up his stuff, so I started taking the set apart.

"Hey, Peter, that was cool, man. I've got some buddies that I play with sometimes. We have a drummer, but you're better than he is. If you could get some drums, we could probably get a group going to play some of the dances at the high school. I know a skate rink where they have dances after the skating is over too."

"I'm working on the drums, but I told you, my Dad isn't too happy with me not playing sax any more. My Mom's okay with it though, so I'm gonna work on her."

"She comes down here with your little brother sometimes. I'll mention it to her that we jammed and that you're a good drummer."

"If we're playing and making a little money so I could pay for 'em, she'd probably go along with it."

"Well, work on her then, man."

Nicky had finished putting his guitar stuff away and went out to check the pool.

I was ready to put the drums on the wagon now, so I loaded the wagon and sat under the cover waiting for the rain to stop.

Nicky came back after a few minutes.

"Nobody's gonna come down this late with the rain, so I'm outta here. I'll give you a ride with the drums, and you can leave the wagon here til tomorrow."

We loaded the drums and his guitar stuff in his car, and he dropped me off at my house. We stuck the drums in the garage.

Nobody was home, so I went upstairs and got changed. Mom would probably be home in a while, and I could ask her about going to the show later. Even with the rain, the day had turned out to be great. I couldn't wait until that night and maybe getting to go to the show with Cathy. I would have to make that happen.

****

Mom got home later in the afternoon and told me I could call Cathy and ask her about going to the show. What were we gonna see? I'd have to look at the paper and see what was going. I could care less what we went to see. I'd be watching her the whole time. I'd gotten a good look at her at the pool and remembered her freckles and soft-looking skin. I bet it was super soft. I loved her long blonde hair too.

When Mom said she'd take us, all I could think of was the time when I could call a girl and ask her on a date and get to jump in my car and pick her up. I'd be sixteen in a few months and could take my driver's test. I'd already driven a few times with Mom and Dad in the car, but I'd need to do some more practicing for the driver's test.

I called Cathy, and she said her mom was okay with us going if she drove us. That was fine with me. I was just glad to be going. We talked about a couple of different movies. I wanted to see the new James Bond movie, but of course I didn't push it. She wanted to see the Beatles movie. I told her I wanted to see the Beatles movie too, so we settled on it. She would pick me up at seven o'clock. Now I had to figure what to wear.

I went through my closet, trying to find something to impress her. We normally went just before school started to get new clothes for the school year, so everything I had was from the last year. I finally settled on some Levi's and a Gant look-alike shirt. I had to polish my penny loafers a little, since they'd been sitting in the closet since school was out, and I put on some of my Brut after shave. I didn't shave yet, but just having the after shave made me feel more grown up.

I hit Dad up for some money for the show and maybe a burger or something afterwards and made a bologna sandwich. The more I thought about the night ahead, the more I felt antsy, so I got a coke and sneaked some of Dad's Jack Daniels into it and went to the living room and put on some records and waited.

Right at seven o'clock the doorbell rang. When I opened the door, there she stood. She had on a flowered skirt and shirt, just the kind I liked on girls, and had her hair pulled to one side with a hair clip. She was so pretty, I just stood and stared at her.

"Hi, Peter." She finally broke the silence.

"Hi." I heard myself stammering.

She took my hand and led me to the car. She got in the front seat, and I followed.

"Mom, this is Peter." Cathy sat in the middle, and I scooted into the seat next to her.

"Hi, Peter."

"Hi, Mrs. Kingman." I was still stammering, but I couldn't help it.

"What show are you two going to again?"

I think Cathy was waiting for me to answer, but when I didn't, she did. "We're gonna see the Beatles' movie, *HELP!* It's at the Park Theatre."

The Park Theatre was on Park Hill and was the place where most kids went on Friday and Saturday nights to see the new movies. The closest theatre from there was in downtown North Little Rock and usually showed more adult type movies. That's where the James Bond movies were usually shown. You had to go across the river to Little Rock to find the other movie theatres.

The drive up the hill to Park Hill was quiet except for a few questions by Cathy's mom. "What does your father do, Peter?" "What are you planning to do after high school?" "What classes are you taking next year?" Cathy and I had no chance to talk ourselves with me answering her mom's questions.

When we got to the theatre, a line of kids was standing at the ticket booth.

"Do you think we'll be able to get in?"

"Yeah. They have a balcony and a downstairs."

"I'll wait to see that you get in, just in case,." Her mom wasn't going to take any chances.

We got out of the car and went to get in the line. It was going pretty quickly, so it didn't take long to get the tickets. We waved at Cathy's mom and went into the theatre. I stopped at the snack counter and got us some popcorn and drinks, then we went to find some seats. The bottom was pretty full.

"Let's go check the balcony." Cathy pulled me up the steps.

We went up the winding stairs to the balcony and went through the double doors. The balcony was not as full. Cathy pulled me to some seats near the back, and we settled in. The cartoon was just starting.

We set the drinks down and put the popcorn between us and dug in.

"I didn't have any supper yet." Cathy was already munching on the popcorn and had downed the drink.

"I had a bologna sandwich, but that was about it."

"Do you like bologna sandwiches too?"

"Almost as much as hamburgers." She was super easy to talk to.

"Oh, I love hamburgers." She screamed and grabbed a handful of popcorn.

Tweety bird was beating Sylvester with a mallet, making us laugh, and then the cartoon was over. The movie started with the Beatles singing the song from the movie.

"I just love the Beatles." The song ended. "I know you must like them a lot too. You were Ringo at the party."

"Yeah, I like 'em too." I wasn't going to let Cathy know that I didn't like them as much as some of the other English groups. At least not yet.

The movie didn't have much of a plot. Just the Beatles singing their songs and running around a lot. It wasn't like the James Bond movies where Bond was fighting all kinds of bad guys and getting lots of beautiful girls. And every time John or Paul was on the screen, the girls would scream their names. Cathy wasn't screaming though, which I was glad of. I wasn't paying much attention to the movie anyway. I was pretty much watching Cathy. She looked even prettier in the light from the screen, and she kept looking over at me, and I'd try to look like I wasn't looking at her and was watching the movie, but after a few times of catching me looking at her, she leaned over to me.

"Do you want to kiss me?"

"Yeah."

She leaned closer, and I leaned in to kiss her. Her lips were warm and soft. She stopped and took my arm and put it around her, and we started kissing again. She was a good kisser. She didn't just sit there and keep her mouth still. She moved her lips and took her tongue and licked my lips. I could feel my dick starting to get hard. Then she pulled away.

"That was nice. You're a good kisser. I don't normally go around kissing boys on the first date. But I like you a lot, Peter. I've liked you ever since I saw you at the party."

I couldn't believe what I was hearing. Here I'd spent all that time trying to get Rhonda when Cathy had liked me the whole time. And Cathy was just as cute but a little bit taller than Rhonda. She might have even been a little taller than me, but I could care less if she didn't care.

I had no idea what to say, but I figured I'd better say something.

"I love your lips. You're a good kisser too."

I leaned over and kissed her again. This time she took her tongue and put it in my mouth. She tasted so good. I moved my tongue with her, trying to match her every move, and I hoped I tasted as good to her as she tasted to me. My dick was getting super hard now, and I wished she would put her hand on it or that I could jack off. What would even be better was if she jacked me off. I didn't dare take her hand and put it on me, though.

My arm was still around her, and I slid my free hand to her stomach and started rubbing her stomach. I wondered if I would be able to feel her boobs, so I moved my hand closer and closer and tried to get a feel with my arm across her chest. I managed to rub my arm across one and felt it through her bra. She wasn't flat chested, but she wasn't big either. I got brave and moved my hand to her boob, and she moved it away. She whispered in my ear.

"Not yet."

I was kind of embarrassed then that I'd tried. I hoped she didn't think I was too forward. I stopped kissing her.

"I'm sorry."

"It's okay. I just don't want my shirt to be wrinkled when my mom picks us up. She's pretty strict about stuff, especially since she caught my sister and her boyfriend in bed."

I didn't feel so embarrassed now that I knew why she didn't want me to feel her.

"What did your parents do?"

"They grounded her forever just about. They can't go out at all. He just comes up and visits her on the weekends, and they have to sit around the house with my parents there. I don't think she's going to go out with him much longer."

"It doesn't sound like much fun for her."

"She hates it. She's used to running around wherever and whenever she wants. But I know she sneaks out sometimes in the middle of the night. I think he waits down the street for her, and they do it in his car."

"What's her name?" I asked.

"Debby. She'll be a junior next year with you."

I knew Cathy would be in the ninth grade next year at Ridge Road, where I had gone to school. I wished now that she would be going to high school with me.

The movie was ending, so we got up and went downstairs to call Cathy's mom to come pick us up. We waited in front of the theatre, talking about the movie, what we saw of it, and about seeing each other again as soon as possible.

Cathy's mom pulled up, and we jumped in the car. She did seem to give Cathy a pretty good looking over when she got in the car.

"Mom, can we go get a hamburger at McDonald's?"

"It's late honey, and we need to get up to go to church tomorrow."

We rode home with the usual questions about how the movie was and if we liked it and all that. Her mom dropped me off, and I thanked her for taking me and letting us go. She said maybe we could do it again sometime, and I said that would be great. Cathy smiled at me as I closed the door. I could still feel her warm lips on mine. I wanted to give her a kiss, but I figured her mom wouldn't like that. I watched them drive away and then went in the house.

Mom was asleep on the couch, and Dad was in bed.

I raided the kitchen, bologna sandwich and chips, Coke, and went up to my room. I turned on the radio and gobbled the sandwich and sipped on the Coke. More British groups were being played on the radio now. The Yardbirds, Herman's Hermits, The Dave Clark Five. The more I heard them, the more I loved the music and wanted to play it. Now, all I had to do was get some drums and start doing some more playing with Nicky and his friends. Monday, I would get on the bus and go to Moses and check out the drum sets. I had about fifty dollars put away now, which should at least be a good down payment for the drums. Then I'd have to figure some other way to get the rest.

I went down to the kitchen and grabbed another Coke. Mom was still snoring on the couch, so I sneaked open the booze cabinet and poured some of the Jack Daniels into the bottle. I went back to my room and sipped on the drink. I liked the warmth of the booze as it trickled down to my stomach. I started feeling light-headed pretty quickly and laid on my bed, thinking of the night's events. I could feel Cathy's warm lips on mine and her tongue playing with mine. I could taste her and could feel the softness of her stomach through her shirt. I wanted to remember touching her boobs but had to imagine what they would feel like. She would have probably let me feel them if we had been alone.

Thinking about touching her started a boner going, and I needed to do something about it. I went to the bathroom and shut the door. It didn't take long to get the boner going to a rock solid hard on. I could feel Cathy's boobs and tasted them. She grabbed my boner and took over for me. It didn't take long for me to come all over her hand, and she just kept rubbing on me with her wet hand slipping up and down on my boner. That kept me going, and I came again. She took my hand and put it in her panties, and I could feel her pussy and the hairs around it. I sank back against the toilet and couldn't move.

I awoke with my hand stuck to my dick and grabbed a washcloth and cleaned the dried come off of my hand and dick and stomach.

I went back to my room and fell onto my bed and began to drift off thinking about drums and Cathy. I would definitely have to do something about both of them or go crazy.

****

Monday came finally, after an almost forever Sunday of rain and more rain. The sun was breaking through the clouds and the rain had stopped, at least for a while. The rain could start again at any time, but I was going to go on my trip to Moses Music rain or shine.

I walked to the bus stop and waited for the Main Street bus. The music store was on Main Street in Little Rock, but the bus would take me to Main Street in North Little Rock, and then I could either catch a bus to take me across the bridge to Little Rock or just walk across the bridge and the few blocks to the music store.

The bus came, and I got on and sat by a window. Not many people were on the bus, so I pretty much could sit where I wanted. I watched the houses and cars and stores and gas stations and grocery stores and all of the trees and dirt lots as we passed through the city. Everything was still wet from the weekend rain, but the sun was starting to dry things out. I decided I'd walk over the bridge when I got off the bus downtown.

The music store was only about five blocks north of the river, so it only took me about ten minutes to walk across the bridge and to the store. The closer I got, the more excited I got. What color would I get? What could I get for fifty dollars anyway? I didn't know much about the kinds of drums, except that a lot of drummers from England used Ludwig drums. I figured that would be a good place to start.

As I stepped into the store, every kind of music and instrument just about could be heard. People were all over the store playing guitars and flutes and saxophones and talking with sales people. I didn't see the drums at first but I could hear drums being played. Then a salesman came up to me.

"Hey, how're you doing today? Can I help you with something?"

"I was looking for the-- "

"Drums." How did he know that?

"Yeah, how did you know?"

"I can tell a drummer a mile away. Just follow the sound up the escalator to the second floor." He pointed to the middle of the store where the up and down escalators were located.

As the escalator carried me closer to the top, my heart pounded harder and harder. The sound of the drums being played got louder and louder the closer I got. Then the floor opened up to a sea of drums, drums of all colors, four-piece sets, five-piece sets, double-bass drum sets. I was in drum heaven.

The first thing I noticed was all the different names of the sets. Rogers. Slingerland. Yamaha. Ludwig. Premier. I hadn't ever heard of most of these sets and felt pretty lost now. I hadn't ever paid much attention to the drums that Gene Krupa, Sandy Nelson, Ringo, or other drummers used, so I figured the first place to start would be to look for colors that I liked and then look at different size sets. I liked blue, so I started looking for blue sets.

My eye caught a blue sparkle that looked pretty cool. It had two bass drums, with a tom-tom on each one, and a floor tom, snare, and a couple of cymbal stands and a hi-hat. I started circling it, checking out the way the light reflected off the blue sparkle, and tapped on the drums as I passed each one. A salesman came up after a few taps.

"Looking for a new set?"

"Yeah."

"I can help you out. My name's Gary." He pushed his hand toward me.

"I'm Peter."

"You wanna try 'em out, Peter?" He handed me a pair of sticks and motioned for me to sit on the drum throne.

"Sure."

It was a lot of drum set. The throne raised me a little too high to reach the bass drum pedals the way I needed to, but I just inched forward on the seat so that my feet hit the pedals right. I lightly tapped the drums, afraid that Gary might not want me to hit them too hard.

"Go ahead and pound on 'em. You won't hurt 'em."

I immediately thought of one of my favorite drum songs, "Let There Be Drums," and started playing my version of Sandy Nelson's song.

Using the two bass drums felt a little weird at first, but I quickly started getting into being able to use the bass drums like the tom-toms.

"Sounds like you've played some before."

"I've borrowed my friend's sets sometimes to play. But I haven't ever had my own set before."

"This would be a great starter set, Peter. It's not as expensive as some of the other brands. And you could always start by just using one bass drum until you get used to the two of 'em."

I took a look at the price tag. Two hundred and forty-nine dollars and ninety-nine cents. Way more than what I had.

"I don't have two hundred and fifty dollars. Do you have any sets that cost less?"

"Okay, Peter. Let me ask you something. Do you like this set?"

"Yeah. This is a real cool set."

"Alright, then. How much money do you have, Peter?"

"Fifty dollars." I pulled the money out of my pocket to show him.

"Well, that's a start. Do you know if your parents have an account here at the store?"

"No. But they bought my brother his clarinet and the sax that I used in band. They might have bought 'em here." I hoped that they had bought them there and not some other music store.

"Let's go check." Gary motioned for me to come with him.

We went to a counter, and Gary gave me a piece of paper.

"Write your parent's names and your address." I wrote the information for him, and he took it and got on the phone.

Customers packed the store now and waited for salesman to wait on them. I moved out of the way of the counter and the waiting customers and looked around through the drum stuff, the sticks, snare drums, cymbals that filled the counter and wall shelves. I couldn't believe all of the different sizes of drum sticks. Some had nylon tips on them. Some had rounded tips. Some had pointed tips. I wondered what the difference was. Which ones should I be using?

Gary found me after a while.

"I talked to our accounting department. They said your parents don't have an account with us. But we can start one, if one of your parents will fill out the application."

"I can't just do it?"

"One of 'em will have to sign it to make it legal. That way we can set up a payment schedule for you and pay your drums off in about twelve months."

I could see now that the drums might have to wait until I could get the money together. That might take another year or so though, unless I could sell something or get a job doing something.

"I guess it'll have to wait. My Dad doesn't want me to play the drums anyway."

"What about your mom?"

"I help her around the house, so she might sign for me."

"Let's go call her." Gary motioned for me to follow him back to the counter.

I called the drug store, and Mom happened to be there. I told her what was going on, and she said we'd have to talk about it at home.

I thanked Gary for all his help and told him I'd let him know what happened with Mom. He gave me a card with the store phone number and his name and told me to call and ask for him.

"I'll save that set for you."

I walked away from the counter and went down the escalator to the front door. The warm, wet air hit me as I left the store and walked out onto the sidewalk toward the river bridge. I stopped at Woolworth's and had a malt and a hamburger and then continued across the bridge to catch the bus to take me back home. It was now afternoon, and I wanted to get home before Mom and Dad. I didn't want to do anything to mess up the evening. I knew that that evening might be the end or the beginning of me being a drummer.

'66

****

Sitting there in the crowded classroom, the teacher droning on about something, maybe English, at the front of the room, I wished I was back in bed. Summer school was not my idea of how to spend my summer, but I had flunked a semester of English and a semester of Economics during my junior year and had to take the summer classes if I wanted to graduate the next year. I didn't give a shit if I graduated or not, but my Mom and Dad weren't about to let one of their sons embarrass them by not getting through high school.

Economics was one of those business classes that Mrs. Billington had said would be good for me to take. And it wasn't that I didn't like English, I had always done pretty well in it, but the first day of class just set the stage for the rest of the year. Mrs. Baumgardner had been my brother's teacher too, two years before, and she recognized the name.

"Peter Bennings. Do you have an older brother?"

"Yes."

"I sure hope you're as good a student as he was."

I can't think of anything worse for a teacher to do than to compare you to an older brother or sister or expect you to be the same as they were. So that blew the whole year for me right there. I could never compete with my brother, not only the pride of my parents but the model student for all his teachers, so why the hell even try.

School was the least thing on my mind anyway. Since I had gotten my drums, I had been constantly playing in bands and enjoying being recognized as a drummer with the kids around school. Girls that would never have even paid any attention to me before were now saying "Hi" to me in the halls between classes or writing notes to me or just talking to me. Even cheerleaders, who any guy in school would have killed to go out with, would smile and say "Hi" to me. Of course, I was too shy to start a conversation with any of them or ask them out, but I felt good knowing that they recognized me.

My favorite hangout at school was the "Smoking Hole," the one area at school, outlined by a rectangle of white paint at the entrance to the football stadium, where those of us guys that smoked could have a stogy at lunch time. No girls ever showed up at the "hole," and the guys who did show up there were not the honor society, drama club, student council BMOC's. The "hole" was home to the '57 Chevy, GTO driving, auto shop, barely able to pass your classes, "bite my ass" regular guys just showing up at school till graduation, when they would be doing exactly what they wanted to do rather than be stuck in school all day long.

Some of the older guys would talk about joining the Army or the Marines after they graduated so they could go to Vietnam and kill "commies" with the thousands of guys who were already there fighting. And every musician in school who played in a rock band could be found at lunch time at the "Hole." After Mom had helped me get my drums, and I'd started playing drums in bands, most of my friends were musicians now, and we would meet at the "Hole" and talk about our gigs or about music in general.

Dad had been pretty mad the day he came home from work and saw my new drums in the living room set up in front of his stereo. I don't know what he said to Mom about it, because they usually talked about stuff like that in their bedroom so none of us could hear, but he didn't take them back, so I figured Mom had smoothed things over with him. I could tell he wasn't real happy about it though. I'd made a deal with Mom that I would pay the $21 a month payment for twelve months and now almost had them paid off.

I'd spent the first weeks after I got them getting used to the two bass drums and practicing with my records on Dad's stereo. Nobody was home during the day, so I could turn the stereo up as loud as I needed and could play as hard as I wanted. I'd start as soon as I got up and ate some breakfast or lunch, and I wouldn't quit until Mom and Dad got home from work. They couldn't have had any idea how much fun I was having, and they probably had more on their mind than what I was doing with the drums during the day anyway. But I was loving it and couldn't have cared less about anyone or anything else.

After about a month of practicing in the living room, I finally got up the nerve to talk to Nicky about playing again. I hadn't been to the pool since I got the drums, so one day I decided to go down for a swim when I knew Nicky would be there.

"Hey, Peter. Haven't seen you in a while." I walked by the lifeguard stand and sat on the edge of the pool.

"I got some drums, so I've been banging around on 'em a lot lately."

"One of the kids told me they thought you'd gotten some cause they hadn't seen you out riding your bike around. What are you working on?"

"Just playing along with my records." I dove down under the water.

The water was warmer than usual and felt good after being away from it for so long. Practicing on my drums had kept me away from swimming and diving every day, and I hadn't gone on my bike to the river with Billy and Darryl to climb the cliffs or up into the woods to fish at Five Mile Creek in ages. I didn't realize how much I'd missed the water though until I was in it again.

When I reached the surface, Nicky waved me over to him. I swam over and rested on the side of the pool in front of one of the water jets, making sure the jet hit right on my dick. "How would you like to come over to my buddy's place up over the hill one night this week and play drums with us?"

This was great. I hadn't even had to ask Nicky about getting to come over.

"Sure. I'll have to work out with my brother or someone to get me over there though."

"Don't worry about that. I can give you a lift. I'll just stop by on my way and pick you up."

Nicky and I worked out the day, and I went home and started working on some of the songs he said we'd be doing. I knew most of them already. I just hadn't worked on those particular ones, because they were more Beach Boy and Jan and Dean type songs. Nicky came by the night of the rehearsal, and we packed my drums into his station wagon and set off for the jam.

We got there and unloaded everything in the back yard where the guitar players were already set up. Nicky introduced me to the other guitar players and the singer, a guy named Eddie. The guys were pretty good guitarists, and Eddie was a great singer, and I fit in super well with them, playing the songs almost exactly like the records. I got a good feeling from being able to just come in and play along with them, almost like I'd been playing in their band for a while already. They noticed that too and told me that they had a drummer but that he wasn't as good as I was. They wanted me to join the group and play with them. That made me feel even better. My first real band practice, and I was already being offered a job. The other drummer was one of the guy's brothers who was just playing so they'd have somebody, so I didn't feel bad about taking his place, and I told them that I'd like to play drums for them.

When we finished, I packed up my drums, and Eddie asked me for my phone number. Nicky and I loaded the stuff in his car, and he dropped me off at my house and helped me put the drums in the garage. I thanked him for the ride, and he told me he'd call me about the next practice.

I went in the house and went straight to the fridge to get something to eat. Mom and Dad had gone bowling, and my oldest brother, who was home from college, was camped out on the couch. I was starving. I'd eaten some of Mom's chicken before I left, but now I was hungry as hell again. I made some bologna sandwiches, grabbed a coke, and raced to my room to scarf down the grub. I turned on the radio and sat at the desk, thinking about the jam that night. I had had a lot of fun, even though the songs we did weren't ones that I'd have wanted to be playing. If it was left up to me, I'd be playing stuff by groups like The Zombies, and The Yardbirds, Them, and the Rolling Stones.

I finished the sandwiches and downed half my coke and sneaked downstairs to raid Dad's Jack Daniels bottle. My brother had The Tonight Show on and had no idea what else was going on in the house, so it was easy to pour some of the whiskey into my coke bottle and go back to my room with it. Before I left, I grabbed a couple of my Mom's cigarettes from her pack on the breakfast counter.

Now I was set. I opened the shades on my bedroom window and lit a cigarette, making sure to blow the smoke out of the window. The cigarette had me getting dizzy before I even took a sip off the coke and whiskey. I wanted to tell somebody how great I felt, how something I wanted was actually happening. For how many years I had wished that I had a set of drums and played in a band and now it was coming true. I had never felt this way when I played sax, except for when I played baritone, and I always knew that if I had the chance that I would be a good drummer. I could just feel it.

The combination of the cigarette and the whiskey was hitting me now. My thoughts raced, and I had to lie down on my bed. I imagined myself playing drums at a school dance. Girls shouted and screamed and threw flowers and notes at me while I played. I could see Cathy in the crowd. She wasn't screaming and jumping up and down like the rest of the girls but looked right at me, smiling and winking at me. We finished playing and left the stage and went outside to our waiting cars. The girls had followed us out and were trying to grab us and pull our clothes off. I jumped in my car, and Cathy was waiting inside for me. She didn't say anything, but leaned over and kissed me and started rubbing my dick. I unbuttoned her blouse and undid her bra and rubbed her tits while she started beating me off until I came all over her hand.

I had a boner going big time now as I lay on the bed, so I got up and went to the bathroom and shut the door and grabbed my dick and imagined that it was Cathy still beating me off. It didn't take long to come. I finished and went back to my room and fell on the bed. I lay there thinking how much I loved being a drummer and drifted off into sleep.

****

A few days after the jam with Nicky and the guys I got a call from Eddie.

"Hey, man, you sounded good the other night."

"Thanks. I had a lot of fun."

Eddie cut right back in.

"I have this band out here in Jacksonville, and we have a drummer, but he's nowhere near as good as you, and I was wondering if you would wanna come out and practice with us sometime and see what you think about our group."

I couldn't believe what I was hearing. Here I'd only had my drums for about a month, and I was already getting asked to join bands.

"What about the other guy?" I hated the idea of taking other guy's places, but if I was a better drummer, why shouldn't I be playing?

"I already talked to him. He's fine with it. He even said if you were as good as I said that he'd like to just hang out with us and help with the equipment and pick up drum stuff from you."

"Sure. But I have a problem getting out there. I don't have a car or anything. My brother usually takes me around in his car, but he's gone to his own stuff a lot of the time too."

"That's okay. I'll come and get you if you need a ride. But, one thing, our band doesn't do the same kind of music that Nicky and those guys were doing."

"I'm not that into surf music anyway. I was just wanting to play my drums. I want to play more rock and roll like the groups from England play."

"That's perfect!" Eddie almost shouted into the phone. "That's the stuff we do. We love that music too."

Well now I thought I'd died and gone to heaven.

So we settled it that I would go to their next practice and see what happened. He told me some songs to listen to for the practice. "Gloria." "For Your Love." "The House of the Rising Sun." "You Really Got Me." "Satisfaction." All the songs were ones I knew already and loved and wished I could be playing in a band. It would be a lot of fun just getting ready for the practice. They also did songs from American groups that I liked. "Louie Louie." "I Want Candy." "Tobacco Road." I couldn't wait.

The day of the practice finally arrived, and I tore down my drums and got them ready to pile into Eddie's car. He had a '61 Chevy Impala, so there'd be plenty of room for the drums and any stuff of his.

Eddie got there about four that afternoon, and we packed up his car and took off. He pulled out a cigarette and offered one to me. It was a menthol, and I'd never had one, so I kind of choked when we lit up, but I covered it by acting like I had to cough. We listened to the radio as he drove along the winding country road to get to Jacksonville, and he told me a little about the group and the guys and what he wanted to do with the band. They had been practicing for a few months but hadn't been able to play jobs yet. He thought a new drummer was just what they needed. I hoped he was right.

Jacksonville was about fifteen miles from North Little Rock, and the house where we were practicing was in the countryside outside of town, set back a couple of hundred feet from the road. The guys must have seen us coming up the driveway, because they came out to greet us, shaking hands and slapping me on the back. They all grabbed a handful of equipment and hauled it into the house as I followed them in.

I set my drums up in the living room, surrounded by their guitar amps and speakers. They played pretty loud, but that was okay, and I followed along easily. Eddie sang the songs almost exactly like the records too. And the guitar players sounded like they could have been the ones playing on the records.

I could tell that they liked my playing. They kept telling me how good it sounded and that we'd be able to get lots of school dances and other jobs playing at the skate rink and youth center in Jacksonville. I couldn't help but be excited.

All I could think about now was that soon I'd be playing drums in front of a crowd of screaming girls. But I also needed to be playing jobs to help pay the monthly payment on my drums.

Eddie drove me home after the practice. On the way he talked and talked about the practice and about how much they liked my playing. He and the guys wanted me to play drums for them, and he said not to worry about being able to get to the 'gigs.' I liked that word, "gigs," and figured I better start using words that other musicians use. He told me that any time I needed a ride I could just call him, and he'd either come get me, or he'd get one of the guys to do it. So, I told him that I'd play for them. I didn't say anything about having to make sure it was okay with Mom and Dad. I didn't want him to think I had to clear things with them, and it didn't matter that much what they said anyway. I was determined to be playing and wasn't going to let anyone stop me. And the deal with Mom was that I'd play to pay back the drums by playing dances and stuff, so it should be okay with them.

Eddie dropped me off at the house and said he'd call me with a list of songs and get any records to me that I might need to listen to. We'd start practicing as much as possible so we could be ready by the time school started to be playing the dances after football games and the holiday dances. We needed to get about twenty-five songs ready to play, at least enough to play for a couple of hours. The dances usually lasted from one to two hours after the football games or other events, and the skating rinks would have bands play after the last skate session of the night. They closed most of the time on the weekends at ten o'clock, so we'd probably play from about ten to midnight at those places. If we got a prom dance or a homecoming dance, we might have to play three hours and would have to add some more songs. Being a night owl anyway, it wouldn't matter how late we played for me.

School would be starting in a couple of weeks. I'd be a junior this year. I almost dreaded it now. Every year up to this one, I'd always been ready for school to start back up after the summer. Even looked forward to it. But now I just wanted to be playing my drums and didn't want to be bothered with having to do homework or take classes I didn't give a shit about. My entire focus now was on learning the songs for the band and getting to play gigs. I'd have to at least do good enough to pass my classes though, or Mom and Dad might try to stop me from playing. I figured I'd be able to do that alright.

****

Before I knew what was happening, I was back in school. The weeks had gone by like a flash with all of the practicing and listening to songs and trying to remember all of the different drum patterns for the songs and the breaks in the music. At least when I was playing sax in the school band I had sheet music that showed where all the breaks were. Now I had to memorize everything. One thing I learned very quickly was to use the words to follow the pattern of the songs. The songs would usually have a verse or two with a chorus in between and then have a guitar solo or organ solo and then have a final verse and a chorus to end the song. That helped me with remembering the songs. Then I just had to work out the snare and hi-hat and bass drum pattern for each song.

I'd always listened to the words to songs and usually liked songs either because of the drum beat or because of the words. But, now that I was having to listen closer to the words, I began to understand better what the songs were about. And the songs from the British groups had great words that had a lot of meaning to me about what was going on with me and about girls and falling in love and about being yourself and not letting anyone tell you what to do. Some of them, like "Gloria," were just stories about going to see a girl or going on a date or to a dance or wanting to be with someone. I liked those a lot and liked playing them a lot.

The band had already gone through some changes over the past few weeks. Eddie had a friend who was an organ player in Jacksonville, Claude, and Eddie had asked him and another bass player to play with the group. So now it was Eddie and Claude, the new bass player, Phil, the guitar player, Mike, from the original band, and me. But it was all okay with me. Claude was great on the organ, and that helped the songs sound more like the originals than just having guitars playing. Claude had twin sisters too - Michelle and Clair - who were super cute and were in ninth grade.

We had learned most of the songs on our list, and Eddie had named the band The Grupe. He wanted something a little different and more like the British bands. A friend of his who would come to our rehearsals and hang out and bring beer had painted one of my bass drum heads with the face of a beatnik guy that looked pretty cool. He painted it to match the blue color, and it fit right in with the rest of the drums.

Our first gig was coming up at the Youth Center at the air force base in Jacksonville. Claude had gotten that gig for us, because his dad worked at the base. His sisters would be there too, which would be great. That would be my first real time to play in front of kids in my own band as the drummer. I was excited but felt a little uneasy. I knew the songs, so that wasn't a problem. I just didn't want to mess up or drop a stick or fall off the bandstand or anything stupid like that. I was kind of glad that it would be in front of kids I didn't know rather than in front of my friends or kids from school. If I screwed up it wouldn't be so bad.

I was starting to let my hair grow out too. All of the bands whose music we played had long hair, and it just seemed to fit. My Mom had always cut my hair herself when I was a kid. She had her own clippers that she would use to shave my head with a crew cut. The past few years though I had been going to the barber shop to get it cut, and it had gotten longer anyway. But now I was letting it grow even longer, and she and Dad were starting to say stuff about it. I didn't care though. It was my hair. I should be able to wear it the way I wanted.

I had been so busy the last part of the summer that I hadn't seen Cathy in over a month. We had gone to the movies a couple of more times, and she had come to the pool to swim, but that was it. Now that I was back in school, and she was still in ninth grade in junior high, I wouldn't see her at all at school. And with the band playing a lot of its gigs in Jacksonville, she probably wouldn't be able to get to them to see me play.

Our last movie date had been a good one. We sat in the balcony in a corner away from the few people who were there. We didn't watch the movie hardly at all. I had kissed her a lot before tonight and had rubbed her tits on the outside of her shirt, and tonight I wanted to see how far we could go. We watched the first part of the movie, and then I made my move. I kissed her and moved my hand around to rub her tits. I started to unbutton the buttons on her shirt, expecting her to stop me, but she didn't. So, I got her shirt unbuttoned and slid my hand inside her bra to feel her tits. They weren't very big, but her nipples got hard real quick. She had a skirt on, and I moved my hand down from her tits to her leg and up to her panties. We were having to be careful so nobody would see us, but I got my hand on her pussy outside of her panties and started rubbing it. She got excited with that and moved her hand up my leg and began rubbing my dick through my pants. I got a boner immediately. I wanted her to take my dick out but was afraid somebody would come by and see us. Her pussy felt wet after a while, and I felt the come oozing out of my dick.

We played with each other for most of the rest of the movie and both had to go to the restroom before we went home. My Dad was coming to get us this time, so we didn't have to worry about her mom giving her an inspection when she got in the car. That was the last time I had seen her, though we had talked on the phone since then and talked about how good it felt with each other.

I wished I could drive so we could just go parking somewhere and do whatever we wanted, but my brothers had had a wreck in my parent's car during the summer and had wrecked it bad enough to have to get a new car. Mom and Dad were so mad with them after that that they pretty much decided that I would never get my driver's license. So I was still riding my bicycle to get places.

Being younger than all of the other kids in my class was becoming even more of a problem now too. Most of the other juniors had already gotten their driver's license and had cars or drove their parent's cars. I wouldn't turn sixteen until half way through my junior year, and my friends who were my age were still sophomores and didn't have their license yet, which meant that we had to get our parents to take us places. It wasn't too great with girls to have to be going places with your parents driving either, and it was embarrassing to be riding my bike places, so I would ride on the railroad tracks to keep people from seeing me riding my bike on the streets. With Cathy that wouldn't matter, since her parents were pretty strict about her going out and all, but it would have been great to go and pick her up and go out on a date to a drive-in movie or to get a hamburger or to just go parking and do whatever we wanted.

****

The Saturday of the youth center gig started like any other Saturday. I slept late and had my usual breakfast of Sugar Pops, toast with grape jelly, and sliced banana on my cereal. I scarfed it down like I hadn't eaten in months and went back to my room to listen to the records of the songs we'd be playing later. I had already had some of the records for the songs before I joined the band, but some I had had to pick up at the store down from the high school. I would wait there for Mom to get me after school. She would come by on one of her drug store deliveries and then take me home.

While I waited for her, I'd go to the magazine or record section and look through the new comic books or find the records I needed. I had gotten good at slipping the records or magazines into my notebook or sliding them into the textbooks and walking out without paying for them. I had to have some use for the books. I sure wasn't opening them to do the homework or to read. And I got a kind of feeling like when I smoked a cigarette or when I drank some whiskey as I was walking out with the records in my books. Once outside I would feel relieved that I didn't get caught, but I still had the dizzy feeling for a while afterwards. My Mom would have died if she had known that I was taking records from the store.

She had caught me stealing one time before when I was a little kid, back in the country. We had a store across the street from our house where Mom would get groceries and sometimes help the woman who owned the store. We kids would go there to get candy and cokes, when we had a few cents to spend. One time I didn't have any money, and I wanted a Zero candy bar. I just took the bar and started to walk out, and the woman stopped me and called my Mom. Mom came down to the store and apologized to her and promised her that I wouldn't do it again. I never did it again cause my Mom took me home and gave me a spanking with a switch from outside. It wasn't the first time I'd gotten a spanking from her, but it was one I wouldn't forget. It was almost as bad as the one I got when I walked home from school instead of getting on the bus. She busted my ass good that time.

So I listened to the records a couple of times each and felt like I knew them about as good as I was going to. I went down to the garage and got my drums ready to go and got on my bike and went out for a ride. I knew Eddie would be coming to get me in a couple of hours, so I had time to maybe go up to the pond and see if anything was going on up there. I had seen the guys at school some and around the neighborhood in passing but hadn't talked to them in a while. The band had been taking a lot of my time. Nobody was at the pond, so I just rode around for a while and then went back to the house.

Eddie came to get me, and we loaded my stuff and took off for the gig. The Youth Center was on the air base and would have dances a couple of times a month for the kids that lived on the base or whose parents worked on the base. Claude's dad was in the Air Force, so it was easy for him to get us the gig. We were only making a few bucks each, but it would be a good first gig for us to play and to maybe get some more gigs out of if we did well.

A bunch of kids were already there by the time we got there and were playing pool and talking and watching us set up. Claude's sisters were there and were looking cuter than I had remembered them looking. They were almost identical, except Michelle's hair was a little longer. They were in a big group of girls who kept laughing and giggling and looking over at us. I wondered what they were saying. Were they talking about me?

We finished setting up and went out back to have a cigarette before we started. They wouldn't let anybody smoke in the Youth Center. I was kind of sweaty now from carrying my equipment and getting set up, so I unbuttoned my shirt and tried to dry off some. Next time I would bring an extra shirt with me to change into. We had decided to wear dark pants and jackets with white shirts and dark ties, because that was the way some of our favorite groups, like Them and The Yardbirds, dressed on their albums. Some of the American groups, like Paul Revere and the Raiders or the Beach Boys, would wear costumes or flowery shirts, but we liked the look of the English groups.

It was time to start playing, so we went back in and got ready. I sat down at my drums and thought about how long I had waited for this moment. The guys made sure their guitars were tuned and Eddie called out the first song, "Gloria." That was a good one to start with and was one of my favorites. The kids had gathered around the stage and were waiting for us to start. As Eddie turned and counted off to start the song, I got that dizzy feeling again rushing through my head and felt like I was going to black out. It was so strong a feeling that I almost forgot the beginning of the song. I quickly remembered how the song started and played right along with the guys. All the kids came down to the front of the stage and began moving to the music. It was just like I had dreamed it would be, except the girls weren't screaming and tearing our clothes off. Maybe that would come later.

We played a couple of fast songs and then played "The House of the Rising Sun." Some of the kids had started to dance to the fast stuff, but now the dance floor was packed.

We had a pretty good mix of songs from British groups and from American groups and got good reaction from both. The kids here were a little different from the kids that might be at other dances, because lots of their parents were in the Air Force and had been to other bases around the world. Like Claude and his sisters had just come from France, where their dad had been at his last base. So these kids were more familiar with songs from the British groups and groups from Europe, so they liked all of the stuff we were doing.

After about ten songs we took a break. When I stepped down off the stage to take my break, I got the answer to my question about what the girls were saying before we had started playing. Clair came up to me and stopped me before I headed out the door to smoke a stogy.

"God, you guys are so good, Peter."

"It's all because of Claude. He's great. Him playing organ makes everything sound just like the records."

She pulled me closer to whisper to me.

"Michelle said she thought you were so cute. You should ask her out."

This was almost as good as the girls tearing our clothes off.

"Yeah? She's super cute too. Both of you are. The problem is I don't have a car." I figured that would put an end to any dates with Michelle, just like with most girls.

"Eddie and I have gone out a couple of times. Why don't you ask her out, and you guys can double date with us."

"She'd be okay with that?"

"Just ask her out. You'll see." Her smile convinced me.

"Okay. I'll talk to Eddie." I headed out the back door.

All of the guys were standing around smoking and passing around a whiskey bottle. I joined the circle and lit up my cigarette. Claude passed the bottle to me, and I took a swig of the whiskey. It was a little stronger than the Jack

Daniels I would sneak from the cabinet at home, but I was still able to drink it without coughing or choking and showing that I couldn't drink it straight. I took a couple of more swigs, finished my stogy, and we headed back in. On the way in I grabbed Eddie.

"Clair said that Michelle wanted to go out with me and that you guys have gone out some. Could Michelle and me go out with you guys some time?"

"Yeah. That'd probably be fun. Me and Clair have been having a good time. She's a great kisser. If Michelle is half as good, you'll have a good time too."

"Is Claude okay with us dating his sisters?" I didn't want to piss him off.

"Shit, he doesn't care. They do what they want, and he does what he wants."

Now I just had to get up the nerve to ask Michelle out. Since she had already said something about me though, it would be a little easier. I just had to pick the right time to go up to her and start talking. How would I start? "Hey, how are you doing?" That was pretty dull. "Hi. You wanna go out some time?" That was maybe too straight forward. How about, "How do you like being back in the United States?" That was pretty good. I'd use something like that to start talking to her.

We played one more hour and Eddie told the kids that it was time for us to quit. Everybody started shouting "No!" And "Play one more!" and "Don't stop." So Eddie called one more song, "The Train Kept a Rollin'." It was a fast number, and the kids loved it. Even the ones who had been hanging out around the walls and in the pool table area got out and danced on that one.

We finished and started packing up our gear. While I tore down my drums I kept an eye on Clair and Michelle. They were still there, standing over by the snack bar. I had to get my drums torn down and ready to load so Eddie could get going, so I didn't know if I'd get a chance to talk to Michelle before we left. I wished I had her phone number. I could feel the whiskey had worn off now, and I was feeling the shyness come over me, even worse than usual. I needed another swig or two on the whiskey to be able to go and talk to her.

Eddie finished and told me he needed to get going. I hurriedly helped him load the car and said I needed to go back and check that I'd gotten everything. Inside, I looked for Michelle and Clair. They were already gone. Shit! I'd missed my chance. I didn't know when I'd see them again, and now I didn't even have her phone number. Why was it that I couldn't just go up and talk to girls? Damn, that pissed me off! I always felt like I was missing out by not being able to talk to girls. Other guys could do it. Why couldn't I?

As Eddie drove me home, we smoked and took swigs off the whiskey bottle and talked about the dance and how much fun it was. He said he was glad I was playing for them and that it had turned out just like he thought it would. He was working on getting some more gigs for us and would let us know when he had something else. The gig today would probably get us some more stuff on the air base too.

We pulled up to the house and unloaded the drums in the garage. Eddie said he'd call me when we were going to practice again.

"Did you talk to Michelle?"

"They left before I got the chance."

"Call her, and we'll set up a date maybe for next weekend, if we're not playing somewhere."

"I didn't get her phone number either."

"Okay, remember this: Yukon 2-2036. Call her and ask her out."

Eddie took off, and I raced into the house and zoomed upstairs and scribbled the number on the first thing I could find, a new Iron Man comic book on my desk, before I forgot it. It was still early, so I'd call her later and talk to her. Hopefully, she'd be there and wouldn't be out on a date or something.

Mom and Dad had gone to their friend's house to play cards, and my brother was out on a date, so I had the house to myself. I was hungry from playing, so I cooked a couple of hamburgers and took them and a coke to my room and turned on the radio to WGN.

As I gobbled the burgers, I thought of the past few months and how I had gone from having no drums to having played my first dance with the band that I played drums for. I don't think my parents could have ever known how I was feeling right then. The drums and music had become my life. The only thing keeping me in school was the fact that my parents would never let me not go. I hated my classes and pretty much just took up space in the desk, in the room. I lived for the next rehearsal, the newest song on the radio, the next dance to play. I'd set up my drums tomorrow and practice on some new songs to play in the band.

I finished eating and went down to the whiskey cabinet and poured some Jack Daniels in my coke. I needed that to make my call to Michelle. I took a big slug from the bottle and went back up to my parents room to make my call. I was feeling the booze now and felt myself getting braver.

I dialed the number, and a woman answered.

"Hello." She had a kind of accent.

"Hello. Is Michelle there?"

"She is. May I ask who is calling?" Was she British?

"This is Peter. I play drums with Claude's band."

"Oh, yes. We've heard a lot about the dance today. I would say that you were a big hit. I will get Michelle for you."

She sounded nice. Not anything like Cathy's mom.

"Hi. Peter?" Michelle's voice was soft and sounded a little like an accent too.

"Yeah, it's Peter. How are you?" That was original.

"You guys sounded so good today. How long have you been playing drums?" Maybe I wouldn't even have to think of something to say.

"I've been kind of playing for a few years, but I just got my set this summer. The Grupe is my first band."

"That's neat. Claude likes the band a lot. He says you guys should get a lot of jobs."

"I hope so. I have to help my parents pay off my drums."

We talked a little longer about school and her being born in England and living in France and how close she and Clair were and living in Europe and liking coming to the United States and all, and then I made my move.

"I was wondering if next weekend you might wanna go out to a movie or something. I think Eddie and Clair are going out, and we could kind of double date with them, if you wanted." Was I being too nice?

"That should be fun. Clair had already said something about that to me."

We finished talking, and I hung up and went back to my room. I felt like watching a movie, so I went downstairs and checked the television schedule. I wished that my new favorite tv show, Star Trek, was on, and that I hadn't missed Lost in Space which had been on earlier, but I saw that Frankenstein was on the ten o'clock movie. That was perfect. Just the thing to end a fantastic day. I got another coke and some Jack Daniels and settled into the bean bag, but all I could think of was Michelle and our coming date. Hey, another first I thought. My first real date.

****

At school the next week, the cheerleaders and jocks and, of course, the principal, Rabbit Burnett, who used to be the football coach, were all getting ready for the Color Day Assembly and the big Homecoming football game. It was still two weeks away, but that didn't matter. Everybody went to the games on Friday night. I would even go sometimes just to hang out with my friends when I wasn't at the skating rink or doing something else. The stadium would be packed for this game though.

I hadn't even thought about the game now that I was playing and hoped we would have a dance to play that night. Then my friend, James, who used to loan me his drums, caught me after class one day.

"Hey, Peter, I heard you got some drums over the summer, and you're playing with a band out in Jacksonville."

"Yeah. Who'd you hear that from?"

"A friend of mine goes to the Youth Center out at the base and said he heard your group and that you guys were good. He knew you from band at Ridgeroad."

"We played out there last Saturday. It was a lot of fun."

"We're doing a drum battle, me and Mark and Lewis for the Color Day Assembly, and we wondered if you would wanna be in it with us."

Shit. These were guys who had been playing drums in band forever, and they were asking me to get up on stage with them and play drums. Did they just want me up there to make them look better?

"We always knew you had it in you to be a drummer." James was nice, so I figured he was being honest. "It'll be fun. Think about it."

He raced off to class, and I stood there, dumbfounded, like a deer in headlights.

I saw James the next day and told him I'd do the drum battle but that I'd never done one before. I'd seen drummers on television, like on the Jerry Lewis show or Johnny Carson or on the Sammy Davis show, doing drum battles and playing songs, but doing one was completely different and pretty scary. He said there was nothing to it, that all I had to do was think of some drum patterns that I liked and play those for a couple of minutes. It sounded easy, but now that I had said I would do it, I cringed at the idea of making an idiot out of myself in front of the whole school.

When I got home from school, I started going through my records, listening to the ones that I liked the drums on, trying to figure out what I might do during the battle. Then I thought about that Gene Krupa song that I liked that had so much tom tom work on it, so I got into Dad's albums and searched for that song. I finally found it. "Sing, Sing, Sing."

Hearing it again, I could remember lying on the floor in the den at our house in the country just listening to the song over and over, getting out pencils or sticks of any kind I could find and playing along with Gene Krupa as he did the song. No wonder I loved the drums so much. I got the same feeling now that I had gotten then listening to it. It was like taking a swig off the whiskey bottle or taking a drag off a stogy. The blood seemed to rush to my head. I couldn't help but move my arms and legs to the beat. The drums were like the ends of my arms and legs making the sounds they wanted to make.

I listened to the song even closer to get an idea about the pattern of it. It started with the floor tom, then the band came in and Krupa changed to playing on the ride toms and the floor tom, still keeping the same rhythm going. The trumpet player, I think it was Harry James, came in and Krupa went from the tom toms to the snare and played the same floor tom rhythm he was playing before during the trumpet solo. Benny Goodman played a clarinet solo while Krupa played some different stuff on the floor tom and the snare and then they both got real quiet. Krupa did some playing around on the cymbals and the snare, and then everything stopped for a couple of beats and the whole band came in again, loud, with Krupa playing a super-fast roll on the snare drum. Then they all ended together.

Okay. I knew how the song went, but I wouldn't have the band there to play along with me. I needed to just figure out which drum I'd play at different times during the solo. I would keep the same general speed and drum rhythm pattern going throughout and work the drums in at different times. So maybe I'd start with the floor tom, like Krupa did, then move to the snare and the ride toms, and then maybe back to the floor tom and then end with the snare. I had a plan. All I had to do was practice and practice until the day of the assembly.

Eddie called a few days later and said that we wouldn't be playing that weekend and that we could take Clair and Michelle out. That sounded great to me, even though I wished we were playing too, so I called Michelle and told her. We could go to the drive in out in Jacksonville or to the Youth Center or to a walk-in movie or whatever everybody wanted to do. I didn't care what it was as long as we went out. She asked Clair what she wanted to do, and they decided we'd just wait until Friday and then figure it out after we all got together.

Eddie picked me up first on Friday so that we could pick up the girls together, in case their parents wanted to meet me. He said he hadn't had to go through a lot of questioning when he had taken Clair out before, so it should be okay. He reached in his glove box and pulled out a bottle of whiskey and took a swig and passed it to me.

"Won't their parents smell it on us?"

"Got that covered." He pulled out a pack of Juicy Fruit.

I took a swig and gave the bottle back, and we both lit up a stogy. I was wondering what Eddie had planned for tonight.

"Where are we gonna go tonight?"

"I don't know what the girls have in mind, but I've been taking Clair to this place I know to park and just listen to the radio and make out. They may wanna do something else since it's both of 'em tonight."

The booze was helping, but thinking of being with Michelle for the first time made my body shake from the inside out. I hadn't ever talked with her in person, only on the phone, and it would be kinda like starting from scratch with her. If it was Cathy, I knew what I could expect.

We got to Jacksonville and drove through this ritzy section of town, like Lakewood in North Little Rock, with big houses and Cadillacs and T-Birds in the driveways. Eddie threw me a piece of gum, so I knew we were getting close to Clair and Michelle's house.

We stopped at this rock and wood house with a yard full of trees, and Eddie hid the bottle under the seat and motioned for me to get out.

"Don't get too close to the parents, if they come to the door. If the dad wants to shake your hand, don't talk to him when you're doing it. Say hello first or back away before you start talking."

Eddie sounded like he had done this lots before. I was glad that he was helping me out with this stuff. Nobody else would, that's for sure. My parents never even talked to me about dating or anything. They never asked me if I had a girlfriend or who my friends were or anything about school. I guess they were too worried about bills or Dad's business. And my brothers were pretty much gone to school or doing stuff with their friends and didn't want their "little brother" butting into their lives.

Eddie rang the doorbell, and a woman answered after a few minutes. I could feel my hands sweating and wiped them on my pants. Didn't want to shake hands with sweaty palms.

"Hello, Eddie." I guessed that it was Michelle's mother. "And you must be Peter." She put out her hand, and I shook it.

"Yes, ma'am." I tried not to breath in her direction.

"Come in, and I'll get the girls." I could see why Clair and Michelle were so pretty. Their mom looked like a movie star, kind of like Esther Williams, and didn't look old enough to have kids, and her accent sounded even stronger in person. French, I thought.

The girls came downstairs with mom following close behind. We went through introductions and instructions on when to be home, "Be back by midnight, girls," and then we made our getaway. I was glad the back seat of Eddie's car was pretty big. I didn't know if I should put my arm around Michelle when we got in or if I should kind of wait and make my move after we talked a little. It was still light out too, so I figured I'd at least wait until it got dark to start getting close like that. But by the time Eddie had pulled away from the house, Michelle had already moved over next to me, so I went ahead and put my arm around her. One less thing for me to worry about.

I didn't have to worry about talking either. Michelle and Clair kept a steady stream of talking going. And we talked about everything. The dance at the Youth Center. The band. Music in general. Songs playing on the radio. School. Living in Europe. Sex was about the only thing that didn't come up, and I wasn't going to be the one to start talking about it.

Most of all, I felt great about the fact that I was finally going out on a real date with a girl. I was in the back seat of a car, with a girl, on a date, doing whatever we wanted to do. No parents driving us around, asking a million questions about everything we did or said or getting us to tell them about the movie or about who was at the skating rink or any of that stuff. The next step would be getting my driver's license and going on a date with just me and the girl in the car. I felt alright being with Eddie and Clair, and Michelle seemed okay with it too, and probably now it was a good thing that it was all of us, and I didn't feel like I had to do all the entertaining.

None of us had eaten, so we decided to go get a burger at Whatta-Burger. We could get them and just eat in the car. The girls just got cokes and fries to split, but Eddie and I hadn't eaten anything, so we both got a burger and fries and a coke. The burgers tasted good, especially since we hadn't eaten in so long, but I liked the ones I cooked better. While we were eating, Eddie grabbed the whiskey bottle from under his seat and spiked his coke with some. He handed the bottle to me, and I did the same. The girls didn't say anything, so I guessed that they didn't care. Eddie had probably done it when he and Clair had gone out before, so she might be used to it by now, and Michelle seemed pretty easy-going about things.

By the time we finished eating, it had gotten dark and the drive-in movie would have started before we got there. We weren't even in any hurry to do anything in particular, which I liked, so Eddie just drove around Jacksonville for a while, going to the teen hangouts and stopping every once in a while to talk with people or get out and take a whiz if nobody could see us. Of course, the girls had to stop about every thirty minutes to get a coke and go to the bathroom, like girls do. Each time they went to the bathroom, Eddie and I would spike our drinks a little more. I felt pretty light-headed by now, but I wasn't about to let what happened with Rhonda happen with Michelle. The burger helped to keep me from getting drunk, and we'd stop and eat snacks and stuff too.

After a while Eddie suggested we go to the parking spot where he and Clair usually went. It was on a hill overlooking the city and never had a lot of people there. We got all of the snacks and drinks and things that we thought we might need for the next little while and headed for the spot.

Now Michelle and I had a chance to talk together more than we had earlier. The back seat kind of gave us a little privacy if we got close and whispered. She seemed to like this a lot, and I liked it too. She was easy to talk with, and now that we could get close, I started noticing more about her. She smelled great and laughed a lot. It was easy to get her to laugh too, and she didn't talk about people the way some girls did. She always had something nice to say about people, the people we saw as we drove along, or the kids from her school or people that she knew in Europe. That made me like her even more.

Eddie drove up a winding road to the spot overlooking the city and the runways at the air base, so while we parked there, we could see the planes landing and cars driving through the city and police lights. The only light on the hillside came from the glow of the radio, playing music from WGN, and no other cars were at the spot, which made me feel like we could do whatever we wanted. Michelle and I talked for a few minutes and watched the lights, and then she got super quiet and looked at me kind of weird, like maybe she wanted me to do something. So I leaned over and kissed her, and she kissed me back. She put her tongue in my mouth and licked my lips and played around with my tongue, getting me more and more excited. If I got a boner, I was afraid she might get embarrassed or mad or something, so I tried to not get one. That didn't work.

The more we kissed, the more excited I got and the harder and harder my dick got till I felt like it would be hard forever. We had been sitting up in the seat, and my dick felt squashed inside my underwear, so I had to move around. When I did that, we ended up moving down in the seat a little with Michelle's tits crunched into my side. She laid almost on top of me now and had wrapped her leg over mine. She was inching closer to my dick with her leg, so I tried to move over a little. That didn't help. Her leg fell on top of my dick.

We had been lip-locked this whole time, and now she seemed to get even hotter. She brushed her leg up against my dick and slowly started rubbing it with her leg, and I felt like I was going to come right then. Then I thought that I didn't want Eddie and Clair to see what we were doing, so I tried to see what was going on with them. I couldn't see them, but it sounded like they were doing the same thing in the front seat, so I didn't worry about that any more. They could probably care less what we were doing anyway.

I wanted to touch Michelle's tits but didn't know if I should try, but then she took my hand and put it on her tit. Her tits weren't huge, but they were a nice size. I didn't want to just feel her tits through her shirt, so I slid my hand inside her shirt, just waiting for her to pull my hand away. She didn't stop me, so I figured that was okay and went ahead and unbuttoned a few buttons of her shirt and put my hand inside her bra. Her tit was so soft and the nipple started getting hard right away. Well that sure got Michelle excited, because she moved her hand down to my dick and started rubbing me through my pants.

We were both sweating. She kept rubbing my dick, and I kept playing with her nipple, and it got super hard, and I started thinking about how her nipple had gone from being soft like my dick to being hard like my dick. I don't know what happened, but suddenly she jerked away and whispered,

"Ow!" and grabbed her tit.

I jumped back now.

She rubbed her tit and whispered again. "Ow, that hurt."

"I'm sorry." I tried to help. My boner that I thought would stay hard forever had become a limp hot dog.

"It's okay. You just pinched it a little hard."

I felt like shit now but didn't know what to do. I had pretty much ruined the mood we had going and figured that was the end of that for the night. Then Michelle squeezed up against me again.

"I think you need to kiss it and make it better."

Holy shit, I thought.

She opened her shirt and pulled her bra to the side of her tit and pulled my face down to her chest. Her nipple had gotten soft, like my dick, but it didn't take much to get it hard again. I kissed the nipple softly, not wanting to ruin this mood, and then put my lips around it and did what she had been doing with her tongue in my mouth.

That turned her on big time, because she immediately put her hand on my dick again and started rubbing. It only took a few seconds for my boner to return. But she didn't stop there. She unzipped my pants and dug into my underwear and found my dick. I just about lost it then. She had my dick in her hand, squeezing it and slowly moving her hand up and down. I froze. I couldn't do anything. Then I had a sudden urge to grab her and kiss her. So I did.

Our tongues fought with one another as we kissed, her hand moving faster and faster on my dick, my hand squeezing her tit. In no time, I came in my underwear, and she pulled her hand out and rubbed my dick again from outside my pants.

I was frozen again, or more like in shock. But I didn't want to stop. I wanted to feel her pussy. So I moved my hand down and started to unbutton her pants, but she grabbed my hand and stopped me.

"Not tonight." I wasn't going to do anything she didn't want me to do, so I went back to playing with her tit. We kissed a little longer, and then we just lay there holding each other, listening to the radio and the sounds of the night.

Eddie and Clair must have finished whatever they were doing too, because I could hear Eddie softly singing along with "The House of the Rising Sun" on the radio.

Michelle sat up and buttoned her shirt, and I zipped up and sat up with her. The come stuck to my underwear and skin, but I didn't give a damn. I had never felt anything like that before, and I sure as hell wanted to feel it again.

I could smell Eddie's cigarette and wanted one too, so I lit up and took a big drink from the coke and whiskey. The ice had melted, but the drink tasted good anyway. I stepped out of the car and went into the dark to take a piss. My dick stuck to my underwear, which the come had glued to my leg. My dick still felt tingly, and I could still feel Michelle's hand on it, wanted to feel her hand on it again. I sure as hell wanted to go out with Michelle again and hoped she wanted to go out with me again. I liked this spot too and wanted to come back here. I stood there pissing, looking at the lights, thinking about the date. If this was how dating was, then I was hooked.

Eddie interrupted my thoughts.

"Hey, Peter, we've got to get the girls home."

I zipped up and went back to the car.

"What were you doing?" Michelle wanted to know.

"Had to piss."

I got back in the car, and Eddie took off. I hated leaving that place. This had been one of the best nights of my life, and I didn't want it to end. I put my arm around Michelle, and she snuggled close to me. We talked about the evening and how much fun it had been. She wanted us to do it again, and I did too, as soon as we could.

We got the girls home and walked them to the door. We had said our real goodbye's in the car and just said bye to them on the porch and watched them go in the house and then took off.

"What'd I tell you, man. Wasn't that cool?"

"Yeah."

I couldn't talk, didn't feel like talking. I just wanted to think about that night and how great it had been. I didn't want Eddie to know what me and Michelle had done and didn't want him to know that that was the first time a girl had jacked me off. I changed the subject and asked him about the band and what gigs we might have coming up. He had talked to the guy at the skating rink and thought we might get a gig there soon, and the Youth Center wanted us to come back there some time. Other than that, we didn't have another gig coming up soon.

Eddie dropped me off, and I went straight up to my room. Mom had zonked on the couch, Dad snored in the bedroom, and I had no idea about my brothers. I didn't care anyway. I just wanted to go to bed and dream about the night.

And dream I did.

****

Without any gigs coming up, I spent the next week practicing for the drum battle. Every day after I got home from school I'd grab my sticks and go through my solo for at least a couple of hours or until everybody got home from work or school. I kept thinking of new little licks to put in and trying out new stuff. I still had the same basic solo, but I knew the other guys had been playing a lot longer than I had, and I'd need some great licks to compete with them. Having played the gig at the youth center and having practiced so much during the summer and with the band had paid off in getting my coordination with bass drums, and I used both of them a lot to make a great, full sound.

One thing I had started working with more was tuning the drums. I had called the music store and talked to one of the drum guys there and found out some about how to tune the drums. I told him what we doing and that I had been listening to the Gene Krupa songs, and he told me how Krupa would have tuned his drums and how the rock and roll drummers tuned their drums. Our auditorium would be packed and could hold a lot of kids, so I wanted the drums to be loud so that everyone would hear them. I tuned everything with a pretty open tuning, the top head kind of tight and the bottom head a little looser. I had learned from the drum guy that the bottom head gave the tone to the drum, and Krupa's drums had a deep tone to them, so I tuned all the bottom heads even a little looser. I couldn't tell exactly how they sounded sitting behind them when I played, but from where I sat, they sounded pretty damn good to me.

School was a lot different that week, not just in the classes but in the hallways, where most of the social stuff took place anyway. Kids who I'd never talked to before came up to me and wished me good luck and said that they couldn't wait for Friday. Each of us had our own group of friends from our classes and from the different junior high schools we had gone to, but with over two thousand kids at the school, a lot of kids didn't know any of us, especially the tenth graders. We were all juniors, so most of our friends knew us from the junior class. I knew a lot of the seniors because they had known my brothers, and Lewis, the only other drummer who hadn't played drums in band, had an older brother the age of my oldest brother, so some of them knew him too.

Girls who had never even looked at me before in class, were talking to me now and saying stuff like, "I didn't know you played drums" and were asking if I played in a band and what kind of music I liked. Being a musician had changed a lot about my life, and I loved it, every bit of it. I couldn't think of any other way I'd want things to be right now. I wanted to play more dances and gigs, but that would come after the band got going a little better.

Friday morning slipped up on me before I knew it. I could barely eat. My stomach turned over and over, it seemed like. This was even worse than before the youth center dance. I could easily make a fool of myself or make a name for myself. I'd already gained a little bit of a name before even doing anything, and now I had to prove that I deserved it. I didn't give a shit if the kids thought I was the best drummer or not, though that would be nice. I just wanted to do a good job.

My brother helped me pack the drums in his car and took me to school that morning. We parked behind the auditorium and hauled the drums up the steps to the stage. He knew everything about the school, so he knew just where to go with the stuff. I would have gotten lost for sure if he hadn't been there, and I could sure use the help getting my drums up the steps. He even saw some old teachers that he knew and went to talk with them after we got the stuff settled. He and Dad could talk to anyone, anytime, about anything. I wished that I knew how they did that.

They had us setting up the drums in front of the curtain but back far enough so that they could use the front of the stage for the cheerleaders and everybody else who would be on the stage. They didn't want to have to take time for us to set up during the assembly, so everything had to be done beforehand. I set up on the end on the left side of the stage next to the guitar amps. I guessed somebody would be playing, maybe Mark's band. I liked that spot. I could look to my right and see the other three drummers all at once and could see the entire audience too. I wondered what I looked like from the balcony. My set must have looked huge from up there with the two bass drums and the tom toms mounted on them. I had borrowed a cymbal from a friend of Eddie's too to go with the couple that I had.

James and the other guys got there a little after we did and began to set up too. Mark was next to me on the other side of the amps, then Lewis, and then James. They had smaller sets than mine, but they were nice sets. It didn't take them long to set up and start practicing. Damn they sounded good. Listening to them practice made me wonder what the hell I was doing up there on stage, but I remembered that I had my solo down pat and knew what I would be doing, and that helped.

The assembly started before classes started so we didn't have to worry about going to class first. We hung around on the stage talking about our drum sets and the bands we were playing with. Mark and I were the only ones playing with a group. He was playing in a group who played some of the school dances and at Lake Nixon and other places and who would play during the assembly. I wished our band could get some gigs doing the dances there at North Little Rock.

The bell rang and students started filling the auditorium. They could see the drum sets on the stage as they came in and were pointing at them and were getting louder and louder. It didn't take long for the auditorium to be packed and for the noise level to raise three or four times. I peeked out through the curtains and about had a heart attack seeing all the students out there who were going to be hearing me play shortly. I wished I had a slug of whiskey to calm me down and thought that I should just put a half pint bottle in my drum bag to always have some on hand. I felt good about my solo though, so I'd be okay.

The cheerleaders went out and got the assembly started, and we were told to get ready to go out to our drum sets. James would go first, then me, then Lewis, and then Mark. The more I thought about it, the more I thought how cool it was that I was playing a drum battle with guys who had reputations as good drummers. Never in my wildest dreams of playing had I thought of something like this happening, especially after only having my drums for a few months. I wished my Dad could be there now to see me. If it had been one of my older brothers, he would have been there.

The cheerleaders announced us, and we all went out to our drum sets. The kids were screaming and hollering our names as we got settled in. They introduced each one of us and then James started his solo. His drumming had a real jazz feel to it. Being a drummer in band, he did a lot of snare work too. That was one thing that I was not as good at, since I hadn't had any lessons and couldn't read drum music. I was glad that I had concentrated on the tom toms for the solo.

James finished, and the kids hollered and screamed, and my turn came. And I felt like I would freeze right there, but I remembered the start of my solo and started my bass drums going and then started on the floor tom. The entire auditorium seemed to disappear, leaving me alone with my drums, banging through my solo. I caught glimpses of the students as I moved from one drum to another, they seemed to be moving in slow motion, but all I could hear was the drums. I followed the pattern of the solo just as I had worked it out. I tried to put in a little more snare but didn't try to force anything.

My whole deal had been working on the tom toms, so I stuck with them throughout. Then I finished like I had planned on the cymbals and the toms and snare all together while I played a roll with the bass drums.

The cheering of the students broke into the trance and brought me back to the auditorium. Here were two thousand students who had watched me play my drums and cheered my solo. It was just like I had imagined it so many times. Now it was for real! I was no longer the short, skinny kid who nobody knew. I was a drummer!

I had done my part and could now relax and listen to Lewis and Mark finish off. I couldn't help but begin to wonder what the students thought about my solo though. I guessed that they wouldn't have expected me to be up there with the other guys if I wasn't at least almost as good as they were. Still, I hadn't played in front of people enough yet to have gotten a lot of feedback.

Lewis and Mark played just as I had expected and just like you'd expect guys who'd been drumming for years to play. They both played more snare, like James had, and had a jazzy feel to their solos. I could never have matched their snare work, but I felt good knowing that I had done something different from all of them and had played more of a rock kind of solo. Lewis had gotten a good response after his solo, but Mark probably got the most cheers and applause of all of us. He had a lot of friends in both Park Hill and Lakewood, the students who pretty much made up the popular crowd at school, and he played a lot of the dances with the twins, so lots of people knew him and knew of him.

Over the next few days I found out what the kids had thought about my playing. Now when I walked through the halls between classes, people who I'd have never had contact with otherwise would stop me or come up to me and tell me how great I sounded or would just pass by and say, "Cool drums, Peter!" and girls were finally recognizing me for something and wanting to talk to me. I had found my place, and I loved the fact that I had a side to me completely separate from the old me who was known for nothing at all.

My drumhead with the beatnik guy on it had been a hit too. People were asking me about it and the band and where we would be playing so that they could come hear us. Some of the seniors who had known my brothers starting acting like my bodyguards too. Joe had especially taken it upon himself to watch out for me, and nobody messed with Joe. Not that people ever messed with me that much or anything, but I thought it cool that people like Joe wanted to protect me.

The only fight I could ever remember being in happened in the sixth grade when we had first moved to North Little Rock. I walked home every afternoon from school and would sometimes walk with Phyllis and some of her girlfriends. One day, this boy had been walking ahead with another girl and was punching on her and looked like he was bothering her. I ran ahead and told him to stop, and that started him doing the same to me. We ended up on the ground with him on top. It hadn't exactly been much of a fight, just some pushing and punching in the arm and stuff, but that kind of taught me that I should never fight, and I'd never been in a fight since. So it was nice to know that I didn't have to worry about guys like that with guys like Joe around.

The next couple of months the band got a few more gigs at the Youth Center, and we started playing fairly regularly at the skating rink on the Jacksonville highway. My brother had taken on being my roadie, hauling me and my equipment around, because I could tell that Eddie had been getting kind of tired of it. Anyway, I think my brother liked the fact that he was with the band too and could try to pick up girls. I hadn't been out with Michelle again either, not having a car and Eddie getting tired of coming to get me, but I had gotten a call from Cathy after the drum battle who told me that her sister had seen me at the drum battle and told her how good a drummer I was. I'd been spending so much time in Jacksonville at the dances and skate rink playing gigs that I hadn't had a chance to see Cathy, but I thought I'd probably try to go out with her or something soon.

Then one night at the skate rink things kind of fell apart. Eddie had gotten to the rink pissed off about something. We usually started about ten o'clock after the last skate session, and he came in right about that time. The rest of us had been there for a while, I had gotten there early enough to skate and do the races, and we had already gotten set up after the final session. Joe and some other kids had been coming out to hear us when we played there, so I had been talking with them and my brother and just waiting for Eddie to get there to start. I had had a few swigs on my whiskey bottle and felt pretty good about then. I was always ready to play.

Eddie finally got there and said we needed to help him to get the P A stuff in so we could get started. We carried the stuff in while Eddie went around talking with the other guys and not talking very much with me. It kind of pissed me off that I had to carry my drums in, well my brother always helped me, and then had to carry his stuff in too while he talked to people. It wasn't that much to set up, just a couple of speaker cabinets and the amp head for the mics, but it was still pretty shitty of him.

We did our first set and then took a break. We still did the same songs we had started with at the first youth center dance, so I had asked if we could learn some new stuff over the past few weeks. I liked The Yardbirds and Them a lot and wanted to do a lot more of their stuff, but Eddie wanted to do more songs by American groups now, because the kids at the skate rinks liked the American groups more than the British groups. During the break I went outside to have a smoke and get a sip of the whiskey bottle. I saw Eddie and a couple of the guys over by his car, but I went around the back so I could piss. When I finished and came back around they had gone in, so I finished my smoke, took a swig off the whiskey and went back in.

We did the second set and finished for the night. I started taking my drums apart and getting them ready to pack up. Eddie was yanking cords out of the amp and the speakers and banging stuff around and was just acting super pissed off. I thought he might hit my drums and moved them so they were out of the way. I asked him what was wrong and he started yelling at me that he wasn't going to hit my drums. I said I just didn't want anything to happen to my drums and he got even more pissed and pushed me and said he wasn't going to hit my drums. Joe had been standing near by and didn't like the fact that Eddie was yelling at me and had pushed me. He walked over and grabbed Eddie and turned him around and without saying a word slapped Eddie across the face. The sound of the slap got everyone's attention in the rink, even over the music playing, and Eddie's cheek turned beet red. You could tell Eddie knew he had screwed up. He stood there kind of in shock for a minute and wasn't about to fight with Joe, so he turned around and went outside. Joe and my brother helped me get the drums in the car, and we all left. That night ended my playing with The Grupe.

I hadn't gotten to know many musicians in North Little Rock, so for the next couple of months I just played my drums at home and kept listening to the music I liked. I had called Cathy, and we talked pretty often, but her parents had gotten even more strict with her and her sisters, so she could never go out anywhere with a guy, but I could go over there and watch television with her, as long as her parents were home.

Jim's Roller Rink became my Friday and Saturday night hangout, and I had met a new friend there named Donnie who was a lot of fun. We'd race in the choo choo race, where I'd sit down on my skates and he'd push, and we'd race other guys that way. We usually did pretty good, and I'd race in the individual races. I had bought a used pair of Chicago skates with the money I had made from playing and loved them.

Jim had bands sometimes on Saturday nights after the skating ended, so Donnie and I would stay and then walk to his house which wasn't too far away. His mom was cool, and he had a younger sister who was cute. His mom would let us use her car sometimes to go get burgers or just run around. We'd usually go out to Rose City and go to a liquor store that Donnie knew about and get booze and go out drinking. Donnie looked older than he was, so it was easy for him to pass for old enough to buy booze. I think he knew the guy who worked there too, or his mom knew him. And he liked school about as much as I did, so we never did homework or worried about classes.

My Mom had found out about me smoking, in a kind of strange way. I had gotten mad at my brother and told Mom that he smoked and instead of getting mad at him, she got mad at me and took a sale sign my Dad had in the garage and broke the wooden stake on it over my back. It didn't hurt that much, but it pissed me off that she got mad at me instead of him. Then my brother told her that I smoked too, and I guess she felt bad that she broke the board over my back, and she started bringing cigarettes home for me about every other day. I thought that was kind of weird, but she and Dad smoked, so why should they tell me I couldn't. Just about everybody did anyway.

Around Christmas time, we had to take an unexpected trip to Pennsylvania when my Mom's aunt who she had been named after and my favorite aunt, Aunt Helen, died. She had raised Mom pretty much when grandma had taken off with one of her husbands, and Mom was very upset over her death. My Mom would always tell the story of how one time when Aunt Helen had come to visit us that my parents were having a poker party with a bunch of the relatives. I was a little kid, about two or three I think, and in the beginning of the evening I was walking around the room and just kind of playing around but that I would always go over to Aunt Helen after I played around a little. At the end of the evening they hadn't seen me for a while and wondered where I was. They found me sound asleep on the floor in the den and they found out that the reason I kept going over to Aunt Helen was because she was sneaking me sips of her Bloody Mary's. Every time I heard that story I always wondered if I had a hangover the next day.

Even though it wasn't a very happy reason to go, I enjoyed the trip and the time away from school and would go walking at night in the snow and cold listening to my portable radio. I loved traveling and loved our trips to Pennsylvania. This time it had just been me and my Mom and Dad and my little brother, so I got to help Dad navigate and stayed up with him while he drove through the night. He couldn't have found anyone better to do that job. We had to get there for the funeral, so he pretty much drove straight through, and we'd stop and get coffee along the way. It was the most time I had spent with my Dad forever, and I felt great thinking that I was helping him with something and that he was spending the time with just me.

The only thing I didn't like about the whole trip was the day of the funeral when Aunt Helen's casket was in the front room of my grandma's house. The casket was open and everybody was there crying and talking about her. Then everybody got up and started moving around the room viewing Aunt Helen in the casket. But they weren't just viewing her. They were all giving her a final kiss goodbye. My Mom said it was a Polish tradition. When I got to her though, she looked so dead and I couldn't stand the thought of kissing someone dead, even if she was my favorite aunt on my Mom's side of the family. My Mom stood behind and said

I didn't have to kiss her, so I didn't. I was glad afterwards that I didn't. I didn't want to remember her as dead. I wanted to remember her as telling her jokes and laughing and drinking booze and sneaking shots of whiskey to us. I wanted to remember the fun stuff.

I spent the rest of the school year hanging out at Jim's on the weekends, drinking and messing around with Donnie, and practicing on my drums. I missed playing a lot, but I had met a few musicians at Jim's, and I knew that before long I'd be playing again, with somebody.

****

Summer school ended the middle of July, and I had only about a month of summer left to try to have a little fun. I had been seeing Cathy again, either at night when her parents were there or sneaking over during the day when her dad was at work and her mom was gone to run errands. I had finally gotten alone with her and had played with her tits and fingered her with her pants on. We hadn't gotten to the point of getting naked or anything, but she had played with my dick with her hand inside my underwear.

I had gotten hooked up with another band during the summer, the only good thing about summer school where I had reconnected with Allan who had sung a little with me and Nicky when we were practicing. He sang with some guys in his neighborhood who met at this guitar player's house during the day. Buddy, the guitar player, had a practice room in the basement of his house that worked perfectly for rehearsing, and his parents worked during the day, so we had the place to ourselves. He had a set of drums there too, so I didn't have to worry about taking mine over. He lived pretty close to my house too, so I could ride my bike over there in a few minutes.

The bass player, Steve, was cool, and we got along great. Allan sang the Stones and soul music just like Mick and James Brown and Van Morrison and loved singing that kind of stuff. We had two guitar players, Buddy and a guy named Edgar who we called "Thumper" for short, though I never really knew where that nickname came from. Buddy would play some keyboard sometimes, which helped with some of the songs, but he mainly played guitar with Thumper. Allan, Thumper, and Buddy all sang, and Steve and I just sat back and kept the rhythm section going. Steve and Thumper had cars, and Allan and Buddy could use their dad's cars when their dads weren't at work, so we didn't have to worry about getting around, and Steve was real good about giving me rides with him. I needed to be able to drive now to get to practices and gigs and haul my equipment, but my parents were still dead set on me not driving.

The soul music we played had great drums to it and was a lot different from the stuff I had done with The Grupe. We still did British music, but soul music had become popular with kids and would get us more gigs. I loved James Brown's music and Sam and Dave and Wilson Picket, and loved playing the drums to their songs. It challenged me more than any music I'd done yet, and I liked that. We did some Beatles songs too, and I was beginning to like them more than I had when their music had first come out. John was my favorite of the group, but hearing Paul sing "Michelle" always made me think of the double date with Michelle and Clair and Eddie.

Donnie was now able to get his mom's car when she wasn't using it, and he and I would sometimes take girls home from the skating rink, after the rink closed, or if he didn't have his car, we'd all walk home. Of course, if we had the car, we would always find a place to park first and would make out or do whatever the girls would let us do, which usually wasn't a lot, but we had fun anyway. Most of the time, we would get his mom's car and pick up a bottle of J. W. Dant whiskey and just drive around or go to a drive-in movie and get drunk and then go back to his house or park the car somewhere and sleep. My parents would always think we were just staying at his house, so it didn't matter where we spent the night. They never checked on me anyway.

School would be starting up again soon, and I couldn't think of anything worse than having to go back, even if I would be a senior doing my last year of school, I hoped. Every time I thought about it, I got depressed and would get drunk to try to forget about it. I hated all the classes they had put me in and tried not to think of what I'd be doing if I was taking classes to be a Microbiologist, which I'd try to forget about by getting drunk too. My biggest hope was that our band would be able to get some of the school dances and would play at Lake Nixon and some of the other places around town that had music. I'd try to finish school to please my parents, but I'd be playing music to please me.

'67

****

Mosquitoes swarmed around us like vultures around a dying cow as we pushed my brother's car to the nearest town, a little place called Hazen. We had played a gig at the "1170 Club," about five miles down a lonely stretch of road from Hazen, and had come out afterwards to find that the car wouldn't start. We had stood around drinking and smoking and talking after we finished playing and had gotten the equipment out, and now everyone had left the club, and we were the only ones there, with no way to call anyone and no one to give us a jump. Each of us took turns sitting in the driver's seat to steer the car, our escape from the swarm of mosquitoes, while the others trudged along in the dark pushing the car with just the lightning bugs to guide the way.

Allan had ridden with me and my brother, and we planned on calling his dad when we got to town to come and get us and give us a jump. His dad worked at night, and my parents would be getting ready for work, so his dad would be the best bet to be able to come and help. We both had to be at summer school at seven o'clock in the morning and nothing was going to stop our parents from getting us there. Going to summer school, again, meant that I would get my diploma, and you couldn't miss any days of summer school and pass. With all the shit our parents had been through that year, they weren't about to let a little dead battery incident keep us from being in that class when the bell rang, whether we learned anything, stayed awake, or whatever happened.

This time it wasn't English. I had done fine in English, especially since my brother was still dating the English teacher, Ms. Patrick. She wasn't going to let her boyfriend's brother flunk her class, and hell I knew all the goods on them anyway, like their stealing tires off of VW bugs and all the screwing they did and running around with my brother's friend Cookie. Cookie was pretty cool but could also be an asshole. He had one of those floating cars that could be used like a boat. You couldn't go very fast in it, but you could cross any water that wasn't moving too fast or wasn't too rough. I think they all used to go out screwing together, just the three of them. That seemed kind of weird. Yeah, I knew way too much on her to flunk English that year.

What I had flunked that year was Bookkeeping and French. I had barely gotten through the first year of French in eleventh grade, and the second year was even harder, because you had to use all the shit from the first year that I had no idea about. I tried to learn all the cuss words and the stuff like "I love you" and all the stuff I might use with girls, but that was about it. I did learn one phrase, vousette en tette demouche, which someone told me meant "you are the son of a fly head," which I thought was pretty funny to say to people. Maybe if I had been in class more I would have done better too.

Bookkeeping was another story altogether. I barely did enough work in my classes to get by as it was, but I never did anything in that class. Of course, it didn't help that I had gotten caught handing in our semester bookkeeping assignment that my girlfriend had done for me. So I got an F for that semester and got a three-day vacation from school. The three-day vacations I didn't mind at all. They thought they were punishing me by kicking me out of school for three days, but I loved the fact that I could sleep late, cook myself some hamburgers or fried bologna sandwiches for lunch, and read comic books or my science fiction novels and listen to my records. Usually a few of us would be kicked out at the same time or someone would be skipping school, and we would gather at one person's house and drink and play poker.

We never did it at my house because my Mom would pop in unexpectedly while she was out delivering drugs, and when I skipped school she'd be out tracking me down. She always knew the right places to look for me, and that was either at Donnie's house or Jeff's house. We didn't go to Steve's or Allan's houses, because they had dad's around. Jeff and Donnie's dads were gone, and it was just them and their mothers, and their mothers worked during the day, so we could drink and play poker and not have to worry about anyone coming in. Except my Mom. If she tracked me down, she'd barge right in and yell at me to get in the truck, that I was going to school even if I was late. Then I'd get kicked out again for skipping school and get to stay home for three more days.

I'd get three-day vacations for my hair too. I wanted it long and wouldn't go and get a haircut on my own. But when it got too long for the principal who we called Rabbit or for the Deans, they'd give me a three-day to get it cut. So Mom would drag me down to the barber shop and have them cut it. Then she'd take me back to school and talk them into letting me back in before the three days were up. They knew her pretty well, not just because of my two older brothers going through and being model students and athletes, but because she had to constantly try to keep me in school and was there every week for something or another. So I guess they felt sorry for her going through all the shit and would let me come back. They knew it wouldn't be long before I got caught skipping again or got caught going across the street to get hamburgers or eat lunch. That was another three-day vacation

The coaches, and that was the principal and all the deans, didn't like me as it was. Whenever we got in trouble for something in P.E. or at school, we were always sent to the coaches' office. They had a paddle there with holes in it, and they would give you licks to try to straighten you out, in more ways than one. I had been sent there one time to get licks, and I had told the coach that he couldn't give me licks. He got so pissed and his face turned bright red, and he said he sure could give me licks. And so I told him that my doctor, Dr. Franks, had written a note to the school and told them about this cyst thing that I had on my ass. If they gave me licks it would make the cyst bust and then I'd have to have surgery, so licks were out for me. It pissed the coaches off like hell when they couldn't treat you shitty or boss you around or give you licks, so they didn't like me too much. They made me run laps instead, which to me was worse than the licks.

With all the skipping school and three day vacations I'd had, the amount of time I spent at school had been barely enough for me to be able to graduate. When you hadn't passed all your classes to graduate yet, they only gave you a blank piece of paper at graduation, and you didn't get the actual diploma until you finished summer school or whatever you needed to finish.

The big worry for us guys on graduation was whether we would go to college or go to the army or some other service because of the heavy fighting that was going on in Vietnam. Since I was only seventeen, I didn't have to worry about it just yet, but most of the guys in my class had already turned eighteen and some had already gotten their notices to go in for the physical. Anybody who had good grades and planned to go to college didn't have to worry too much about the draft, but guys who had barely squeaked by and didn't have any plans for college or couldn't afford college scrambled to join the week-end warriors or just went ahead and signed up for the Army to get it over with. It was just two years, but when you got drafted or joined the Army, you knew you were on your way to Vietnam. Some guys got married because they would take single guys before they would take married guys, and some guys would take off for Canada or Europe.

My friend, Donnie, hadn't done too well in eleventh grade and was already eighteen before our junior year had ended and so after a few months into the school year he got his draft notice and had gone into the Navy. I missed him and all the fun we had going to Jim's and parking with girls and going to the drive in and getting drunk. The Navy or the Air Force was where a lot of guys would go if they wanted a better chance of not going to Vietnam and coming back in a body bag, and I think he liked the idea of getting to travel

The band had gone through some changes since our meetings at Buddy's house and now consisted of me on drums, Allan singing, Steve on bass, and Thumper on guitar. Thumper had a cool house up in Park Hill that sat on the side of a hill and had a basement area where he had his bedroom and had den with a pool table and a poker room with a bar where his dad would have parties. We'd practice in the den and play pool and drink and smoke. He had all of the latest music and would regularly go to Memphis to buy records. His wall shelves were filled with albums, he must have had over a thousand, and he had his own bathroom off the bedroom. On top of that, he drove a cool sports car that I loved.

With so many records to choose songs from, we played some of the newest music that no one else around town was playing. We loved The Who and The Yardbirds and Them and played a lot of their stuff, like "My Generation" and

"Substitute" and "Shapes of Things" and "I Can Only Give You Everything," but we still did some of the James Brown songs and other stuff that we had been doing with Buddy, like "I Feel Good" and "Papa's Got a Brand New Bag." We just liked the music that had stronger guitar parts and drums, and I loved Keith Moon's drumming more than just about any other drummer now. Allan could sing the shit out of those songs too, so our group was getting well known around school, and we were being asked to play dances after the football games and at the rec center down from the school.

The rec center had become my favorite hangout after school each day. I'd go down there and play pool until Mom came and picked me up when she had a run that way or was going home. I had gotten to be a good pool player and always had somebody challenging me to a game. They had regular pool tables and snooker tables too, so I had learned to play regular eight-ball, nine-ball, and snooker. Snooker and nine-ball were my favorites, and I'd spend hours playing after school. We'd also take classes there, like when Donnie and I took classes in jui jitsu. We had had a lot of fun with that and would make my Mom laugh, even though she didn't like that we always got in trouble when we were together, by doing fake fights or playing "napkin man" or some other stupid stuff. I sure missed him.

I had met some other guys through Allan and Steve, and I spent a lot of time hanging around with them. Most of them were juniors too, like Allan and Steve, but two of the guys, Jeff and James, were seniors. Well, James would have been a senior, but he had had a skiing accident at the end of the summer and had broken his neck and was now living in the big rehabilitation center in Hot Springs. Jeff was my age, his birthday was four days after mine, so we got along great being the same age. We'd go over to his house after school a lot with Reggie and Bob, two juniors, and drink and listen to

Frank Zappa and the Mothers of Invention. We loved the new music from Zappa and Jimi Hendrix and Cream and would buy any new albums or forty-fives by them. Jeff and Bob and I would skip school sometimes and drive down to Hot Springs and visit James at the center. He always got a kick out of the fact that we were skipping school just to come see him.

I had kept going over to Cathy's house whenever I could during the summer and had finally gone almost all the way with her. Her parents had gone to some church deal and had left her home for the afternoon, and so she called me and asked if I could come over. I jumped on my bike and raced over along the railroad tracks, hoping that the guys from Wood Street wouldn't be out on the tracks hitting rocks. We had rock fights with them sometimes and if they had seen me they probably would have bombarded me.

It was hot that day when I pulled up to the side of her house. I never parked in front of her house, in case her parents came home while I was there and I could take off through the back yard. She opened the side door and let me in, wearing shorts and a button shirt and looked cute as ever. We hung around in the garage talking and started kissing and playing around. I unbuttoned her shirt and played with her tits, and she put her hand down my pants and played with my dick. I had a boner going from her playing with me, and I moved my hand down to her shorts and unzipped them and put my hand inside her panties and started fingering her. She got super excited with that and pushed my pants down and started jacking me off. I pushed her pants down, but she wouldn't let me pull them off and kept fingering her, and then I moved over on top of her and stuck my dick between her legs. I didn't get inside her pussy, but I could feel her pussy against my dick and came on her legs.

She got embarrassed and said her parents would be home soon and that I'd better go. We cleaned up, and I took off. That was the last time I saw her through the summer. When school started I didn't see her very much, since she was in sophomore classes, but her sister, Debby, who was a senior and was super cute too, had been talking with me and was being extra friendly with me. She had been grounded forever and could only see her boyfriend when her parents were home, and I guess he had gotten tired of driving the two hours to get there to see her and have to sit in the front room and not be able to screw, and now she wasn't going with anyone. With her long straight blonde hair and the flowered dresses she wore she reminded me of Marianne Faithful, who I loved and thought was beautiful, and so I started calling and talking to her on the phone, and we had made a date for her to come to the next dance to see me play. Her mom would drop her off and pick her up, but she could stay afterwards until her mom got there and would be there when we took breaks. I couldn't wait for the dance because it was also the first one we would be playing for the school and the first time that most of the kids from school would be seeing me play with a band. I was determined to put on the best performance of my life, even better than the drum battle, and to see just exactly what Debby thought about me.

****

The band, we were The Things now, got together as many times as we could before the dance to learn a few new songs and stay tight on the ones we would do at the dance. We had learned a few new songs especially for the dance, ones that had just come out and a couple of older ones that kids had asked if we did. We learned a new Stones song for Allan called "Paint It Black," and some of the kids had asked if we did the new songs "Wild Thing" and "Good Lovin'," so we worked those up too. I loved the group Love, and we were already doing "My Little Red Book" by them, but we worked up a new one by them called "7 and 7 Is." By the time we got through, we had added six new songs to our list and had all the ones we would need for the two hour dance. We could always play a couple of others from our regular list if we played a little longer too. If we'd had Claude playing the organ for us we could have done a bigger variety of songs, but Thumper played great guitar and could play any of the guitar parts on any of the songs and sounded just as good as any of the guitar players on the records.

Even though I loved the songs we played, a lot of the songs that meant a lot to me because of the words and the tunes were songs we couldn't play, usually because of the instruments or the singing. I listened to groups like The Association and The Left Bank, The Four Tops, The Hollies, Peter and Gordon, because the words in their songs fit with what was going on with me a lot of the time or fit with what I wished would happen, like when they would sing about losing a girlfriend or meeting someone and then never seeing them again or wishing that someone loved you as much as you loved them, and the words just seemed to find a place inside me to rest and cause my emotions to react.

I'd listen to songs like "We'll Sing in the Sunshine" or "A Summer Song" or "You Were On My Mind" or "Walk Away Renee" or "Windy" and wish that I knew those girls or think about girls I knew that those girls in the songs reminded me of or think about the situations those guys were in. It would embarrass me sometimes when I'd hear those songs and other people were around, and I could feel the tears coming and would try so hard to hold them back until the feeling stopped or would stop talking because I'd get choked up. So, those were the songs I listened to at night, alone, in my room, with the lights off or in front of the stereo in the dark living room, while everyone else was watching television downstairs or in bed upstairs and couldn't hear or see me crying, because that was what the words did to me.

I went to school every day until the day of the dance, because I didn't want to get in trouble and not be able to play that night, and I was seeing Debby more and more between classes and walking her to class sometimes, so I didn't mind going to school as much now. I wished that we had some classes together, but she took more high level classes than I took. She had Bookkeeping but had it during a different period with the same teacher, and she started helping me with the homework in that class. Besides being super cute and super smart, she was super nice too. I could talk to her about anything, and she loved that I played drums in a band, and she knew that I hated my classes, so I guess that was why she wanted to help me with my homework. Well, she wasn't just helping me with it, she was doing a lot of it for me. After a while it got hard to leave her at her class, and I couldn't wait for class to end so that I could meet her and walk her to the next class.

My oldest brother had moved back into the house over the summer and had again taken on being my roadie, especially since we were playing high school gigs, and he could go there with Ms. Patrick. When my brothers had wrecked our station wagon, Mom and Dad had bought a Ford Custom, kind of a cheap Galaxie, which had plenty of room for my drums, and my brother would pretty much load the car himself, and all I had to do was just put in some of the littler stuff and my stick bag. He didn't care if I drank or smoked or what I did either, so that worked for me.

We got to the Rec Center about eight o'clock, while the game was still going on at the stadium across the street, so that we could get set up in plenty of time to start after the football game ended. The stage at the center was pretty much like the one at the school auditorium, raised about four feet off of the ground, except it didn't have any seating in front of it. We set up on the front of the stage in front of the curtain, and it had a little platform that I could set my drums on. I felt funny being so far above the dance floor, but I figured everyone would sure be able to see us and to see me too. Allan moved around the stage a lot, but his mic stand was always in the middle of the stage and Steve and Thumper would set up on the sides of him and me. I always wished that I could hear how we sounded from out front though. All I ever got was a kind of echo of the sound after it hit the walls and the floor and bounced around the room.

Debby got there before the crowd from the game and looked great with her long, shiny blonde hair and wearing one of my favorite flowered dresses. She stood over to the side of the stage and just stared at me while we finished getting the sound adjusted and practiced a few of the songs. I felt a little funny with her staring at me like that, so I would kind of watch Allan and Steve and would sneak glances at her. Steve and I played off of each other a lot with the bass and bass drums, so we were always looking around to see what the other one was doing and got into the music together.

We finished getting ready, and I hopped down off the stage and went over to Debby.

"Hi. I'm sure glad you could come tonight." I thought I sounded stupid.

"Your band sounds great, Peter. I knew when I heard you in the drum battle that you were a good drummer, but you sound even better with the band." I thought I would melt right there.

"We've been practicing and getting ready for tonight. We wanna get more gigs here."

"You shouldn't have any problem with that, not with the way you sound."

"I wanted to go out for a smoke before everybody gets here. You mind?"

"I'll go with you." She had the sweetest voice.

We walked out the back door into the dark alley behind the center. I lit a cigarette and offered one to Debby.

"I don't smoke. But it's okay if you do."

I took a swig off my whiskey bottle. I offered her a drink.

"I can't drink whiskey unless it's mixed with coke or something."

"I'll go get you a coke." I started back for the door. She stopped me.

"I'm okay. I don't want my mother to smell it on me when she picks me up. I'm just now able to get out again. I don't want to screw it up."

"I heard about what happened." I hoped she didn't mind me bringing it up.

"I think everybody has. It's been hell."

I didn't want to embarrass her or anything by talking more about that, so I changed the subject.

"Any songs we can play for you tonight?"

"No. I'm just here to hear you play the drums."

She inched closer to me with that, and I got the idea that she wanted me to do something the way she was staring at me. I put the bottle in my back pocket and put my arm around her and kissed her, and she kissed me back big time. Our tongues found each other quickly and had their own wrestling match going on. She could kiss great and must have been getting turned on, because she put her leg between my legs and started rubbing against my dick. I already could feel my dick getting hard, and so I rubbed it against her leg. She moved one of her arms from around my neck and moved her hand down to rub my dick. About that time I wished we were in the back seat of my brother's car, in the huge back seat, and I thought about going to get the key from him, but Steve burst through the back door.

"Hey, man, we're going on now."

I think we surprised him as much as he surprised us. We finished our kiss and followed Steve back inside.

Kids had started filling the center and kept coming in from the game. We could tell who had won by the excitement of the kids and the horn honking and cars racing around in front. That would be good for us. Everybody would want to have a good time and dance and probably have bottles of booze to mix with their cokes. It was pretty easy to sneak booze into the dances. The chaperones were usually busy talking with each other, and with chaperones like Ms. Patrick and my brother, anybody could get away with anything at the dances.

Debby settled into her spot down by the stage where she could stare at me and where I could see her, and we started playing. We wanted to get things going right away, so we started with "Paint It Black." The cheerleaders and pep squad girls filled the floor and got everyone going. It was great having them there to get people fired up and get the shy guys out on the floor. We played our usual three or four fast songs and then played a slow song. We could tell they enjoyed the music, because they applauded after every song and kids kept coming up to the stage and requesting songs and saying that we sounded great. That got us even more buzzed and probably made us play even better.

Guys kept going over to Debby and, I guessed, asking her to dance, but she didn't dance with anyone and they didn't stay around long, so I figured she wasn't interested in talking with them either. I liked that a lot. I didn't want to see her dancing with other guys or other guys holding her, especially on slow songs. I wanted her all to myself. I kept feeling her hand on my dick and her leg between my legs and wanted to go outside with her and kiss her again. I wished that she wasn't being picked up by her mom and that we could take her home. Maybe I'd have her call her mom during our break and ask her if we could take her home. We could always try. What could it hurt?

At the break, I told my plan to Debby. She didn't think it would work but said she would call anyway. She went to the pay phone and called her mom while I went outside to have a smoke and a swig off the whiskey bottle. Steve came out with me.

"Didn't mean to barge in on you guys earlier."

"It's okay. This is our first real date."

"She's cute. She's been staring at you all night. I think she likes you."

"I like her a lot."

"Why don't you guys go out with Debbie and me some time?"

"As long as we don't get 'em confused. Her name's Debby too."

"No shit?"

"That'd be great." I didn't want to say anything about her parents being so strict, so I just let it drop right there.

Debby came out the back door.

"She said she was already ready to come get me. So not tonight." We were both disappointed at that. Debby moved over to me, and I put my arm around her.

"Steve, this is Debby."

"My girlfriend's name is Debbie too." Did Steve realize what he had just blurted out? Debbie and I looked at each other. She grinned.

"Does she spell her name with a 'y' though. Most girls spell it with an 'ie.'"

I took it from her grin and from her not saying anything about Steve's comment that she was okay with him calling her my girlfriend.

"We better get back in there." Steve left us in the alley. Debby turned around to face me.

"Is it okay with you that Steve thinks I'm your girlfriend?"

"I like it a lot." We kissed and went back into the center.

The rest of the night I couldn't think of anything except Debby. She kept her spot by the stage and didn't take her eyes off me all night, and guys had stopped coming over to her, which made me feel better. We played all the songs we had planned and had to play a couple of extras, because the kids didn't want to leave. But the chaperones cut us off when it was time to close the center, and they started herding everyone out while we took down our equipment. I hated that I couldn't spend time with Debby, but I had to get my stuff packed up and get out of there.

Before her mom got there, we went out back for a last kiss and decided we'd get together as soon as we could. Maybe we could go to a movie or something and have my brother take us. I told her that my parents wouldn't let me drive because of my brothers wrecking the car, and she said she didn't care as long as we got to see each other.

I watched her leave with her mom and got the rest of my stuff packed up. My brother and Ms. Patrick had been getting all the kids out of the center and were ready to go by now. They dropped me and my drums off at the house and took off, I guessed out to steal more tires or go to her place and screw.

I wanted to call Debby and talk to her, but I knew she wouldn't be able to talk that late. I'd just have to wait until tomorrow, if I could. I thought I could get on my bike and go over to her house and try to talk with her through her bedroom window maybe. But if we got caught, she'd never be able to go out with me. I decided I better just stay there, so I fixed a couple of bologna sandwiches and had a coke with some whiskey in it and went to my room. I turned on the radio and scarfed down the sandwiches in no time. Playing always made me so hungry, and I could never get to sleep after I got through playing.

I lit a cigarette and lay down on my bed in the dark listening to the radio. "Good Vibrations" played on the radio, and all I could think of was Debby and how good she made me feel. Not just rubbing my dick and kissing me, but making me feel like she for real liked me and being so sweet and everything. I'd never felt like this about anyone before, and it was a strange feeling to know that a girl felt about me the way I felt about her. Strange, but something I could definitely get used to.

****

If only my Mom had known why I suddenly started spending more time at school. She thought, at first, that I had finally gotten my shit together and had gone back to being the old Peter who loved going to school and learning. Then she found out the real reason and didn't like it one bit.

"Peter!" She yelled up the steps with the scream that had terrorized department stores, grocery stores, the neighborhood, little animals in the woods, my Dad, forever. I cringed every time I heard it. I knew what followed like no one else, and it always meant that I better run, hide, or have a good excuse for whatever had caused her to use it.

"Come down here! Now!"

I slinked down the steps.

"Yeah, Mom." She had a letter in her hand, waving it at me as she began.

"Your counselor says that you are only passing English and P.E. and that your other grades are D's and F's. What is going on with you? You've been going to school every day, so how can you be doing so badly?"

"I don't know. I'm going to all my classes." But I wasn't doing shit in any of them, and I couldn't tell her that. The dance we played had gotten the band some more gigs playing dances after the football games, we might even get the Homecoming dance, and I didn't want to miss any of those or mess that up for the guys.

"It's that Debby girl, isn't it? I've heard about her down at the drug store. She doesn't sound like a good girl to me."

Mom had heard me talking to Debby on the phone and knew that she had come to the dance that night. I had been spending a lot of time talking to Debby on the phone when I got home from school and in the evenings, while Mom and Dad would be downstairs watching television or would be bowling or something, but they didn't know exactly how much time I was spending on the phone and probably would have been pissed if they'd known. But it pissed me off that that was what she thought about Debby.

"They don't know what they're talking about! Debby's one of the nicest girls I've ever met! She's the reason I'm going to my classes and trying to do better!" The last part, of course, was only partially true, but it sounded damn good.

Now I got the mother stare, trying to figure out if what I was saying was the truth or was me just trying to get out of trouble with her. It didn't take long for her to come around. After all, I was her baby who almost died at birth, and she hadn't had to drag me back to school in at least a couple of weeks, so that had to be helping.

"We'll see what happens with your report card, but you better get these grades up if you want to graduate."

I knew what she was getting at here, but I didn't care as long as I got to see Debby.

Debby's parents had become more lenient with her the past few weeks, and I had been slipping over there in the evenings, racing along the railroad tracks on my bicycle, to spend a little time with her. We'd sit in the kitchen and do homework and talk and when no one was around would sneak kisses, and damn she was a great kisser. When I saw her at school now, I would start getting a boner just watching her, thinking about kissing her, feeling her hand on my dick, wanting to touch her.

She had gotten to go with me to rehearsal once, with my brother taking us, and we had finally talked her parents into letting us go out to a movie. We were going out with a friend of mine from English class, Johnny, who was also a singer and who we were talking to about maybe joining the band for some gigs. He was a good friend of Joe's too, so he had been around some of the dances I'd played even in Jacksonville. He and his girlfriend, Jenny, and Debby and I were going to go to a movie, maybe, at least that's what the parents thought, on Friday night. I couldn't wait.

Friday was the day from hell. I walked around like a zombie all day. I wanted everything to be perfect for our first real date. Johnny had picked a movie he already knew, so in case we wanted to do something else, and we'd still be able to tell our parents what the movie was all about. Mom had taken me to Sears to get some new clothes for school, so I planned to wear one of my new shirts, a Gant look-alike, and some Levi's and my penny loafers, so it would look like we were actually going to a movie.

Johnny and Jenny picked me up about seven, and then we went to get Debby. He had a '58 Chevy Impala which was pretty slick and had a big back seat. At Debby's house, we went through the interrogation with the parents about where we were going, when we'd better be back, and all the other twenty questions, and we finally got away.

Once we got a few blocks away from Debby's house, we couldn't help but plant a huge kiss on each other. This had been a long time coming, and we were both ready for it. I felt like tearing her clothes off right then but controlled myself. It didn't help matters that she had put her hand between my legs right next to my dick either. I didn't want her to think that I wasn't experienced or that I was too anxious though, so I held back the urges I felt.

We decided to get something to eat and went to Park Hill to the Whatta Burger and ordered burgers and fries and cokes. They had root beer floats and stuff there too, but that didn't mix too well with the booze that Johnny and I mixed in with our cokes. Jenny mixed some with her coke too, but Debby didn't want any right then.

Johnny finished eating and was ready to go. "What are you guys up for?"

We looked at each other, and we definitely knew what we were up for. "You're driving." I answered for the both of us. I knew Johnny had something in mind.

Debby and I settled into the back seat while Johnny took us to all the cruise streets in North Little Rock. We went down the hill to our part of town, first to Pike Avenue, then hit Main street, and then Broadway. Broadway was a little rougher area of town, probably where the term "dog town" for North Little Rock had come from, but it was great to cruise and see all the different people and bars and stuff.

Debby and I would kiss whenever we went through a dark section of town or when we weren't talking with Johnny and Jenny or watching what was going on around us. I could feel an electrical feeling between us, like a spark waiting to set off an explosion. Her hand hadn't moved from my leg, and my arm around her shoulders held her as close as I get her to me. After we kissed we would just stare into each other's eyes, almost in a trance. I wondered what she was thinking.

We cruised Broadway a couple of times, and Johnny was ready for something else. "You guys ever been to Lookout?"

"What's Lookout?"

"It's this place up on the side of a hill by a park in Little Rock. You can see the whole city from there." Johnny looked back and grinned. "It's really dark." Jenny giggled.

"You're driving."

We crossed the river and got on Cantrell Road which followed the river up into the Heights area of Little Rock. I had gone that way lots of times to the Razorback Drive-in on Cantrell and on up into the Heights to visit my aunts and uncles who lived up there. It was a pretty drive during the day and was dark at night, so Debby and I took advantage of the dark and made out some more. Her hand had inched up my leg against my dick now, and I touched her tits. She had one of the flowered dresses on that I liked which had buttons up the front, and so I unbuttoned a few of the buttons and put my hand inside to play with her tits outside her bra. Her nipples got hard, and I put my hand inside and played with them. We got interrupted when Johnny pulled into a store, and so Debby and I stopped what we were doing.

"I'm gonna get a coke before we go up there. Anybody want anything?"

We all got cokes and took off up a street by the park at the bottom of the hill off of Cantrell. I'd never gone that way in all the times I'd been to my relatives houses. That dark and windy road through the woods ended at another two-lane road with a drop-off in front of us that looked like it went down forever.

Johnny turned left onto the two-lane road which curved around the hill with houses on our left side and the drop-off on the right side lined with trees. After a few minutes the trees were gone, and we could see the lights of the city. Johnny was right. You could see the whole city from up there. It looked bigger than I thought it was, but the buildings downtown looked huge with the lights on them. You could also see the lights from Fort Roots and the cliffs where Darryl and I used to climb.

We pulled off of the little road onto a lookout spot built onto the side of the road. The spot was big enough for a bunch of cars, but we had it to ourselves right then. The only light came from the city lights. Johnny was right about it being so dark up there, especially since the moon wasn't out tonight.

We all got out and went to the wall and sat and looked at the lights. Johnny and I mixed some booze with our cokes and lit up cigarettes. I couldn't believe how peaceful it was there, with the lights twinkling from the city and no traffic on the road. We were up high enough that we didn't get any of the noises from the city, except for an occasional distant siren, but only the sounds of the night, crickets and grasshoppers and dogs barking down the hill. Debby sat next to me on the wall with her arm around me. It was getting a little chilly out, so we decided to get back in the car.

We nestled back into the back seat and resumed our kissing from before. We had to get warmed up again, but it didn't take long at all. Her hand went back between my legs, and my hand went back to her tits. Then she started rubbing my dick, and it got hard, and I didn't even try to hold back. I moved my hand from her tits to her leg under her dress. Her legs were so smooth and soft, and I followed up to her panties. Her hand was inside my jeans now holding my dick, then she unbuttoned the jeans and unzipped my pants and pulled my dick out. We had been slowly moving down in the seat and had pretty much laid down now. She had my dick out and was moving her hand up and down on it, while I had my hand down her panties and had started fingering her. Her pussy was so warm inside and was so wet, my finger slid in and out so smoothly. Her hand had begun moving up and down my dick faster and faster with me fingering her, and I knew that it wouldn't be long before I came. I didn't want to come on her hand or on the seat though, I wanted to come in her, I wanted to feel my dick inside her and feel the come go into her like I'd always dreamed of, like I fantasized about when I beat off. And this time it was with someone who liked me and who I liked a lot, which made it so much better.

We had gone this far, and Debby didn't seem to be holding anything back, so I made my move and pulled her panties down one leg and moved over on top of her. I was so close to coming now that I could barely hold it back and tried to get inside her, but I couldn't tell if I was in her or not. So I started moving up and down anyway. She squirmed a little, but the way I had laid on top of her, she couldn't move around much. I felt my dick starting to tingle with the come and moved faster. Then I came. I was so surprised by the fact that I had come for the first time from fucking a girl, that I didn't know if I had come inside her or had just come between her legs. It had felt warm and wet on my dick, but the come had gotten on the seat and on her dress, so I wasn't sure if I had slipped out or if I had ever even been inside her.

I laid there with her, feeling the stickiness of the come on my dick and on her leg. My dick had gone limp and was resting on her leg, and she was lying pretty still and just staring at me. I knew that she knew that it was my first time to do that with a girl, but she didn't say anything about it and just held me. I felt a little weird not knowing if we had fucked for real or not, but I wasn't about to ask her if we had. She had been with at least one guy, that I knew of, who was older and probably very experienced at those things, and I didn't want to look even more weird than I already felt. And she was older too, already seventeen and I had a couple of months to go before I turned seventeen.

I suddenly felt like a little kid and got mad at myself for being so stupid about those things. Here I was with a girl who wanted to be with me, who was willing to let me go all the way with her, and who I thought wanted me to do those things with her, and I had no idea what the shit I was doing! Why didn't anybody tell you about those things! Why was it supposed to be such a secret and you were supposed to just learn it on your own with no help from anyone! Even my brothers would never tell me anything about it, and they had been with enough girls to at least be able to tell me the basics of fucking. It made me madder and madder the more I thought about it.

I sat up and started cleaning myself up, and Debby did too. I thought she could tell that I was mad or uncomfortable about the situation, but she didn't say anything. I was glad that she wasn't asking me anything or talking, because I didn't want to talk at all about it right then. I only hoped that she didn't feel funny about it. At least she wasn't laughing at me or being mad at me or acting disgusted.

Johnny and Jenny had been in the front seat, probably doing the same thing we'd been doing and had popped their heads up, and Johnny was smoking a cigarette. I felt like having one too and lit up. I grabbed my coke and stepped out of the car and went over to the wall. I stood there looking out over the city, wondering if Debby would want to go out with me again or if she thought that I was a little kid too. If she would give me another chance, next time would be better. I at least had an idea now of what to do. I heard the car door open and close, and she stepped up beside me, straightening her dress. She gazed out over the city too and just stood there beside me. I didn't know if she was waiting for me to say something or do something or what, and then she took my hand and pulled my arm around her shoulders, and we both stood there silently, watching the lights, and listening to the crickets and the sounds from the woods, barely hearing the radio from Johnny's car. And I knew that everything was okay.

****

Thanksgiving seemed to come earlier than usual. Football and turkey and dressing was on the menu, and Debby and I had made plans for her come to my house to have dinner. We had been seeing each other steadily but had not gone out on any real dates since the one with Johnny and Jenny. Mom would be busy with cooking and cleaning up and girlfriends and with my little brother and any friend he had over. She had gotten used to the idea of Debby being my girlfriend and had even taken us on some dates to the movies, but Debby and I hadn't been alone at all. My Dad and older brothers and their friends would be glued to the television all day watching the football games, especially the Cowboy's game, giving Debby and me a chance to spend some time together.

We had gone on one date with my brother to see The Yardbirds. They were playing with Gary Lewis and the Playboys and Sam the Sham and the Pharaohs and some other groups on a tour. I went to see The Yardbirds mainly, but the rest of the groups were good too. I had only been to a couple of concerts before that, and those were smaller ones on the smaller stage at Robinson Auditorium. I hadn't seen this many groups at one time before or this many kids at a concert before either. I remembered seeing the Beatles and the Rolling Stones when they played on Ed Sullivan with all the girls shouting and screaming in the audience, but these girls surrounded us and people were throwing stuff on the stage, and at first I got pissed, and then I saw that they were throwing flowers and notes at the stage, especially at the guitar player, Jimmy Page. He had on a pink suit with a ruffled shirt and played great. I about died when they played "Shapes of Things" and "The Train Kept a Rollin'." They all sounded fantastic. I couldn't believe I was actually seeing and hearing my favorite group live. Debby loved it too.

My brother and I went about noon to pick up Debby for Thanksgiving dinner. Every time I had to have someone drive me somewhere, like to pick up a girl or just get something from the store, it pissed me off that my brothers had caused me to not be able to get my driver's license. Here all of my friends had their licenses and drove their parent's cars or had their own cars, and I still had to get a ride to do things or had to sneak around on my bicycle so that none of the kids from school would see me riding it. I sure didn't feel like a senior in high school very much. I felt more like I was still in junior high. What would have been so wrong for me to drive the few miles to get Debby and bring her over to the house or go out to a movie? I hated that shit so much about my life.

We got back to the house and did the introductions with the girlfriends and our other guests. Mom was stuck in the kitchen cooking, but Debby made her way in there. She was trying so hard to get on my Mom's good side, and Mom was coming around little by little.

"Hi, Mrs. Bennings." Debby sweetly greeted my Mom.

"Hi, Debby. We're sure glad you could come for dinner today. That's such a pretty dress."

"Thank you. And thank you for having me over today."

We went down into the family room with Dad and the guys hollering at the teams on the screen.

"Hello, Mr. Bennings." Debby tried to get a word in between the shouts and screams.

"Hello, Debby." My Dad barely took his eyes off the screen. He'd only met Debby one time before when he took us to a show, but I was sure Mom had talked to him about her.

Nobody else noticed us so we went up to my room, closed the door, and kissed right away. She tasted so good, maybe even better than the turkey and dressing Mom and the girls were fixing for dinner. I waited all year for Mom's turkey and dressing, mashed potatoes, gravy, sweet potatoes with marshmallow topping, pumpkin pie, and all the rest of the foods that would completely fill our dining room table and the breakfast bar. But that would come later on. Right now I could only taste Debby's sweet kiss and played twister with her tongue.

We moved to my bed and continued the kiss there. It had been so long since we had been alone that we couldn't stop. I wanted to touch her all over and feel her up against me and feel my dick inside her, but I didn't want her to feel uncomfortable at the house so I kept my hands from roaming all over her body. I moved my leg over in between her legs and rubbed my dick against her leg and my leg against her pussy. She seemed to like that, so we kept that up while we kissed. A knock on the door interrupted us. It was my brother's girlfriend. We sat up on the bed as she poked her head into the room, smiling.

"Dinner's ready, you guys."

We got ourselves back together and went down to the meal. We didn't have enough room for everyone to sit at the dining room table, so everyone was pretty much taking a plate and, if it was a guy, going down to the family room to continue watching football and eat, and if it was a girl or a little kid, finding a place at the table or at the breakfast bar to eat. Debby and I hung to the back, until everyone else had gotten plates packed with food, and then we found two seats at the table. Mom and the girlfriends had made places for themselves at the breakfast bar, so we had the table mostly to ourselves, except when someone came up to get seconds. I piled my plate full of dressing and mashed potatoes and gravy, turkey and cranberry sauce, peas and sweet potatoes, and threw a couple of rolls on top. Debby barely put any food on her plate.

"Don't be shy. Everybody eats plenty around here."

"I got all I wanted." Her plate would have barely been an appetizer for any of us.

"Mom will think you don't like something if you don't get a little of all of it."

"She'll understand."

We sat down and dug into the meal, or at least I dug in. Debby kind of picked at hers and kept looking over at me and grinning, I guessed wondering how a skinny thing like me could put away all that food and not weigh more. I had never had any problem with eating as much as I wanted and not gaining weight. Playing drums kind of kept me in shape, along with riding my bike, swimming any chance I got, and all the walking I had to do up and down the flights of steps at school. I guess I needed all that food for the energy to do all of those things.

We finished eating and decided to have pie a little later. Mom always had at least two or three kinds of pie for Thanksgiving. Pumpkin. Pecan. Dad's favorite, chocolate. Dad's other favorite, lemon meringue. Everyone else was still eating and had gone down to the family room to watch the Cowboy's game. We didn't care about football and wanted some time alone anyway, so we put on our heavy coats and went for a walk.

The weather was typical November in Arkansas, overcast, cold, perfect for Thanksgiving, and with the football game going on, we would be the only ones on the street for the next several hours. We walked along holding hands, talking about the food and about the concert and school and the band and just about everything. I still had my moments when I couldn't think of something to say or didn't know what to say, but Debby didn't seem to mind when we didn't talk. Even though we'd been going together for a couple of months now, I still didn't feel sure of myself with her. I kept thinking that maybe she'd get tired of not being able to go out together alone in my car or that I was younger than her and would want an older guy or that she wanted to be having sex and I wasn't experienced enough for her. I worried about all that a lot. I didn't want anything to happen to us.

We walked up the street next to my house which ended at a field and followed a dirt road beside the pond and up into the woods. Some of us guys had built a tree house to use as a hideout a few years back, and when we saw it, Debby wanted to check it out. It wasn't too high up into the tree and had a ladder from the ground up into the floor, so it wasn't like we had to climb the tree to get into it.

I climbed up first and helped Debby climb up. It was pretty big inside, big enough for a couple of people to sleep comfortably, so we had plenty of room to move around. It had a window which could be blocked off by a piece of plywood, so we put the plywood in the opening to keep it a little warmer, but it also made it fairly dark, except for the light coming in through the floor opening. We settled against the wall close to each other, my arm around her and her hand on my leg. We sat there for a few minutes just holding each other. Debby finally broke the silence.

"Kiss me."

I kissed her and her hand immediately moved up my leg to my dick. It didn't take any time for me to start getting a boner, and the harder it got the more she rubbed it. She grabbed me and pulled me down on the floor beside her. We still had our coats on which made the floor a little less hard, and I opened hers and unbuttoned the buttons on her dress and played with her tits. She unzipped my pants and put her hand down my underwear and grabbed my dick. I was hard as a rock now. I moved my hand to her leg and followed up to her panties and ran my hand over her pussy. She started squirming and opened her legs, and I put my hand inside her panties and fingered her. That turned her on big time, and she unbuttoned my pants and pulled my dick out of my underwear.

"Take your pants off." I liked her telling me what to do.

I kicked off my shoes and pulled my pants off as she pulled off her panties. She pulled my underwear off and pulled me over next to her again, running her hand up and down my dick. I fingered her some more and then she pulled me over on top of her and spread her legs and put my dick inside her. I could feel the warmth of her pussy surrounding my dick, and it was so wet. I had no doubt now that I was inside her and started moving in and out of her. She pulled me to her tight and moved her pussy toward me as I kept moving in and out of her. In no time I was feeling the tingle in my balls that meant I was getting ready to come. She must have felt it too, because she began moving faster against me, her arms wrapped around me pulling me tighter to her, and then I felt the explosion of the come inside her and she strained up against me one last time till I finished and then it was over as quickly as it had started.

We lay there forever, her arms wrapped tightly around me, me lying between her legs. My balls still tingled. My dick was still inside her, the boner had gone, but it still felt great being inside her warm pussy. I didn't want to move and ruin the feeling I was feeling, so I just lay there and waited for her to make the first move. I closed my eyes, and when I opened them again, it had gotten pretty dark out. I didn't have a watch on, but I knew it got dark around five o'clock. She had noticed how dark it was too.

"We'd better get going. I have to get home soon."

We started getting dressed, but I wished we never had to leave, that we could stay like that forever, that my dick would get hard and stay hard, and we could just keep fucking. All the times I had dreamed of being with a girl, that I had masturbated thinking about screwing so many different girls from magazines and from real life, and none of that even closely compared with the way it had actually felt. Not just the fact that I had come, but that I had been inside her, that she had wanted me to be inside her, that we had been holding each other so tightly and so close, that she was the girl that I cared about and wanted to be with. I had had feelings before for girls, Rhonda especially, that I thought was the way love felt, but now I had felt the physical side of it too. I wanted to tell Debby that I loved her, but what if she didn't love me? I didn't want to hear her say she didn't love me or just not say anything, so I didn't say anything either.

We finished getting dressed and climbed down the ladder. It was still light enough for us to see the way back to the street and the street lights, but it had gotten colder, and the air felt like snow coming. We walked down the street glued together to keep warm and made it back to the house. The game was in the last quarter, so no one had even wondered where we had been or how long we had been gone. We stood by the fireplace to warm up a little, and just kind of took in what was going on, but we'd look at each other every few minutes and just grin, both of us knowing that the other was thinking about the treehouse.

I had gotten hungry again and grabbed Debby and took off for the kitchen and fixed a plate of some turkey and dressing and mashed potatoes. We would be eating that for the next few days, unless my brothers pigged out and ate it all or brought their friends over to eat. Debby had a piece of pumpkin pie with whipped cream while I devoured the turkey and dressing. Then I had a piece of each one of the pies. I usually would take a little piece of each one rather than take one big piece of one. I liked tasting all the different flavors that way. Mom's homemade whipped cream added just the right touch to the pumpkin and pecan pies, and I always loved the lemon and chocolate meringue pies. Now that I thought about it, I couldn't understand why I didn't get fat like my brother from eating all that food. Of course he didn't get fat until after he got injured in football. That was also why he didn't get drafted. I think he did something to his eye, so they wouldn't take him. He was kind of pissed about that, because he wanted to go to the Army Engineers, and they would have paid for him to go to college too.

By the time we finished our food, it was time to take Debby home. That was the last thing I wanted to do just then, but if she got home late she might get grounded again. She said her goodbye's to everyone and we got in the car and took off. She always sat in the middle and would talk to my brother. They got along pretty well and talked about math and stuff. Her ex-boyfriend had been a football jock too and was about my brother's size, so I kind of worried sometimes that she might start liking him, since he was older and had a car.

We dropped Debby off and headed back home. Everyone had gone now, and my brother took up his position on the couch, while Dad snoozed in his chair by the fireplace, and Mom kept guard at the kitchen bar. The food had been put away, ready for reheating tomorrow and the next day as leftovers, and maybe the next day, if I was lucky. I couldn't end the night without one more piece of Mom's pumpkin pie though, so I cut a big slice, spooned some whipped cream on it and took it to my room. My brother wouldn't have even gotten a plate out, he'd have just scarfed it down straight from the pie pan in one or two bites. I liked to eat it slow and enjoy it.

I turned on my radio and sank onto the bed. I took my first bite of pie and then stopped dead. It finally hit me that I had fucked for sure for the first time that afternoon. I could now tell anyone who asked if I'd ever done it, that I had. I wouldn't go around telling everyone that Debby and I had, but I wouldn't deny it either. Then I started to worry that maybe she didn't like it so much and was just being nice about it. Maybe she wanted an older guy like my brother and would get tired of being with a kid who didn't have his driver's license yet. I didn't like thinking about that and just wanted to forget that I had even thought of it. I'd get some coke and some whiskey and that would help.

I finished the pie and took the plate down to the kitchen. Dad had gone to bed, and Mom had gone downstairs and taken his spot in his chair to watch television now. My brother still camped on the couch. I put the plate away and got a coke out of the fridge. I took a couple of drinks and then sneaked the whiskey bottle out of the cabinet and filled the coke bottle back up with the whiskey and returned to my room. I turned off the light and lit a cigarette and sat at my desk, staring out of the window at the drizzle that looked like sparklers in the glow of the street light. If it got any colder tonight, we might have a little snow on the ground in the morning, but it was still a little early in the year to be getting snow on the ground.

The whiskey and cigarette had started to calm me down. I took the last puff on the stogy and put it out and lay on my bed, the radio playing "Here Comes the Night." That didn't help matters much hearing Them singing about a guy losing his girl and watching her walking down the street with another guy. I tried to think of something else, so I thought about this afternoon, holding Debby and feeling my dick inside her. I started to get a boner that got harder and harder the more I thought about fucking Debby. I couldn't help but jack off thinking about my dick in her and making it with her and came on the bed. I lay there soaking up the feeling and didn't even have the energy to get up to clean up, so I downed the rest of the coke and lay back down, still holding my dick, listening to Them, fucking Debby over and over again.

****

Between Thanksgiving and Christmas, having school was pretty much useless. Nobody wanted to do anything, and all anyone could think about was Christmas vacation and what they wanted for Christmas or where they were going during the time off. The teachers probably thought about it even more than the kids did, and we'd watch lots of films through those weeks and did lots of stupid projects.

One project we had in Bookkeeping, the only for real project, was to keep a log of accounts payable and accounts receivable for an imaginary business. The teacher gave us all of the information we needed for our log book, and of course everything had to equal out in the end for us to get a good grade on the project, and it counted for a lot of our grade for the semester. This class had to be the class that I hated the most through my whole twelve years of school, not just because I didn't like math that much and couldn't see myself spending my life writing numbers in a log book all day long, but because my brother went to college to study accounting, and I had no intention of being anything like him, like my parents and teachers wanted me to be. I pretty much refused to do the work, and so Debby decided she would do mine for me.

I went over to her house every night during those weeks to help her, though all I did was try to kiss her or feel her up whenever no one was in the room. She wanted to do well in school, and she wanted me to do well too, so it irritated her whenever I wouldn't do my homework or would do poorly on tests. I had never told her that I had wanted to be a Microbiologist, I didn't talk about that at all, with anyone, so she couldn't understand why I wouldn't at least try and would always tell me she knew I could do it if I would just try. Even my parents never gave me that much encouragement. The one thing she knew for sure was that I loved music and wanted just to play my drums.

The band had played a couple of gigs at the youth center, but we hadn't gotten the Homecoming Dance because they wanted a soul band for that dance, so Thumper thought that maybe we should add some people to do gigs like that. We had talked with Johnny and another singer we knew, Frankie, and Thumper had talked with Claude and another guitar player about playing with us. Thumper wanted to get us some college fraternity gigs, so we would need a fuller sound for those gigs. We would still play gigs with our basic group of me, Thumper, Steve, and Allan, but we would be able to play a lot more gigs with the other guys.

One gig I was looking forward to big time was an afternoon gig at the music store where I had bought my drums. Thumper had gotten hold of an album by a new group from England called Cream, and we had worked up a couple of songs from it. The drummer, Ginger Baker, was my new idol on the drums. He played double bass, like Keith Moon, and had a great style. One of the songs on the album was called "Toad," a drum solo song that lasted about five and a half minutes with Ginger playing the shit out of the drums. We had worked up that song which kept me busy practicing every day to get all of his licks just right. We could only do about a set worth of songs at the gig, and that was one of the ones the guys wanted to do, which was fine with me.

I found a copy of the Cream album and loved the whole thing and loved the way the guys were dressed on the front cover. They were wearing pilot clothes that looked like World War II stuff, and, being a guy, I'd always had a kind of interest in the army and had had army men and cowboys and Indians that I played with as a kid and would set up battle fields and would blow up the soldiers with fireworks. So, seeing the band dressed that way made me want to get something like that for the music store gig. I searched through an Army-Navy store and found a pilot's cap and had a jacket that looked like a flight jacket and got goggles and a scarf and ended up with an outfit that looked close to what they were wearing on the album. I was set.

Playing the drum battle and the dances at school had helped me become a lot more confident about my playing, but the music store was a different story. I would be playing in front of people who didn't know me and maybe didn't know some of the songs we were doing. Debby would be there, which would help, but this would be in front of a new crowd and would be heard over the radio. That kind of upped the stakes for me.

The store had set up a great stage with a drum stand and lights all around and a huge sound system. They had drums available, but I wanted to use mine, especially since their set was only a single bass set that couldn't be set up the way I set up my drums. I didn't want to be playing on a set that I wasn't familiar with for this gig. Everybody else had the amps and mics and things that they needed and just brought their own guitars to play. We would play first too, which helped with getting my drums set up without having to rush to get set up like the next drummers would. I'd have to get torn down quickly, but that wouldn't be too bad with my brother there to help.

People had already been arriving for the show before we finished getting set up and seemed to be getting anxious for us to start playing. A local radio station that played rock, KAAY, had set up the show to promote the concert tonight by the group The Outsiders and would broadcast from there while the show was on, so people had heard about the show on the radio all week long and would likely invade the store that afternoon. We weren't getting paid anything to play, but we were getting free tickets to the concert and were hoping that we'd get some other gigs from this one too, maybe even at the Lake Nixon concerts, which were also sponsored by KAAY. My drums were ready, so I went behind the stage and got into my pilot's outfit, took a big slug on my whiskey bottle, and went out to the stage.

Debby took up her position beside the stage, but now my brother joined her there. They had been talking more lately, and it was starting to piss me off. He was smart like she was, and they were getting more and more comfortable, it seemed to me, around each other. I started imagining him going by and picking her up and taking her to go parking and fucking her in the back seat of his car. He would be feeling his dick inside her like I had and would be coming in her pussy like I had. Maybe they were doing other things too. I had heard guys talk about blowjobs, even though I had no idea what the fuck they were. Maybe they were doing that too. Maybe that was what Debby had wanted all along, a guy who knew about all that stuff and would know what to do with her. I felt like a little kid again and got more and more pissed off each time

I looked over and saw them laughing about something together.

I had to stop looking. I couldn't think about that right now. I needed to concentrate on the songs we would be performing, especially "Toad." We had Christmas vacation coming up at school soon. That would give me a chance to spend more time with Debby and maybe sneak out my brother's car sometime after he fell asleep on the couch. I could go pick up Debby and take her out to park myself. If we spent more time alone, we'd be able to explore each other more, and I'd learn more about that kind of stuff.

Thumper gave us the signal that we were getting ready to start, so I stopped thinking about Debby and looked out front and just concentrated on the first song, "Shapes of Things." We wouldn't do "Toad" till the end, which would give me a chance to warm up. The crowd had grown a bunch now and kids had crammed against the stage and onto the floor around the stage. We were upstairs, so I had a great view of the outside and the entire upper floor of the music store. Just over a year ago I had been here buying my first drum set, and now I was playing a gig with a band here that was being heard on the radio by anyone listening here in Arkansas or in the surrounding states. Then the DJ started his introduction.

"Okay. Are you guys ready for this?" The crowd roared back its approval.

"And for all of you listening out there to the Mighty 1090, we're here at Mose's Music Store in Little Rock to welcome that "Time Won't Let Me" group, The Outsiders, tonight to Robinson Auditorium." The crowd roared again.

"Now to kick things off, from North Little Rock, The Things!"

Thumper counted off and we started the song. The crowd immediately got into the song, clapping and waving their arms in the air. We were playing the best we ever had. Thumper was playing the shit out of his guitar, and Allan would get down close to the girls and sing to them and jump around the stage like Mick Jagger. Steve didn't do a lot of jumping around or anything. He was more like Bill Wyman and just played the hell out of his bass guitar. I loved playing with him and keeping my bass drums playing along with his bass lines. We were putting on a good show and could tell from the way everyone was reacting.

We finished the first song to cheers and started right in with the rest of our set. By the time we got to "Toad," I was more than warmed up and gave my best imitation of Ginger Baker playing the solo. I got so into the solo that my goggles fogged up, and I yanked them off and threw them into the crowd. They loved that. The girl that caught them waved them around and put them on. We finished "Toad," and we wanted to end with a bang, so we went right into our last song, "The Train Kept a Rollin'." That one would give Thumper the chance to show his guitar playing with the solo in the song, and Allan would get to play the harmonica on it. We had seen Jimmy Page do it at the Yardbird's concert and thought it would be a great one to end the set with. And it was.

We finished the song, and the DJ cut right in.

"Let's hear it for The Things! From North Little Rock!"

Hearing our name like that made the blood rush through me, and hearing the applause and cheers of the crowd sent a shiver up and down my spine. It was something I wanted to feel again, a lot. The DJ continued.

"Be looking for them at the Lake Nixon concerts in the coming months." That was good news to hear.

The day had worked out just the way we had wanted. I didn't want that afternoon to end, but we had to get our stuff torn down and get off the stage so the next band could get going. I quickly began taking my drums down. I looked over to where my brother and Debby had been standing to see if he would come and help. My brother wasn't around, and Debby was talking to a guy. I wanted to share my excitement with her, but the old feelings started coming back as I packed up my gear, keeping one eye on Debby the whole time. What was going on with us? With her? I wished she would just tell me if something was wrong.

At the concert that night, Debby didn't seem to be there. I asked her if anything was the matter, and she said nothing was, but I still couldn't help but feel that something wasn't right. We talked and held each other and kissed on the way home, but it wasn't the same kissing that we had had at the start, and when we dropped her off, she didn't say anything about the next weekend or Christmas vacation. I had made plans to go to my older brother's frat house to a party with Debby and wanted to make that our night to get things back together. Then we could spend the rest of Christmas vacation being together. My parents would be working through the vacation pretty much since Christmas and New Years were on the weekend, and her dad would be working at the railroad yards and her mom was always out running around doing stuff, so maybe Debby could come over to my house during the day when everyone was at work and busy and no one else was around, at least that was what I had hoped would happen.

****

Christmas Break started out to be the best one ever. Christmas was on a Sunday, which meant that school would be out the week before and the week after for New Years, and we would get a few extra days after New Years, because no one wanted to go back to work or school the day after

New Years, so we actually got about two and a half weeks instead of the usual two weeks.

My birthday was during the week before Christmas, and my brother had told me to come up the Friday before to party with him and his girlfriend and his house buddies. My friend Jeff, whose birthday was on Christmas eve, had gotten an old '54 Chevy from his brother for a birthday and Christmas present, and we were going to take his car and him and his girlfriend were going to go with us to my brother's. It would be the last party for his frat house before they all went home for Christmas break, so it looked to be a lot of fun.

We picked up the girls on Friday and headed out for Conway, where my brother went to college, about thirty miles from North Little Rock. I hadn't met Jeff's girlfriend, Shelley, yet, a junior at an all-girl's Catholic school, St. Mary's, in Little Rock. She seemed real nice, and she and Debby got along okay, but Debby seemed to be a little annoyed by her, or by something. Jeff and I had gotten some booze from the drive-through liquor store that would sell to anybody and were drinking whiskey and coke. Whenever we had to buy it ourselves, we would get the stuff we could afford, like J. W. Dant, but we preferred to get my Dad's Jack Daniels when we knew he wouldn't miss it. Shelley drank too and was getting fairly silly from the booze, which annoyed Debby even more. I guessed from the way Shelley was acting that she didn't drink very often, or get out very much or something. Maybe that was just the way girls who went to all-girl schools acted though.

We got to the house, and the party was already going strong. My brother welcomed us and introduced us to his buddies. I already knew some of them from high school and from them all running around together before they graduated. I liked his friend Butch who was there with his girlfriend. He had always been nice to me, like his own little brother, since he didn't have any, even better than my own brothers treated me. I couldn't understand why my brothers had been so mean to me when we were kids. They were better now that they were older, but I couldn't help feeling pissed about how they, especially my oldest brother, would chase me around and hit me or tell Mom when I did something Mom wouldn't like.

So guys like Butch I didn't mind coming over, but a lot of their other friends would treat me the same as my brothers or would tease me. Of course that changed somewhat when I started playing in bands, another advantage to being a drummer. Debby wasn't too thrilled to be at the party, since she wasn't drinking and thought Shelley was so "immature" and just wanted to get away from everyone. I found my brother and some of his friends talking and asked if it was okay to go to his room.

"Top of the stairs, then all the way around to the left. Don't make a mess." They all grinned at each other.

Debby hadn't liked their grins, and I thought she was going to want to leave, but we went upstairs and found my brother's bedroom. I could see why he said not to make a mess. It was just like his room had always been at home, everything in its place, everything labelled and categorized and just right. We left the bedspread on the bed and grabbed a blanket from the hutch and laid on the bed and started making out. I started running my hand over her body, and she kind of tensed up, so I stopped and sat up.

"What's wrong?" I couldn't understand what was going on with her.

"I just don't feel too much like a party tonight. I wish we could be alone sometimes and just do what we want instead of what someone else is doing or always being around other people."

"This is kind of like my birthday party. I thought you might wanna help me celebrate tonight."

"I do. But I'd like for it to be just us and not a bunch of drunk college guys or Jeff's drunk little friend." That kind of made me mad when she said that.

"Even when you go to play and I go with you, I just sit there while you're playing. Then you get a break and go out and drink and smoke with the guys and come back and spend a few minutes with me before you go back to play."

I was glad she was telling me all this, but I didn't know what I could do about it. I didn't want her to be unhappy, but I couldn't, wouldn't, quit playing.

"I love to hear you play, but I want to spend time with you there. I love going to concerts with you because you love music so much, and we can both enjoy the concert and the music. But I get tired of just sitting there while you're rehearsing or playing."

I finally had to ask. "What do you want me to do?"

"Can we just go?" Well, that wasn't what I had wanted to hear, and she must have been able to tell.

She took my hand. "I don't want you to do anything. Just come here."

She pulled me down onto the bed and kissed me and put my hand on her tits. We undressed each other while we kissed, and she started beating me off while I fingered her. Then she pulled me over on top of her and put my dick in her. We had never been in a bed before when we screwed, so having all the room to stretch out and move around made this time different than the other times. It didn't take long for me to come, but I didn't want to stop, my dick was still hard, so I kept on screwing her, which she seemed to enjoy. We didn't stop for what seemed like a long time until I came again. We had both gotten sweaty and were kind of sliding around on each other. We finished and lay there in the sweat and the come. Even though it was winter and cold outside, the room felt like a locker room during the showers after P.E. I lit a cigarette.

After we lay there a while, the cold started to creep up on us, so we got up and cleaned up and got our clothes on. We didn't say much during all of this, but I didn't have much to say anyway. I was still thinking about what Debby had said before we screwed and was thinking about our screwing. It had definitely been different and a lot better in bed by ourselves, not in the back seat of a car with some other couple in the front seat. I hoped I'd be able to talk her into coming over to the house during the break so we could screw in my bed with no one else there. That might give her the time alone she was talking about wanting.

We finished dressing, put the blanket back, straightened the room, and went downstairs. The party had slowed down a little. People had split off into little groups around the rooms, laughing and drinking. I looked around for Jeff and Shelley but didn't see them anywhere. We walked around the bottom floor looking for them and found the kitchen and the booze. I grabbed a coke and whiskey and Debby got a coke, then we kept searching.

Walking around the house gave me an idea of what college would be like. It looked like it would be a lot of fun, having parties and studying stuff you liked, being around friends that liked the same things you liked. If only I could study music in college and play in a rock band. That would be perfect! Jeff and Shelley were coming down the steps as we made our way back to the living room. They looked like they'd been doing the same thing we'd been doing.

"Where's the booze?" It sounded like they were singing harmony.

I pointed to the kitchen. Debby wandered into the living room and found a chair away from all the groups. I followed and sat down on the floor beside the chair. I suddenly felt like a puppy following its mother around waiting to get to suck on a tit.

Jeff and Shelley found us and sat down on the floor with me. Jeff seemed to know that something was wrong between Debby and me, how could he not, but didn't ask about what was going on. Shelley didn't seem to notice anything except her drink. We sat there quietly, except for Shelley running her mouth about how great the party was and trying to get Jeff to take her upstairs again, then Debby cut her off.

"I have to get going. Now!" Shelley didn't like that.

"Ahhh. Do we have to go." She smiled at Jeff. "This is fun." Jeff looked at me and I looked at him. He knew what to do.

"Yeah. We better be heading back home. The later we wait, the more drunks will be on the road."

"We can be the first!" Debby didn't even wait for the rest of us and just got up and walked out the front door.

Jeff gathered Shelley up off of the floor and headed for the front, and I followed them out the door. Jeff was trying to get Shelley to the car, but she kept falling and pleading with him to stay and fuck her again. I helped him carry her to the car and get her into the front seat and sat in back with Debby.

The car radio kept the drive back from being totally silent, along with Shelley who would occasionally ask Jeff to "come on, fuck me again." Debby kept silent and to one side of the seat staring out of the window into the darkness of the lonely two-lane road. I didn't dare put my arm around her for fear that she would pull it away and make me feel even worse than I did already. I was trying to understand how she felt but was also trying to figure out what I could do about it. My parents were dead set against me driving, nothing I could do about that, so I pretty much had to rely on my friends who had cars or on my brother to get around. I hated that I had to depend so much on other people. I wanted to be able to do things for myself, but that didn't look like it was going to happen for a long time yet.

We got to Debby's house first, and I walked her to the door. She wasn't going to say anything, so I did.

"My birthday's next Tuesday. I was wondering if we could do something."

She hesitated. I figured my Mom wouldn't have anything more than just a cake maybe. No big deal. I never had had a true birthday party since my birthday was so close to Christmas, so Debby and I could go to a movie or something.

"Sure. Call me." She looked at me for a moment, didn't say anything else, opened the door and was gone.

I got back in the car, in the front seat, with Jeff and Shelley, who was now asleep with her head in Jeff's lap, and we drove off. We dropped Shelley off at her house, fortunately her parents were already asleep, went by my house and picked up some more booze, and drove to the Old Mill. Some other kids were there, so we sat in the car and drank the booze and waited until they left.

We took Jeff's flashlight and made our way to the Mill and climbed the steps to the second floor. We lit up cigarettes and passed the bottle back and forth as we sat in the window and watched for cops who sometimes patrolled to make sure no one was messing around at the Mill.

"That was nice of your brother to get you that car. I wish somebody would get me one. Even if I had the money to get one, they wouldn't let me get one."

"He got it for me so I'd move up to Missouri with mom. It wasn't being nice. Shit. I'm just glad I got it."

"What are you gonna do for your birthday next week?" Mine was before Jeff's, but I was hoping to do something with Debby.

"I don't know. We might be going to my brother's for Christmas."

"We should do something before you go. We oughta drive down to Hot Springs and see James. I haven't seen him in ages." Debby and the band had been keeping me pretty busy.

"I saw him about a month ago. He's getting to where he can move his hands a little. Yeah. Let's go. He'd like that for Christmas. Let's see if Bob and Reggie wanna go too. Maybe Wednesday."

"Yeah. Wednesday would be good." My thoughts went back to the party. "Shelley's cute. Doesn't take much to get her drunk."

"She's okay. She doesn't normally drink that much. Just likes to go out and fuck. Was Debby on the rag or something?"

"I don't know. Wasn't on the rag. Just wasn't in too good a mood." I did know but didn't want to get into right then. I'd call her tomorrow and see how she was doing, maybe go over and see her.

We finished off the bottle and smoked another stogy, then Jeff had to go, so we got back in his car, and he took me home. We decided we'd go to see James for sure on Wednesday, and if I wasn't doing anything on my birthday to give him a call, and we'd go to the drive in and get drunk or something.

I called Debby the next day, but she was gone somewhere. I called again in the evening, but she was still gone. Where the shit was she? My brother had been out all day too. Were they off somewhere together? Now, I was getting pissed. I needed to know where she was, but I didn't have any way of finding her. It was already dark, but I jumped on my bike and raced along the railroad tracks to her house. Her mom's car and her dad's truck were there but no others.

I sneaked around to the back of her house to peek in the window and see if she was there. The light was off, so I figured she wasn't there, but I tried to look into the family room and see if she was doing something there, maybe playing a game with her dad her something, I hoped. Someone was in the living room watching the television, but I couldn't tell who it was. I hid across the street in the dark and watched the front of the house for Debby to get home, but after about thirty minutes I got tired and hopped on my bike and went back home.

The ride had been cold, so I poured some whiskey into a glass and got a coke from the fridge and went to my room. I opened the window and lit a cigarette and downed a swig of the whiskey. I could feel the whiskey travel down my throat to my stomach, warming my insides as it passed through. Each time I took a swig of the whiskey I'd follow it with a slug of the coke. Even the cigarette was warming me from the chill of riding in the cold night air to Debby's house. Where could she be all day long? Had she just gone somewhere by herself? Her parent's cars were there, so she wouldn't have been gone with them. Who was it? All I could imagine was her with some other guy, in bed putting his dick in her, then in the back seat of his car parked out in the woods somewhere, fucking. I kept putting different faces on the guy. My brother. Her ex-boyfriend. Jeff. Everybody but me! And I was the one who was supposed to be fucking her! But I could only see them fucking her!

I didn't want to think about it anymore and tried to think about us at the party, in bed, her putting my dick in her, but I couldn't keep the thought of her with the other guys out of my mind. I got a boner thinking about all of it and went to the bathroom to beat off. Even the thought of her with other guys and them coming in her pussy made me excited, and it didn't take any time for me to come. But I couldn't stop. I got excited all over again and beat off again. This time when I came my nuts hurt. It felt like I had strained them or something. I cleaned up and went back to my room, lit another cigarette and finished the booze. I turned off the light and sat at the window, listening to the radio. It was going to be a long night.

A couple of days later, I found out what I had wanted to know. Debby called and told me that she had decided that she wanted to go out with other people and that it was okay if I wanted to go out with other people too. I didn't want to hear that. I told her I didn't want to see other people. I wanted us to stay together. She said she had made up her mind already and that she didn't want to hurt me but that she wanted to go out with other guys. I could feel the tears welling up but I didn't want her to know that she'd made me cry.

"Can't we just go out one more time?" I thought if I took her out again and did things differently that she'd change her mind. But what would I do differently?

"One more date won't make any difference. I don't think we should see each other for a while. It'll be easier that way."

"Not for me! I don't wanna see anyone else. I love you!" That was the first time I had told her that, and it surprised me that it had slipped out, though I knew I had felt that way since the night we had first screwed.

She was quiet for a moment. I started getting pissed now.

"Who have you been going out with?" She was quiet.

"Nobody yet."

"Where were you Saturday?"

She was quiet again. "I went running around with some people."

"Some people or a guy?" So many different feelings were running through me now that I couldn't separate them.

"It doesn't make any difference --"

"It does to me!"

"I've got to go. My mom is waiting for me to go with her to the store."

I calmed down a little now. "Can I call you later?"

"I don't know when we'll be back."

"I'll call later."

"Okay. But I can't promise we'll be here. I have to go. Bye."

The silence on the end of the line was deafening. All I could hear was the nothing that Debby had left me with. My mind raced. What would I do now? She wanted to see other guys. That meant she wanted to fuck other guys. She had gotten tired of me being so inexperienced, being unable to drive and not being like the other senior guys. Shit! Even junior guys drove and had their own cars! I had never felt so pissed before, so much like a little kid! Why were my parents ruining my life like this! I wanted to hit something and keep hitting it! I ran to my room and slammed my fist on my desk and kept slamming it until I just started crying. I fell on the bed and couldn't stop crying. I was glad no one was there to hear me or see me. After a while I stopped and just lay there, so much confusion running through my head. I felt exhausted and dozed off.

****

Dark outside. I had slept into the night. My life was over. I was glad it was dark. I didn't want to be in light, to have light on me, to be seen. I wanted it to stay dark, to always be dark. I would never be happy again, so I would live in darkness forever. I couldn't keep the tears from flowing again. Would I ever be able to stop crying? I didn't think I ever would. I had never felt that helpless or that hopeless in all my life. I wanted to call Debby, but it was past eleven, and

I didn't want to get her in trouble. I could go over there and maybe get to talk to her through her bedroom window. I had done that when we first started seeing each other.

I took a huge slug on the Jack Daniels bottle, hopped on my bike, and took off for her house. I didn't want to chance the railroad tracks that late at night, so I took the side streets to get there. I pulled around to the back of the house and left my bike in the shadows. Her light was off, but I scratched on the screen to try to get her attention. Finally the shade opened, and I saw her. She opened the window. She was in her nightgown and when she bent down to talk to me I could see her tits through the gown.

"What are you doing here? You must be freezing." I didn't even feel anything except the booze going to my head.

"I didn't wanna call this late and wake up your parents. I wanted to talk to you. I wanted to see you."

"Don't do this to yourself."

"You're doing this to me!" I couldn't hold back.

"Shhhhh! You'll wake up my parents!" I quieted down.

"Okay. I'm doing this to you. I take the blame. But that's it." Her 'that's it' sounded way too final to me.

"Tomorrow's my birthday. Can't we go out one more time?"

"I have plans already." That hurt way down.

"A date?"

"Yes."

I felt my blood boiling again and the tears following.

"Okay. Bye."

I stormed off, pulled my bicycle out of the shadows and rode as fast as I could back to the house. I went straight to the whiskey cabinet and poured a glassful of whiskey and coke, took a big slug off the bottle and went into the living room. I got one of my Yardbirds albums out and put it on the stereo. Maybe listening to some of my favorite music would help me forget everything. I laid down in the dark in front of the stereo and tried to think of playing drums or seeing the Yardbird's concert, but everything I thought about had Debby in it, and my thoughts would always go right back to her. The Yardbirds weren't helping, so I put on another album, a new one by The Blues Magoos called "Psychedelic Lollipop" that I loved. One of the songs, "Love Seems Doomed," fit the way I was feeling perfectly. It was a slow song about a guy whose girl has left him after they have had a happy time together. He keeps saying things like, 'she was the only girl for me' and 'she was the one in a million for me,' all the things I felt about Debby. I kept listening to it over and over, drinking the whiskey and coke, filling up my glass when it was empty, getting more and more drunk, crying more and more.

I woke with the needle scratching at the end of the album, shut off the stereo, and tried to make it up the steps without killing myself. I fell onto the bed and didn't move the rest of the night.

My birthday, the next day, started with me taking a handful of aspirin to try to stop the pounding in my head. Each time I breathed I felt like my head would blow up. I drank some coke to see if that would help, but it only made me feel like I was drunk again. The bacon and eggs I fixed myself after I had gotten awake a little bit finally did the trick, and I started feeling at least a little bit myself again. But always at the back of my mind was the thought of Debby, and the fact that she had a date that night. I kept picturing her in the back seat of some guy's car with her legs spread out and the guy fucking her. That's what the guy would probably expect, even on a first date, if it was a first date, and as much as Debby liked it and had fucked before, I couldn't imagine her not letting him or not wanting him to fuck her. I had to stop this. But what could I do? I couldn't stop thinking. No matter what I did to try to get my mind off her, I kept seeing her. I thought if I beat off, maybe I'd stop thinking about her for a while, but when I tried to beat off, it made my head hurt worse, so I stopped. I wished that the band had something going on, but the guys were off with their families during the break and wouldn't be around until next week, and we didn't have any gigs lined up for a while. I decided I'd take Jeff up on his offer to go to the drive-in movies. Mom would have cake when she got home from work, but other than that we wouldn't be doing anything special or having any kind of celebration or anything. My brothers always had some kind of party or celebration. Jeff and I had gotten screwed by being born so close to Christmas. We always missed out on the birthday party.

I called Jeff, and we decided to go to see two spy movies, "Our Man Flint" and "Agent of H.A.R.M.," that were playing at the Razorback Drive-in. He said he would call Shelley and see if she had a friend who might want to go with us, if I wanted, which was fine with me. If Debby could go out with other guys, then I would go out with other girls. Jeff called back and said that we would be going with Shelley and her friend, Beth, and to be ready for a good time.

"What does that mean?"

"You know Shelley likes to fuck, and she likes to give blow jobs, and maybe her friend will too."

"Okay, what the fuck is a blowjob?" I had to ask.

"You don't know what a blowjob is?"

"Come on, just tell me." I felt like a little kid again.

"Well. It's when the girl kisses your dick and takes it in her mouth and sucks on it. If she's good, and she gets off on giving 'em, she'll suck on you until you come. Believe me, you've never felt anything like it."

It sounded weird, but I was game for anything.

Mom brought a cake home, and the two of us and my little brother had cake and ice cream, and she gave me some money and a new shirt and jeans for my birthday. She also had a package that she said Debby had left with her at the store. She seemed surprised that Debby hadn't given it to me herself, and so I told her that Debby had broken up with me. "It's probably best. I never thought she was that nice a girl anyway." Normally that would have pissed me off, but right now I was feeling pretty much the same way about her.

I took Debby's package upstairs to my room and opened it. It was a navy blue sweater that was just what I had wanted and had told Debby that I would like to have. I started to cry but managed to hold back the tears. I'd wear it tonight to think about her, though I didn't even need anything to keep her on my mind. What I needed was something to keep her off my mind.

Jeff came by, and we went straight to the liquor store and got our regular bottle of J. W. Dant and went to pick up the girls. Beth was at Shelley's house and had told her parents she was spending the night with her, so we pretty much had as much time as we wanted to go to the show and do whatever else after. Beth was cute and was a junior, like Shelley. She went to St. Mary's too and seemed to be as wild as Shelley. They were both grabbing for the bottle and taking gulps of the whiskey before we got a block away from Shelley's house. I could see we were in for a different type of night.

"Shelley says you're a drummer."

"Yeah. I play with a group called Night Child." We had changed the name of the group when Johnny and Frankie and Claude joined.

"I like that name. Does that mean that you're a child of the night?"

"I've always been a night owl. I can hardly get to sleep at night so I stay up and listen to music and read or work on models or something."

"I can't sleep at night either. I love to read, so that's when I get my reading done. What kind of books do you like?"

"Science fiction is my favorite. But I also collect comic books."

"I have to read a lot for school, but I like romance, not the kissy, kissy stuff but the novels from the nineteenth century, like Jane Austen and Emily Bronte'." I had no idea what she was talking about. "Do you like poetry?"

"I did when I was in the ninth grade, but I haven't read much since then." That was when I liked school.

"I love poetry, especially Emily Dickinson and Sylvia Plath." Had we studied them in English class?

"What kind of music do you guys play?" She wanted to know everything. I liked that.

"Lots of British groups like Them and The Who and The Kinks and--"

"Oh, I love those groups! I wanna come hear you play some time. Can I?"

"Yeah. Anytime. Maybe you and Shelley and Jeff can come to our next gig."

"It's a date." This was going great.

We went to Whatta Burger and got some burgers first and cokes to mix the booze with and headed for the drive-in. Shelley and Beth kept talking and laughing and kept us laughing and having a good time. Once I got a good look at Beth I saw that she was damn cute and had a nice body. Her tits were pretty big too, and she had a nice shape. The more I looked at her the more excited I got that maybe we would be doing something later.

The first movie was funny. Flint was a secret agent like James Bond, except he had a lot more girls and all of the people around him were pretty stupid. We were all laughing at the stupid stuff that was going on in the movie and were comparing it to the James Bond movies we had seen. Beth liked James Bond too and had seen all of the same movies I had seen. About half way through the movie, I leaned over and kissed her, and she French kissed me back. I took a chance and put my hand on her tit, and she didn't stop me, so I played with her tits while we kissed. I had never felt tits as nice as hers before and could feel my dick waking up.

The intermission came, and we all went back to get popcorn and snacks and more cokes to mix with the booze and to use the bathrooms. We were all feeling pretty good about now. I went to take a piss and thought about Debby. Was she doing the same thing? Had she already fucked the guy? Did she do blowjobs? Why hadn't she done a blowjob with me?

We got our snacks and drinks and went back to get ready for the second movie. While we were waiting for the movie to start and watching the intermission, the girls pulled out a Hostess Cupcake with a candle on it, lit the candle, and they all sang Happy Birthday to me. I have to admit that it was one of the best birthdays ever. Even my own family didn't go to that much trouble for me. Jeff made a toast to "Many more happy birthdays," and we all drank a big gulp on our drinks.

The movie started out a little weird and was more like a bad science fiction movie, so we weren't as interested in it and started making out instead of watching it. Beth and I lay down in the seat, and I unbuttoned her shirt and played with her tits. They were so soft and the nipples got hard right away. She undid her bra, and I moved it out of the way and started kissing her nipples. She got turned on with that and reached down and started rubbing my dick. She unzipped my pants and took my dick out and ran her hand up and down it. I put my hand in her pants and found her pussy and slid my finger inside and fingered her. Her pussy was so hot and got wet from that, and she ran her hand up and down my dick even faster. Then she bent down and began kissing my dick. I about shit my pants I was so surprised. She kept kissing it and then took it in her mouth and started running her mouth up and down on it. I had never felt anything so great in my whole life. She was licking on it like it was an ice cream sandwich, moving her lips up and down. It felt so good that I didn't want her to stop, ever, but I started feeling the come building up, and I tried to pull her head away so we could fuck, but she kept sucking on me until I couldn't hold back any longer, and I felt myself explode into her mouth, and she kept sucking until it had all come out. I couldn't stop. I wanted her to suck everything out of me, and it felt like she was.

My dick was still hard, and I was too excited to stop, so I pulled her up to me and laid on top of her, and she put my dick in her, and I started fucking her. I could feel her tits against my chest and her warm pussy around my dick. She felt so great. And she didn't just lie there like Debby had, she kept moving and bending up to meet me. I came again, and she pulled me close to her as I finished coming inside of her. I moved off of her, but she wasn't done yet. She grabbed my hand and put it on her pussy and started rubbing herself with my fingers at the top of her pussy. She got off big time on that and whispered to me.

"Finger me and rub me there."

Her pussy was so wet by this time, and she was bending up and opening up her legs. She took my fingers and moved them around on the spot and began breathing harder and harder and was getting wetter and wetter. Then she arched her back and buried her face in my chest and kind of bit me and her whole body shook. Then she relaxed and went limp, like my dick when I finish masturbating. I didn't know what

I had just done, but she had loved it, and that was all that mattered.

We lay there and ran our hands over each other. We were exhausted, but I wanted to feel every part of her, her toes, her fingers, her hair, her knees, everything. This was what I had dreamed about forever, the feelings that I had imagined that sex would be like. I had been beating off for years thinking about this, and now it was happening for real, and it felt even greater than I had imagined. I knew what to do now and didn't feel so much like a little kid like I had with Debby. I had mixed feelings about Debby and probably always would. I hated her for breaking up with me, but I loved her too, or thought I did, and I couldn't help but wonder what her night had been like.

We sat up and pulled the rest of our clothes on and noticed that Jeff and Shelley had been busy too and were now sitting up and dressing. We asked them if they wanted anything and went to the bathroom and to the snack bar before it closed and got drinks and candy bars for all of us. We got back to the car and all piled in the back seat and scarfed down the bars and made new drinks. The movie was still going and had gotten even more weird, but we watched and laughed and just talked and had fun. I had to admit that this was the most fun I'd had on a date, not just the sex but everything about it.

With Debby, I always felt a little uncomfortable and like I had to be a certain way with her and for her. And it always seemed more serious and planned, and whatever we did depended on how she felt. This date had been anything but planned and serious. Jeff just liked to have fun like me and was always game for about anything, like me, and Beth and Shelley seemed like good matches for us. I hoped we'd all be able to do this a lot more.

The movie ended, and we sat there and waited for the traffic leaving to die out a little and then took off. We didn't need to get back for a while yet, so we drove around in Little Rock, then cruised Broadway in North Little Rock and ended up at the Old Mill. We ran around playing chase and hide and seek until a neighbor came out and yelled at us that we weren't supposed to be there that late and that she had called the cops and they'd be there any minute. We jumped in Jeff's car and took off around the lake and into a side road and hid in the floorboard. We waited there until we thought the cops had had enough time to get to the Old Mill and see that no one was there and leave. We all decided we would be back to that woman's house on Halloween to give it a good egging.

We dropped the girls off at Shelley's, made plans to go out again as soon as we all could, maybe next week since we would all still be out of school and back in town from visiting relatives and other Christmas stuff, said our goodbye's with our last wet kisses of the night, and Jeff and I took off. I had told my Mom I would probably spend the night with him, just in case we wanted to stay out late or all night, and we were both pretty beat, so we just headed on over to his house. His mom would be in bed and asleep, and we could stay up as long as we wanted in his room and listen to Frank Zappa and finish off our bottle of J. W. Dant and anything else we could find there.

This had turned out to be a damn good birthday. Even though I still missed Debby and wondered what she had done that night on her date, I liked Beth a lot and loved the sex we had had and wanted to see her again. Being with her and Jeff and Shelley had helped keep my mind off Debby, but I wondered how long that would last and if I would miss Debby as much again when I was alone in my room with no one there to keep me from thinking of her.

****

The rest of Christmas vacation could have never happened, and it would have been fine with me, even though I didn't have to get up and go to school each day. I wasn't looking forward to the return to school at all anyway, especially after I had heard that Debby had been going out with a guy I knew, kind of a friend who was a junior, and that he had fucked her in the back seat of his car while a bunch of guys had watched. I still had the mixed feelings about her and didn't want to have to face her or any of the people that knew what had happened with us and with her new boyfriend.

Jeff had gone to his brother's house in Missouri and Beth and Shelley had gone off to visit relatives, so I was left pretty much alone through the remainder of the vacation. My thoughts kept going back to Debby, and I couldn't help but picture her in the back seat being fucked while guys were standing around staring and laughing. I had sat in the dark in front of the stereo night after night, crying and listening to "Reach Out" by The Four Tops, over and over. The words to that song just fit everything I was feeling, mainly the first verse when they said "if you feel that you can't go on, because all of your hope is gone."

Not only was Debby gone from me, but I had found out that Beth was moving to California as soon as her dad found a house for them, which could be any day. When I tried to get to sleep, I would just lie there and cry and try to think of something else besides Debby and Beth, or I'd beat off thinking about both of them until my dick hurt and nothing would come out, but the only thing that helped was to drink until I passed out from being drunk.

By the time school started back, I still felt as bad as my dick hurt, but I could see the bruises on my dick. I did everything I could to delay going to school that day. I stayed in bed until my Mom practically had to drag me out of it. I acted like I was sick, but my Mom wasn't falling for that act.

"You've been home for over two weeks. You're going to school today." Period. No argument.

I tried to hide out as much as possible at school. I knew all the hallways that Debby would be taking to her classes, so I was late to all my classes trying to avoid her. Luckily, I didn't have any juniors in my classes, so most of the people in class didn't know or care about what had happened with Debby, and I didn't have to worry about them staring at me or laughing. At lunchtime I went across the street to the burger place and got caught by Monty and managed a three-day vacation out of it. But when my Mom found out, she called and talked them into letting me back in. She knew this game well by now and was determined to keep me in school, almost as determined as I was on not being there.

Jeff had gotten back from his visit to his brother's and was feeling the same way about school as I was. He was pissed that his mom was going to move to the little town in southern Missouri where his brother lived, and she said if he got in any more trouble that he would be going up there before she did.

"There's nothing to do in that little shithole."

Shelley had gotten grounded from seeing him when her parents found a note she was writing him about wanting to fuck him and suck his dick on their next date, so we'd go out every night and get a bottle of J. W. and sit on the dirt road where they were building the new mall on McCain up in Lakewood and get drunk and throw rocks at the construction equipment and rant and rave about how much we hated it there and hated school and hated parents and hated what was going on in our lives and how we didn't "give a fuck!" about anything or anyone, except Shelley and Beth.

Jeff missed Shelley and I missed Beth, so Jeff and Shelley worked out a way that they could get together. Shelley had a friend named Linda who went to our school and whose sister was a senior who we knew, so Shelley would tell her parents she was going to spend the night with Linda and then Jeff would go to pick up Linda and Shelley, and we would all go out screwing around. Shelley's parents and Linda's parents weren't friends or anything, so Linda's parents didn't know that Jeff and Shelley weren't supposed to see each other, and they thought Linda was going out with Jeff and Shelley was going out with me. Linda wasn't near as cute as Beth and wouldn't do anything more than make out and let me finger her and play with her tits, but shit, that was better than nothing.

We went out like that a few times. We'd go down to the river on the sandbar sometimes and start a fire and get drunk and make out. We didn't dare go in the water, but we'd throw stuff in, like the night Jeff bet me he could throw his senior ring farther than I could throw mine. We never knew who won that stupid bet. Then Linda's parents said Linda couldn't be around me anymore, that I was a bad influence, because Linda's sister told them about some of the stuff that was going on with me at school. We still wanted to go out together, so we had Reggie go with Jeff to pick up the girls while I waited for them at a school down the street, and then we'd drop him off or pick up his girlfriend and go to the drive-in or the sandbar or just cruising. Then Jeff would take the girls back afterwards.

One Friday night, the shit hit the fan. We were well into our plan, Jeff had gone with Reggie to get the girls, and I was waiting at the school. Reggie had started drinking beer early and was feeling pretty good. Jeff and Reggie got back with the girls, and we sat there in the school parking lot trying to figure out what we were going to do that evening. Reggie was drinking a quart of beer and finished it and wanted to see if he could hit a tree across the parking lot, just wanting to show off. We told him not to, but he threw it anyway and missed and hit the sidewalk, and the beer bottle exploded into a million pieces and sounded like an M-80 going off. We tried to get Reggie to get in the car, but he was laughing and acting crazy, and then a guy came running out of his house next to the school and started hollering at us that he had called the cops, and they would be there any minute. We jumped in Jeff's car and started to take off, but the cops pulled into the parking lot and stopped us from leaving. We all got out and stood beside the car. One cop watched us while the other asked the questions.

"What are you kids doing up here?" We hoped Reggie would keep his mouth shut. Luckily he did and Jeff answered.

"We just stopped in here for a minute to check my tire and were getting ready to go." We were glad we hadn't been by the liquor store yet, and Reggie had finished the only bottle of beer he had. Maybe they didn't know anything about the beer bottle.

"This is your car?"

"Yes, sir." Jeff pulled out his license and showed the cop.

"We had a report that some kids were up here making a lot of noise and drinking."

"No, sir. We were just talking and laughing about a joke we heard. We weren't drinking anything." Jeff sounded very convincing, so maybe they'd just let us go.

"Okay. I need to get your names for my report." He looked straight at Reggie.

"What's your name son?" What we heard next wanted all of us to commit murder.

"Mick Jagger." Reggie was such an idiot.

"And where do you live, Mick?"

"Thirty-four twenty, west fourteenth street."

The cop stopped writing and looked at Reggie.

"You sure that's the right address?"

"Yes, sir." The cop put his pad and pencil away. Things weren't looking too good. He pointed toward the cop car.

"All of you get in the car." He looked at Reggie. "There is no thirty-four twenty, west fourteenth street, Mick."

Shit! How could Reggie be so stupid? Even if the cop didn't know who Mick Jagger was, he would know every street in North Little Rock! We all piled in the back seat, the girls crying now.

The ride to the police station was quiet except for Linda and Shelley crying, but Reggie didn't need to hear us to know what we were thinking from the looks we were giving him and from the boo-hooing of the girls'. I could just hear Linda's parents when they found out about this, and Shelley could just as well forget about ever seeing Jeff again. And who knew what would happen to Jeff and me. Jeff was my best friend. If his mom shipped him off to Missouri, everyone I had ever cared about would be gone from my life.

The cops led us guys to a cell and locked us in. The girls stayed in the front room with the rest of the cops. Jeff and I were so pissed at Reggie that we wanted to bust his face, but we couldn't hit our friend, so we started belting the cinder block wall instead. We had had some to drink before we left my house, so we weren't feeling any pain, and after the first hit our hands were numb anyway. Then we started competing with each other to see who could hit the wall the hardest. Reggie just sat back and watched us, probably thinking we were more stupid than he was.

It didn't take long for our parents to get there to pick us up. When the cop opened the door to come and let us out, I saw Linda's dad in the outer office, and he saw me. He didn't look at all happy. If we hadn't been in the cell, he might have tried to see how hard he could hit us. I was glad the cops were there, but then I saw my Dad through the doorway. He didn't look very happy either. He had never hit me, my Mom had been the one to do the spanking and hitting, but I figured he probably wanted to about now.

He didn't say a thing as I followed him to his car and he unlocked the door to let me in the front seat with him. I was ready for him to start yelling at me, but he just sat there and drove the car in complete silence. We got about half way home, and I looked over and saw that tears were rolling down his cheek. I'd never seen my Dad cry before, but now he was crying, and I felt like shit. I would have rather he belted me than do that.

"Your mother couldn't come with me. She was too upset." What he meant was that she was too embarrassed. Maybe he thought he better come because she would have killed me right there.

"What are you doing? Why can't you just get through school and do something with your life, like your brothers."

There it was. I should be like my perfect brothers. That's all they wanted, for me to be like them. But I wasn't them and didn't want to be them or anything like them.

He didn't say anything else the rest of the way, and I had nothing to say. When we got home, he noticed my hand, which had now swollen and had bloody scrapes from the block wall. He said they'd have to take me to the doctor in the morning and get it checked and asked what the hell we were thinking to be hitting the wall like that. I still didn't have anything to say and just walked upstairs to the bathroom and washed my hand off and went to my bedroom and shut the door. My hand was hurting some now but I wouldn't be able to get anything to drink to deaden the pain until Mom and Dad went to bed. I hoped that I would be able to play drums okay, though I wouldn't have to worry about that since my parents weren't going to let me do anything for the rest of my life.

My Dad took me to Dr. Franks, who was also a friend of my Dad's, the next morning, even though it was Saturday, and the doctor didn't normally work on Saturdays. Dad didn't tell him what had actually happened, but my Dad knew too many people in town for Dr. Franks not to find out the real story in time. He checked my hand and said he didn't think anything was broken but told us to go to the emergency room and get it x-rayed anyway, and he gave me some pills to take if it started hurting too bad. We stopped by the emergency room and got the x-rays and then Dad dropped me off at the house. I went straight to my room and fell on the bed.

Mom still hadn't said anything to me. That was her way of letting me know that she was super-pissed about what was going on. I wished she would just haul off and slap me or grab a two by four again and smash it across my back and get it over with. She had stopped hitting me though as I grew older and had reverted to this silent treatment. I couldn't understand why either, because I wasn't that much bigger in size than I was when she was still bashing me, and it wasn't like she was afraid of me. Shit, she was at least five foot eight, and I was a measly five foot five, and she wasn't a weakling at all, not with all the washing and cleaning and stuff she did around the house. She could have competed with the Polish weight-lifting team in the Olympics if she wanted.

I wanted to call Jeff and see what had happened with him, but I didn't want to get him in trouble for calling if his mom answered, so I just lay on my bed and tried to figure out what was going on with me. Whenever I did what I felt like and what felt good to me I got in trouble, and when I did what everybody else wanted, things went fine, but that didn't even feel good to me. I tried to think of something in-between the two, but all I could think about was the night before and Debby and the drive-in with Beth. Damn, I wished Beth was there right then and was in bed with me, kissing on my dick and sucking on it until I came in her mouth again. I got such a boner thinking of that, but I didn't feel like beating off right then and my hand was hurting some anyway. I needed one of the pills the doctor gave me. I got up and found the bottle and went to the bathroom and got some water and took one. It didn't take long for the pill to take effect and for my hand to stop hurting. Those pills were pretty good. I'd have to try and get some more of those.

I fell asleep and woke up later that evening. I was hungry as hell but I didn't dare go downstairs and have to face my Mom and the silent treatment, so I stayed in my room and smoked a cigarette. Then I saw Jeff's car pull up in front of the house, so I sneaked down the steps and out the front door and jumped in his car with him.

"My mom is gonna send me to Missouri."

"Shit, man, what are we gonna do?"

"I'm going to California. You wanna come with me?"

"Damn. How are we gonna get there? I only have about twenty-five bucks."

"I've got a couple of hundred that I was saving. That should be enough to get us out there."

"Let's go. I know where Beth lives. At least we know somebody who lives out there."

Jeff pulled out, and we went straight to the liquor store and got a bottle of J. W. and got some cokes and went to McCain to plan our trip. Jeff had already figured that we could take Interstate 40 pretty much all the way there and could find our way to Los Angeles after we got there. That's where everything we liked was going on anyway. The Jefferson Airplane and Frank Zappa and The Byrds and a lot of the groups we liked were all out there. We could get gigs and maybe I could get a gig playing drums in a band.

We needed some clothes, and we couldn't leave without our records, so we stopped by Jeff's house before going to get my stuff. When we got there, he saw his brother's car parked in the driveway.

"Damn. He's here already."

No lights were on, so we figured everyone was in bed. He got out and sneaked around to the back of the house, where his room was, and opened his window and climbed in. Stuff started pouring out of the window. A big wad of clothes hit the ground. Then records flew out. A bag of something hit the ground. Then a light went on in the front of the house, and Jeff fell out of the window onto the pile of clothes and records and stuff. He grabbed as much as he could in his arms and raced to the car, threw the stuff in the back seat.

"Shit! My brother woke up!" He jumped in the front seat and started the car and peeled out. We didn't stop for anything till we got to my house. Jeff stopped the car up the street from the house and let me out. I ran through the back yards of the other houses into our back yard and climbed up to the bathroom window and slipped in. I peeked out into the hallway and saw the light from the television downstairs but saw that all the other lights were off.

I moved as quietly and quickly as possible to my room and grabbed a bag to throw my stuff into. I had a hard time deciding what I truly wanted to have with me. Clothes were no problem, but I would never be able to get all of my records in the bag and my books and comic books, my skates, my model cars. And my drums. I'd have to buy a new set when I got to California. How would I do that with no money? I'd have to leave most of the stuff behind, but what could I live without?

I heard a car stop in front of the house and a door slam and looked out the window and saw Jeff's brother and mom getting out of his brother's car. My worrying was over. I grabbed my clothes and a stack of records and ran down the steps and out the back door as the doorbell rang. I jumped down the steps and ran into the yard next to ours and hid in the dark and watched as the lights in the house came on. Then I heard a commotion out front and Jeff's brother hollering for him to "Stop!" We were caught.

I moved further into the dark and kept an eye on the house. The back porch light came on, and my Mom stepped out onto the porch.

"Peter!" She waited a moment.

"Peter!" They could have heard her in Little Rock.

Lights came on in the houses around ours. Nobody was going to tell her to "Shut up!" or "Keep it down!" They didn't dare say anything. They'd just be nosey enough to look out and see what was going on and then decide to go back to bed or whatever they were doing. I didn't dare move. I sat back and waited.

After a while, the lights went off in the house. I waited a little longer and then made my way to the house and checked the back door. It was locked, so I climbed on the roof and got in through the bathroom window again. The house was quiet and dark which made it easy to sneak through the hallway to get to my room without getting caught. I'd love to have had a bottle of whiskey about then but didn't want to make any unnecessary noise. I looked out the window and saw Jeff's car parked in front of the house. That wasn't a good sign. I guessed that his brother and mom took him with them and would come back to get the car. I had a bad feeling about this. I was cold and tired. The grass had been wet, and my pants were soaked. I pulled them off and put on some dry shorts and fell on the bed and was asleep in no time.

I tried calling Jeff's house when I got up the next morning but got no answer. They probably wouldn't have let me talk with him anyway and were probably keeping him from calling me. I went downstairs to see what was going on and get whatever was going to happen with my parents over with. I had left my stuff on the back porch and found it in a pile inside by the back door and took it upstairs and threw it on the bed. My parents had let me sleep and had gone on to do their stuff that morning. I had no idea what I was in for when they got back, but I didn't even give a fuck by this time. What could they do? If they tried to ground me, I'd just sneak out and go do what I wanted. They couldn't take my car away from me or keep me from driving. They could take my drums away, but then they'd have to give me money for stuff. All they wanted for sure was for me to graduate, and I was getting by enough to do that, even if I had to go to summer school again, which I probably would. I forgot about that and made a couple of fried bologna and ketchup sandwiches and got a bag of chips and a coke and went back to my room to eat. I was starving. I downed it all in a flash and had to go back to make another sandwich. It only took a couple of bites to finish that one off too.

I found out later that Jeff had been shipped off to his brother's house to finish up the school year. My best friend gone. Fucking parents! Why couldn't they just let us alone? Why did they always have to fuck up our lives? All I could think of was getting out of there, getting drunk, forgetting about everything.

After Jeff left, I concentrated on the band and started hanging out more with our bass player, Steve. We had doubled a couple of times but hadn't hung out much while the band wasn't working. We were getting ready for some big gigs at frat houses and for the end of school and for the Lake Nixon gig and were rehearsing a lot, so he was giving me lifts to the rehearsals a couple of times a week and rides to the gigs. He wasn't any happier with his parents than I was with mine, and we both pretty much stayed in trouble constantly for something or other with them or at school or just in general, like when we took the fifth of whiskey from Thumper's dad's bar and found out later that it was some old expensive bottle of booze that his dad was saving. Thumper was actually the one who got in trouble over that one, but we knew his dad thought we had done it. The big difference with Steve was that he liked school okay and made good grades, so his parents didn't get on him quite as much about that, just other stuff like his car and playing music so much.

I wasn't dating anyone regular since the night at the jail, but Steve and some of us would go out sometimes and pick up this girl named Shannon and go to Burn's Park or to some parking spot or somebody's house if their parents were gone and gang bang her. She was a ninth grader who was kind of homely looking and just would fuck any and all of us. I always got sloppy seconds or thirds, but I didn't care cause at least I was getting some pussy, and we didn't have to spend any money on taking her to a show or on buying food or anything like that. She didn't drink or smoke either, just fucked. She didn't do anything else, she'd just lay there and wait for the next guy to get on top of her and get his rocks off in her. I always wondered how she didn't get pregnant with all us guys fucking her.

Steve and his Debbie were kind of off and on again, and he would bring her to the gigs sometimes when they were on. Whenever I saw her sitting over at the table I would think about when my Debby would come with me to the gigs. It wasn't that long ago but it seemed like ages since we'd dated. I hadn't talked with her since the night at her window. I'd seen her at school walking in the halls to her classes or in the lunch room and would just turn around and go the other way or act like I didn't see her. She didn't try to talk to me, and I probably wouldn't have stopped to talk to her even if she had. No matter what I did to try to forget her, nothing helped. One thing I knew for sure was that I couldn't imagine ever not feeling empty any time I thought about her.

****

Allan's dad wasn't too happy about being woke up so early in the morning after he had worked until after midnight and then would have to drive to Hazen to get us. But at least the reason was something that we couldn't have helped. It wasn't like we had gotten drunk and rolled our car like one of the guys from school who had rolled his Karmann Ghia coming down Snake Hill in Lakewood. He always drove with his head kind of sticking out of the driver side window, kind of like he was always looking in the rear view mirror. When he rolled the car it did a number on his head. Killed him.

We tried to jump the car to get it started, but that didn't work. My brother stayed behind to get the car checked when the service station opened, and the rest of us took off back to town to try to get to school on time. We rode in absolute silence, I think me and Allan were actually asleep since we hadn't slept very much and wanted to grab a few winks before we had to face the class. And Allan's dad was a lot like mine, quiet and hard-working, a little younger, but had grown up in the same time period when guys had to work to support their families a lot of the time. Allan, being his only kid, was pretty much able to get away with a lot and had about everything he wanted. I sometimes wondered how things would be for me if I had been an only child.

We made it to school okay and got through the morning pretty much without any hassles. I think the deans were just happy that I would be leaving soon for good and that my Mom wouldn't be showing up every day asking them to let me back in school. But no one was happier than me that I would be done with that place. I had barely made it, but at least I had done what my parents had wanted and would be graduating.

The school year had ended pretty calmly. Everybody in my classes was talking about where they were going to college or whether they were joining the Army or Marines or about the jobs they would be working at or about prom or the graduation party. I just sat there and listened. I hadn't gone to prom. I hadn't thought that much about it and didn't have anyone I wanted to go with anyway. Jeff had talked his brother and his mom into letting him coming down for the weekend and go to the prom. He was supposed to go, but we ended up going to McCain and getting drunk and hitting rocks at the construction equipment. It was great to see him, better than going to prom. He hated being at his brother's. It was a little town in the Ozarks in southern Missouri, and it was boring as hell. He couldn't wait to graduate and maybe get to go into the service or go to college somewhere. His mom would be moving up there too when she sold their house.

The night of the graduation party was about the same. I sneaked out my brother's car and just drove around drinking and cruising. I had been sneaking out my brother's car a couple of times a week. It was easy. It was a stick shift on the column, and our house was uphill from the main street going out of the neighborhood. My brother slept like a log, so I'd let the car glide down the driveway, then push it, if I needed, to get it started down the hill and would pop the clutch and get going. I did it later at night, so the streets were not as crowded either, and he always had gas in it, so I didn't have to worry about stopping to get gas or anything. It always made me feel very free to be driving around on my own like that, and it made me even more anxious to get my driver's license and get my own car. Who ever heard of a senior in high school who didn't drive anyway? Shit! My parents had sure fucked up high school for me!

The band was playing fairly steady and had a big gig coming up on Friday night. Steve and Debbie had broken up again, and Steve's parents had taken his car away from him for something stupid, so he was pretty pissed at them, and with Debbie breaking up with him again too, he wasn't happy at all with the way things were going. Johnny was giving us rides to rehearsal. We had one more rehearsal before the gig. We played a game of pool during a break.

"I'm tired of this fucking place." Steve had a way of being pissed without sounding mad. "I'm thinking about going to Florida."

"When?" I liked Florida. We had gone there once on vacation to Panama City.

"I don't know. Whenever I can get a ride down there I guess. You wanna come along?"

"What're we gonna do down there." I had another couple of weeks of summer school, but I didn't care if I finished or not at this point.

"Same thing we do here, play music, get drunk, play pool." Steve already had it worked out.

"We have a gig on Friday, so we get money for that. We can sell our records and anything else we don't need to take with us."

"I know where my Mom keeps her bowling money." My Mom was treasurer of her bowling team and kept the money in a drawer in her bedroom. My Dad kept his rubbers in another drawer with his underwear.

"We should be able to get maybe two hundred bucks each with what we make Friday night too."

On the way home from rehearsal we told Johnny about our plan and made him swear not to tell anyone. He said that he would take us as far as Baton Rouge if we'd buy him gas.

That sounded good to us, so after the gig on Friday night, we'd pack our stuff into Johnny's car, no Joe's car was bigger, so Johnny would ask Joe if we could go in his car. They'd drive us down to Baton Rouge, and we'd get a motel room and find a way to get down to Florida, probably ending up in Miami. We shouldn't have any trouble getting gigs playing music once we got there. We could even work our way down to Miami playing some of the places along the way.

The rest of the week, we secretly sold everything we could think of to sell. Records. Clothes. Comic books. School books. My record player. Anything anyone would buy. Anything but our drums and amps and guitars and stuff we would need to work. Mom would be bowling on Thursday night, so she would probably have some money from that. Maybe this time I'd finally get out of there for good. The thought of not having someone always running my life and telling me what I could and couldn't do was getting me excited.

By Friday we had about four hundred bucks between us, that wasn't counting what we would make that night and what we would get from the bowling money. That would get us a pretty good start. We could even maybe take a bus or train the rest of the way. It couldn't be that expensive. We hadn't told anyone the real reason why we were selling our stuff, just that we needed some money. I think Steve was telling them he wanted a new bass guitar or something like that. Only Johnny and Joe knew the real reason, and they had promised not to say a word to anyone.

The gig was at a club outside of Pine Bluff, about thirty miles south of Little Rock, on the road going to Baton Rouge. It worked out perfectly that we would already be a little ways toward our destination after we got through with the gig. We'd pack our stuff in Joe's car and take off. I was only using one bass drum for the gigs with this group, so that would give us more room in the car. It was about a three-hour drive to Baton Rouge on a two-lane road that went through the farm land of southeast Arkansas and the bayou country of northern Louisiana then through part of Mississippi and back into Louisiana. Since we were travelling so late at night, we probably wouldn't hit much traffic and could maybe make it even faster than that. Our parents wouldn't expect us home too early either, but we had taken care of that by telling them we were going to spend the night at each other's house.

Before leaving for the gig, I snuck into my parent's bedroom and raided the bowling money drawer. The money was in a big yellow envelope with a bunch of forms and some pictures of my Mom with her bowling friends. Seeing my Mom and her friends made me feel kind of bad about taking the money, so I put the envelope back in the drawer and went back to my room.

I had finished putting the stuff I wanted to take with me in my bag and looked around the room for anything else I might need or want. Nothing there. I wished I could take my stacks of comic books from the closet, but too many there. What about my desk? I opened each drawer and rummaged through. In the second drawer, under a stack of papers, I found the booklet on Microbiology I had gotten years before. I sat at the desk and stared at the cover. My eyes began tearing up as I opened it and started looking through. I felt myself getting angrier and angrier with each page I turned. I stopped at the page with the researcher at the microscope and remembered how I used to dream about being that guy, sitting at my microscope exploring bacteria and microbes. I would be going to school next year to start on my career as a Microbiologist if my Mom would have just taken up for me and made them let me take the classes I needed. Those last few weeks of school, I'd have been telling my friends where I was going to school and what I would be studying instead of sitting quietly and just listening to all of them talk about their plans and their excitement at going away to college. I'd have probably even felt more like going to the prom and to the graduation party and other senior stuff if I'd have known that something would be following that last year of high school, something to look forward to, something that I was excited about, something that I had planned for myself.

At first I felt like ripping the book apart or burning it, but I decided to keep it to always remind me of what could have been. I tossed the booklet into my bag and went back into Mom's bedroom, pulled the bowling envelope out and took all of the money that was there. I almost wanted her to catch me doing it so that she could see how much I hated what she had done. Had she ever even thought about what she had done? Would she even make any kind of connection now when she found the money gone? One hundred and eight dollars and some change. A pretty good haul. That would add nicely to what we already had.

Johnny and Joe picked us up about six, and we grabbed some burgers and headed for the gig. We knew we were on our way to Pine Bluff when we started smelling the stink that came from the paper mill there. It was hard to describe the smell, but when the wind blew just right you could smell it all the way to south Little Rock, and it got even worse once you were on the road between the two cities. Pine Bluff was much smaller than Little Rock, but it had a little college and had the mill and a lot of farming around there, so they had some pretty good little clubs and parties for bands to play. We would be playing a club near the college and would probably get college students who wanted the soul music we played and that Johnny and Allan and Frankie could sing the shit out of.

We hadn't told the guys that we were leaving after the gig that night, and while we were playing, I started feeling a little empty inside, that I would miss playing with the guys. I was ready for something different, to be on my own and away from the constant control of my parents, my mother actually, but I would sure miss playing music with Allan and Thumper. We had been together for almost two years now and had been through a lot of shit and had had some great times. I had to think of what might be ahead for me and Steve. Maybe we'd get with a group who was making records and would come back to Little Rock playing at Robinson Auditorium or Barton Colosseum? That would show my parents, and Mrs. Billington and all those teachers who thought I wasn't able to do anything, that I was smart, that I could do something if I wanted to do it. Maybe they'd see that they should have listened to me a little and to what I loved and wanted to do rather than thinking they always knew what was best for me. My parents had never even come to see me play a gig, but they'd have to be there if I was coming back to town playing in a famous rock band. I'd make sure they knew and would send a limousine to get them. They couldn't refuse then.

The gig was a lot of fun. Lots of girls who looked to be about our age, but lots of guys hanging around them too. Older guys probably from the college. They danced a lot, and since it was a private club, they could drink too, so lots of booze was being passed around. The guys kept coming up to the bandstand and offering us beers and shots from their bottles, and of course we didn't refuse. By the time the gig was over, we were pretty well smashed and were ready to hit the road. We loaded our equipment into Joe's car, as much as we could in the trunk and the rest in the back seat, and squeezed in for the ride.

The road to Baton Rouge was pitch dark and was straight at first but began to get windy and scary after we got to Louisiana. The trees along the side of the road didn't help much with the moss and stuff hanging down from the limbs and made us think of the stories of swamp creatures and of scary movies like "The Creature from the Black Lagoon" and "The Fly." Joe kept the car moving at a pretty good clip, so we made good time, but it was still a good ways, farther than I had thought.

By the time the sun was coming up, we were pulling into Baton Rouge. We found a motel right away and got a room and unloaded the equipment. The room was packed by the time we finished getting all of our stuff in there. We gave Joe money to get gas on the way back and thanked him and Johnny for bringing us. They told us if we needed anything to just give them a call and took off. We went to the room and crashed.

I awoke later that afternoon to Hank Williams on the radio and Steve sitting on the bed with his hand down the back of his underwear, picking dingleberries out of his ass. That was quite an eye opener, though a cup of coffee would have been better, then I looked over on the side table and saw the coffee cups.

"You ever ride a motorcycle?" Steve had grabbed a paper from the table.

"No." It was too early to be answering questions. I reached over and grabbed one of the coffee cups and took a big gulp.

"We're never gonna get to Florida with all this equipment. I say we sell the equipment and get a motorcycle and go on to Florida."

It was still too early to try to think. "You think we could get enough for it?" Did that come out right? We'd both had a little experience selling stuff lately.

"There's a pawn shop down the street, and I found a couple of ads for motorcycles for sale in the paper that we can call about. We just need to find out how much we need to get for the equipment." He sounded like he'd been up for hours. Maybe he hadn't even gone to sleep.

I was starting to wake up a little now.

"Maybe we could trade some of it too for the motorcycle." I had to take a shit.

"I'll start calling some of these ads." I didn't know if I wanted to touch the paper after Steve had been handling it and his dingleberries.

I was kind of wobbly trying to get to the bathroom but made it and rested my head on the counter while I took a dump. I could hear Steve through the door talking to someone about a motorcycle. It still hadn't hit me that we would be riding all the way to Florida on a motorcycle. I'd never ridden on a real motorcycle before, only on Petey's motorbike. That would be a completely new experience for me to ride on a motorcycle, especially that far. My head was still woozy from all the booze from the night before, but the coffee had helped to wake me somewhat. I finished up and went back out to see how Steve was doing.

"This guy's got a bike and wants to trade for our equipment." Steve was a real dealer.

"What kind of motorcycle is it?" I didn't know the difference in them anyway but wanted to sound like I knew something.

"It's a Triumph Bonneville. It's a good bike. My brother had one."

"What do we have to do?" I was ready to get it and get going.

"He can't do anything today. But he said he could come by in the morning with it and let us see it and look at the equipment."

"Whadda we do until then?"

"Let's go get something to eat. I'm hungry as shit. We can get something to drink too. The drinking age is eighteen here."

We got dressed and walked down the street looking for a place to eat. The street was pretty busy with trucks with boats hanging out the back of them. We found out later that they called them pirogue's down there, not boats. It must have been the main drag cause lots of cars were passing through with license plates from Mississippi and Alabama, plus all the Louisiana plates too. We saw lots of bars up and down the street and thought it might not be a bad place to stay for a while if the motorcycle thing didn't work out. We might be able to get some work playing gigs around there. We found a restaurant and got these sandwiches called Po' Boys. I'd never had one, but Steve had, and he said if I liked fish I'd like it. It was so good, with shrimp and crab meat and coleslaw, all stuff I loved anyway. We gobbled them down and had a beer with it, the guy didn't even check our licenses or anything to see if we were old enough. This was the first time I'd ever been out on my own like this knowing that I didn't have to answer to anyone, and it was great being able to just walk around and decide what I wanted to do and what I wanted to eat and drink and what I'd do and where I'd go tomorrow.

We got some Po' Boys to go for later and walked back to the room. We didn't want to leave the equipment in there for too long, so Steve went to a market nearby and got us some beer and cigarettes and cokes for the evening. He picked up some cards too so we could play poker or something else and got a couple of magazines. We were pretty set for the night and just turned on the television and the radio and played cards and ate our Po' Boys and drank the beer and smoked our cigarettes and did whatever the shit we wanted to do, and it was great!

****

The pounding on the door at two o'clock in the morning would have woke up the dead and scared the shit out of the two of us. We jumped up from our beds and threw our pants on. The room didn't have windows that would open, so we were stuck there with no way to escape.

"Baton Rouge police. Open up in there."

What the fuck? What had we done?

"Shit." Steve was the first one dressed and to the door. He opened the door and two of the biggest cops I'd ever seen stepped into the room.

"Which one of you is Steve?" How the hell did they know who we were? Where we were?

"I'm Steve."

"You two get your clothes on."

We finished dressing, and they put us in the back seat of their car and didn't say a word as they took us to the city jail, an old two-story building with the jail cells on the top floor. It wasn't anything like the jail in North Little Rock. We were stuck in a tiny, run down, dirty cell with an old cot and a hole in the floor to piss or take a shit. I lay down on the cot, wondering what we were doing there and what was going to happen to us next, and fell asleep while Steve sat by the bars and talked to the guy in the cell next to us who was wondering what two teenagers were doing there.

I woke up a few hours later, sweating from the heat, wishing I had a drink of water. Steve was still sitting in the same spot, now smoking a cigarette the guy next to us had given him. Steve's clothes were sticking to him too, and I could now smell the piss hole and the smell of sweat like in gym class after we'd played dodge ball all period. No, this was nothing like the jail cell in North Little Rock. This felt like the kind of jail you thought of when you heard about somebody going to jail, a place you wouldn't want to go to. Ever.

"What do you think they'll do to us?" I hated not knowing why we were there as much as I hated the place itself.

"We didn't do anything. Shit. I can't even figure out why we're here. Want a drag?"

Steve reached over with the cigarette. It was so strong but kind of sweet and didn't have a filter on it, and it felt like the smoke was burning my lungs. I coughed and choked on the smoke while Steve just sat there grinning at me.

"Barnard's been here for a month already this time." That must be Steve's new friend in the next cell. "They say he stole a car. He says he didn't. They also say he murdered somebody. He says he didn't. He says it doesn't matter much what he says down here. Just what they say."

"Hey. You 'bout done over there? Pass that thing back." A gigantic black hand appeared from the other cell with its fingers opened up for the cigarette.

Steve took another drag and handed it to me. I took another, coughed my lungs up again, and placed it in the fingers of the black hand. My hand looked like a puppy's paw against the outstretched fingers.

"Barnard's country momma makes the cigarettes for him. He has a momma in the city and one in the country. He stays with the city momma when he's out of jail and with the country momma when the cops are looking for him." Steve seemed pretty pleased with himself that he'd learned so much about Barnard.

I was beginning to feel a little light headed, like after I'd drank a shot or two of J. W. Dant, and lay back against the wall. Music filled my head. The Yardbirds were playing "Shapes of Things." Cream was playing "I Feel Free." Zappa and the Mothers were playing "Wowie Zowie." The Kinks were playing "I Need You." All of the music was mixing and stopping and starting and repeating. Flashes of Debby in the tree house with me on top of her ran through, then we were in the back seat of Johnny's car the first time we fucked. Then I was with Beth. She was sucking on me. I had her tits in my hands. And the music kept playing.

Breakfast came. Oatmeal and black coffee. It was kind of dry, but I ate it anyway. I was hungry. Steve seemed pretty hungry too. We hadn't had anything to eat since the Po' Boys the night before. Ummm. Just thinking about those made me even hungrier. Then I started wondering when we were going to find out why we were there. Would they keep us there forever. Would we be like Barnard and be there until next month, waiting? What about our equipment? Had they taken it as evidence? Would we ever get it back? I couldn't stop thinking all of the questions and hearing all of the music and seeing Debby and Beth and everything that was running through my head!

The oatmeal and coffee helped. I started waking up and remembering what had happened the night before. We hadn't done anything, so they had no real reason to hold us there. It wasn't like when Reggie had broken the bottle and given his name as Mick Jagger. What a dumb shit! No. It must be something else. The beer we bought? Steve picking dingleberries out of his ass?

After what seemed like hours, another huge cop came to get us. We said our goodbye's to Barnard and thanked him for the cigarette and followed Goliath down the steps to the main office of the jail. Standing at the counter was Steve's mom and older brother. Now at least we knew what was going on.

"We were worried sick about you two. What were you thinking, Steve?" Steve's mom just stared at him. Then she looked at me.

"Steve is going back with us. Your mother and father said if you want to stay, you can. They won't make you come back, but they want you to come home. You can ride with us if you want to go back." Everything was fucked now.

"I'll go back with you, if that's okay."

Steve's mom finished with the cops, and they gave us their speech about running off and worrying our parents, and we left. Our equipment was already in the car with the rest of our stuff from the room. We squeezed into the back seat and sat quietly. Steve's brother pulled into a burger place, and we got burgers to go and hit the road back to Little Rock. Steve's mom told us that all of the parents had been worried to death when they found out we hadn't spent the night at each other's houses. They had called Johnny and Joe to find out what happened, and the guys told them about taking us to Baton Rouge. I couldn't blame them for not wanting to get in trouble for taking us down there like that. We were both only seventeen, and they were both over eighteen and could have gotten in big trouble if our parents had pushed it.

The ride back was quiet and gave me plenty of time to think, something I didn't seem to have been doing too much of for a long time. I'd be finishing with summer school and would be completely done with high school in a couple of weeks. What would I do then. I had no idea what I wanted to do any more. I wanted to keep playing drums, but the band would be going different ways with guys graduating and going off to school, and after this Steve's parents probably wouldn't let him play any more. I was pretty much on my own with music. I'd be draft age soon, but I sure didn't want to go to Vietnam and come back in a body bag like was happening to so many other guys. I didn't even care to join the Army or Navy either, so I'd need to go to college to keep from being drafted, if they'd even let me into college after I had done so bad in school the last couple of years. What would I study anyway? I didn't even know what I liked anymore.

Seeing the trees pass by as we drove through the bayou's wasn't as scary during the day as it had been late at night. What scared me now was wondering what to expect when I got back home. My parents had said they wanted me to come home, but I couldn't understand why. I had been nothing but trouble for them lately, had stolen Mom's bowling money, had sneaked Dad's whiskey and done nothing but get drunk and fuck around my whole senior year of school, had barely graduated only because my Mom had forced me to go to school. What was it? I guessed I wouldn't ever know the reason.

I laid my head back against the seat and closed my eyes. The words to "We Ain't Got Nothin' Yet" ran through my head. *"One day you're up, and the next day you're down. You can't face the world with your head to the ground."* I was definitely going to need a plan when I got back. For whatever reason my parents said I could come back, I would at least have a place to stay and wouldn't have to worry about going to school and would be free to start something new, and it'd be another six months before I had to worry about the draft. I could take a few weeks and think, have some fun, go to the river, maybe go to the lake and do some fishing. I didn't have to be anywhere or do anything in particular for a while. That felt good and felt scary at the same time. Allan had told me about this girl, Betty, that lived next door to him at his new house. He had made out with her and said she had nice tits. Maybe I'd give her a call and see if she wanted to go out.

Steve was asleep on the other side of the seat. He'd been up all night with Barnard. I relaxed and curled up next to the door, the sun beating through the window warming me and making me drowsy. The whirring of the tires on the pavement filled my head and felt soothing, and I could feel myself drifting off into sleep. I didn't know where I'd be when I woke up. I didn't know who I'd be. I only knew that whatever I did, from now on, it would be me making the decisions. If I fucked up, I had nobody to blame but myself.

I didn't know why, but I felt a little better now. I wanted to tell someone, not Steve's mom or brother or my parents. Somebody who really knew me and who I really knew. Somebody who understood. Was there anybody who could understand for sure though?

I knew the first thing I'd do when I got home was make a couple of fried bologna and ketchup sandwiches and have a coke with some of dad's whiskey and flop down in front of the stereo. After that, I had no idea, but it was summer, and that'd be a good start.

Nosedive

Also by **B. R. Fleming**

The Secret People follows Lesley Whitney as she enters the realm of Native American Spiritualism and encounters the Inorganic Beings on her search for her missing father in the Four corners region of the US.

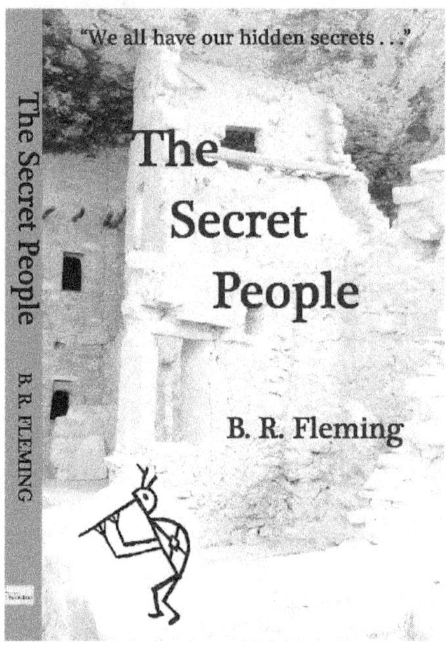

Available from Amazon and other book retailers.

ABOUT B. R. Fleming

B. R. Fleming grew up in the '60's reading sci-fi novels and watching sci-fi movies and was a musician in rock bands that played psychedelic rock and the music of the British invasion. After serving in the US Air Force as a Technical Instructor during the Vietnam War, he returned to civilian life and began a career in teaching. He lives in Southern California and still plays music. He finished the Screenwriting Program at the University of California, Irvine, and has completed five feature-length film scripts. His screenplays have been marketed to Sony Pictures and Walt Disney Studios Pictures Marketing. *Upping Peter* follows *Nosedive* in *The Peter Saga.*

Mr. Fleming's next project, *The Colony Trilogy: Torus I; The Colony;* and *The Coming,* presents a fact-based sci-fi series revolving around colonization of the solar system.

Follow B. R. Fleming:

Twitter: @BFScreenwriter
Instagram: brfleming_write_play_shoot
Facebook: www.facebook.com/bruce.fleming49
Website: http://brflemingauthor.wix.com/brfleming
Email: brflemingauthor@gmail.com